Malcolm Richards crafts stories to edge of your seat. He is the author mystery novels, including the PI Bla nominated Devil's Cove trilogy, and the Emily Swanson series. Many of his books are set in Cornwall, where he was born and raised.

Before becoming a full-time writer, he worked for several years in the special education sector, teaching and supporting children with complex needs. After living in London for two decades, he has now settled in the Somerset countryside with his partner and their pets.

Visit the author's website: www.malcolmrichardsauthor.com

BOOKS BY MALCOLM RICHARDS

PI Blake Hollow

Circle of Bones

Down in the Blood

The Devil's Cove Trilogy

The Cove

Desperation Point

The Devil's Gate

The Emily Swanson Series

Next to Disappear

Mind for Murder

Trail of Poison

Watch You Sleep

Kill for Love

Standalone Novels

The Hiding House

PI BLAKE HOLLOW BOOK ONE

Malcolm Richards

CIRCLE OF BONES

StormHouse

First published in 2021 by Storm House Books

ISBN 978-1-914452-00-0

www.stormhousebooks.com

The first one is always for Xander.

1

THE FRONT DOOR flew open and crashed against the wall as Blake Hollow came hurrying in. Her face was pulled into a scowl and her shoulder muscles ached with tension. Setting her mother's carry case on the floor next to the coat stand, she stepped to one side as her father struggled to get the wheelchair over the front doorstep.

"Careful, Dad," Blake said. "Mum doesn't need another broken leg."

The wheelchair came over the threshold with a bump and Mary Hollow's extended left leg almost smacked against the wall.

"Dad!"

Blake's mother held up her hands. "Honestly, will you leave your father alone for one second? He's doing the best he can. And were you born in a barn? Close the front door before we lose all the heat."

Blake did as she was told, then watched her father awkwardly wheel her mother into the dining room. Mary had reached the age of sixty-one with a vibrant youthfulness and just a few silver strands that were only starting to peek through her dark brown hair. But the accident and her time in hospital had aged her. 'You can't sleep in those places,' she had complained on the journey home. 'All those sick people moaning and groaning, it's any wonder you don't die from exhaustion.'

Two weeks ago, Mary had been carrying a basket of dirty laundry downstairs when she'd slipped on the top step and tumbled head-first to the hallway, snapping her femur in the process. The injury had required surgery, and now her leg would be in an immovable cast from hip to toe for at least two months, which meant upstairs was off limits and someone else needed to take care of the household. Dressing, bathing, and just about any practical act of self-care would also require assistance.

Blake had done her best to convert the dining room into a temporary bedroom for her parents. She had dismantled the table and propped it up against the wall, stacked the chairs neatly in the corner, and then single-handedly dragged the sofa-bed from the living room into the dining room. Now, her gaze settled on the sofa-bed, which was still upright, the sheets and pillows draped over one of the arms.

"Dad, you were supposed to make the bed! That was the one thing you were meant to do."

Ed had positioned Mary in front of the window and now he stared out at the rear garden. At the age of sixty-two, he was developing a slight stoop. His skin was lined from years of outdoor work. His hands were still strong, but starting to show telltale signs of osteoarthritis. Even so, at just over six feet tall he was still an imposing figure. He rolled his shoulders and let out a deep sigh, before settling his icy blue eyes on Blake.

"There wasn't time. I had paperwork to finish."

Blake crossed her arms over her chest. "So, I'm supposed to

do everything, am I? I literally got here six hours ago and I haven't sat down for a second."

"It doesn't matter," Mary said. "It won't take five minutes now. Ed, why don't you make a cup of tea while Blake makes up the bed?"

Ed's face softened as he leaned over to kiss the top of his wife's head. He left the room. Blake's eyes burned into his back. A moment later, running water could be heard, followed by cupboard doors opening and mugs clinking together.

Snatching up cushions and dumping them on the floor, Blake reached inside the sofa and pulled out the bed frame. She grabbed the cotton sheet from the arm and shook it out.

"Oh, bird," Mary said. "You're so short tempered these days."

Blake shot a glance over her shoulder. Since she'd arrived that morning, her father had barely lifted a finger in preparation for her mother's return. Blake had cleaned the house from top to bottom, converted the dining room, and even scrubbed the toilets. All she had asked of her father was to make up the sofa-bed. She knew she could have done it, but it was the principle of it all. And yet he'd failed.

Blake grabbed a pillow and stuffed it inside a pillowcase.

Mary rubbed her plaster cast, as if it would somehow soothe the pain. "Anyway, I'm glad you're here. Are you sure you can afford the time off work?"

"What work?" Blake said. "I've had one case in the last six weeks. One. It's a good job I have savings or I'd be shafted."

"Do you have to talk like that?"

"Yes, I do."

"Have you tried getting more work?"

"You don't just go out and find private investigator work, Mum. You advertise or you're hired. It comes to you."

Finished with the pillows, she set them down on the sofa and started on the duvet.

"Maybe it's just a quiet patch," Mary said.

"I don't think so. Since Axis Investigations arrived on the scene, they've been snapping up every job in the city. Even my regular insurance gigs. I can't compete with their prices."

"But a place as big as Manchester, surely there's —"

"There isn't. A big agency like that will eat us independents for breakfast. Anyway, I'm here for a few weeks and it's fine. Maybe I can use the time to think about a career change."

She threw the duvet on the bed and brushed out the creases.

A career change. The idea of it filled Blake with horror.

She was thirty-seven years old, and had been a private investigator for most of her adult life. What else could she do? She was sure she had transferable skills, even if she didn't know what they were. What she did know was that she enjoyed the solitary nature of private investigation and the unsociable hours. The work for hire she did for criminal defence lawyers was varied and sometimes even exciting. The routine insurance jobs not so much, but there was the occasional case that involved more than sitting around in a car for days, slowly destroying her spine.

Then there were the private cases. Men and women who suspected their spouses of cheating. Missing person cases when initial investigations had dried up and families were desperate to find their loved ones. And very, very occasionally, a years-old cold case, such as an unsolved murder. They were so infrequent that each time one landed on Blake's desk, her pulse would start to race. She knew she should turn them down, but the client was always desperate and out of options. For Blake, a cold case was always a challenge to test her skills. A challenge that she had so far failed every time.

She wasn't a bad private investigator. In fact, she was a damn good one. But if the British police force couldn't solve a cold case with entire criminal investigation departments and forensic specialists at their disposal, not to mention a vast arsenal of computer technology, including the famous criminal database HOLMES, then how was Blake going to solve it when all she had was an internet connection and her own ingenuity?

Blake glanced at her mother, who had grown a shade paler since they'd arrived home.

"Have you heard from Alfie?" she asked.

A smile lit up Mary's face. "Dear of him. He called the hospital yesterday morning. He feels terrible he hasn't been able to visit, but you know what those city jobs are like. He works all hours, and with the baby on the way and Violet about to go on maternity leave, he's got his hands full, bless him."

Blake turned away and rolled her eyes. Her brother could take a weekend out of his busy London life if he wanted to. Besides, there were still two months until the baby was due. But as usual, it was Blake who had come to the rescue, driving down from Manchester to Cornwall, and giving up her life for the next few weeks. She tried to remember the last time she'd talked to Alfie. A month ago, maybe. It wasn't as if he ever called her, either.

"So," she said. "You want to get into this lovingly made bed?"

"Not just yet. I've been in bed for days. Besides, I need to keep this leg elevated."

"Do you need the toilet?"

"Heavens, Blake. Stop fussing. Anyway, you need to go to the supermarket."

"I thought Dad was doing that."

"He's got to go into work."

Blake clenched her jaw. "He's meant to be taking the whole day off."

"It's just for an hour. One of the boys called this morning. Something about building materials not showing up. They can't build houses out of air."

"So, I just leave you to fend for yourself? What if I wasn't here at all right now? What if you have an accident?" She crossed her arms again. This time she couldn't stop shaking her head. "Why can't Dad pick up the shopping on the way home?"

"Honestly, the way you talk about your father it's like he's some sort of monster. He tries his best, you know."

"Well, his best isn't good enough."

As if on cue, Ed returned carrying a tea tray.

"There you go, love." He put it down on the side table next to the sofa-bed. Blake stared at the single mug and the spilled tea pooling on the tray. "Let's get you into bed before I head out."

"Mum said she's had enough of being in bed for now."

"I'm fine, Blake. Stop fussing."

She watched her father scoop her mother up as if she were made of paper, then gently deposit her on the bed and bolster her plastered leg with pillows. Mary smiled at him. Ed brushed a strand of hair from her forehead.

Blake glowered at them both. If there was one thing that she had learned about people over the years, it was that they were creatures of habit, governed by rules and routines. Ed and Mary Hollow were stuck in their ways and nothing would ever change them. It didn't mean that Blake had to like it.

Pulling her car key fob from her jeans pocket, she expelled a deep breath. "I guess I'll go to the supermarket, then."

"There's a list on the fridge," Mary said.

Of course there was.

"What about you, Dad? You want a lift to work?"

"I'll take the van," he said, then smiled at Mary. "I'll be an hour. Two at most."

Blake glanced at her father, who was still avoiding her gaze, and headed for the front door.

———

A weight pressed down on Blake's shoulders as she drove into town. Now that she had confessed her lack of work to her mother, she couldn't stop thinking about the future. She had never bought her own house, so there would be no missed mortgage payments to worry about, and her rent was paid in advance for the next six months. Despite having lived in the same tenth floor flat at the heart of Manchester's metropolis for eight years now, she didn't feel particularly attached to it. That was the downside of renting; it never truly felt like home. The same could be said about Manchester. Blake liked the city well enough and enjoyed living there, and although she'd never established any deep-rooted friendships, she knew enough passing acquaintances to not feel lonely. But there was an emptiness at the centre of it all. A pit needing to be filled. With what, she didn't know. At least her lack of emotional attachment would make it easy to leave if work continued to dry up.

Her parents' house stood alone in half an acre of land. The nearest town was Wheal Marow, which was a ten-minute drive along a winding, tree-lined road flanked by fields and meadows.

As a teenager, Blake had found living on the peripheries difficult. The bus to Wheal Marow would stop just once an hour on a good day, or longer on a bad day, which left Blake at the mercy of her parents' schedules whenever she wanted to meet friends. By the time she'd reached womanhood boredom had set in, and she'd had her suitcases packed and ready to go before her university application had even been accepted. Now, driving along in her dented blue Corsa, she was amused by how perception shifted with age and experience. Eighteen years ago, Blake would have barely looked up. Today, she glanced at the crisp blue sky, which was a rarity for winter in Cornwall, and at the flashes of fallow fields flitting between the trees. She smiled, momentarily forgetting her worries.

With a population of just eighteen thousand, Wheal Marow was a small town. Located inland, it went unnoticed by millions of tourists flocking to Cornwall during the holiday season. Growing up, Blake had envied the coastal towns and villages that buzzed with energy and a multitude of fresh faces come the summer. Wheal Marow remained insidiously quiet. No one wanted to come to a dying town, even if it did have a rich history connected to mining.

As Blake drove through the one-way high street, she noted closed-down shops and boarded-up windows. Pedestrians milled up and down, most of them in their later years. It was a far cry from the busy streets of Manchester. Pulling into the supermarket car park at the far end of town, Blake switched off the engine. The weight on her shoulders grew a little heavier.

Well, she thought, let's get this over with.

Grabbing a shopping trolley from outside, she made her way through sliding doors and squinted in the harsh glare of the overhead strip lights. The supermarket was reasonably busy, with food shoppers trawling the aisles and toddlers stuffed into trolley seats. Adjusting her jacket collar, she took out her mother's handwritten shopping list and headed for the fruit and vegetable corner. She shopped quickly and strategically, heading down each aisle at a brisk pace and throwing items into the trolley. She had managed to get a third of the way down the list when a sing-song voice called her name.

"Blake, darlin'? Is that you?"

Blake brought the trolley to a halt, then let out a breath. "Hello, Mrs Moon. How are you?"

"It is you! I thought it was, after all this time. And what's all this Mrs Moon business? You know well and good you call me Tina."

Tina Moon was a large, squat lady, with an apple-shaped face and grey-white hair that was gloriously unkempt. She smiled widely and planted a kiss on Blake's cheek. "It's good to see you, flower."

Blake smiled. Sometimes she missed the host of affectionate terms the Cornish used to greet each other. *Flower. Bird. Me luvver. My 'ansum.* And it wasn't just reserved for friends and family. Go into any shop and the chances were you'd be addressed just as warmly by the shopkeeper. Unless you weren't born in Cornwall. Then you were just an *emmet*.

"How's your mum?" Tina asked. "She get back home all right?"

"Oh, yes," Blake said. "She's currently propped up in bed and hating every minute of it."

Mary and Tina had been friends since school, and they had run the textile shop in town together for decades, until Mary had taken an early retirement. Although they saw less of each other these days their friendship hadn't waned.

"You come home to take care of her then, have you? Dear of you. I expect she can't do much for herself right now. How long are you here for?"

Blake shrugged. "Until the cast comes off, I suppose."

"Well, I'm sure Mary will be happy as pie to have her girl home for a bit. 'Ere, you should give Judy a call. She'd love to see you."

Judy was Tina's daughter. Just like their mothers, Blake and Judy had gone to school together and grown up as friends. But unlike their mothers, their friendship had grown distant over the years.

"Judy still working for The Cornish Press?"

Tina smiled proudly. "Writes the farming news now, you know, and an occasional feature. A few weeks ago, she even got to write the front-page story!"

"Good for her," Blake said.

In truth, the front-page story of The Cornish Press was never more salacious than 'Pair of Spectacles Thrown from Car' or 'Sheep Attacks Man'. Not that she was knocking Judy's success, but Blake did wonder at times why Judy had never aimed for one of the big newspapers in the city because she was more than qualified. But that was small town folk: some couldn't wait to get away, while others were happy to stay put. Blake had been the former. She glanced down at the shopping list in her hand, then at the items in the trolley. But Tina wasn't quite ready to let her go.

"How's Manchester? Still being a fancy private detective? It sounds so exciting!"

"Believe me, it really isn't."

"Judy's been married for seven years now. There was a minute there I thought she would end up on the shelf, until she met Charlie. He's a lovely lad, even if Judy refused to take his surname. Mind you, can't say I blame her: Judy Cock doesn't sound too good, does it?" Tina laughed. "Don't even get me started on her girls' last name. Moon-Cock, indeed! But they're beautiful angels and growing up far too fast."

Blake smiled. The last time she'd seen Judy's daughters, the youngest had still been a toddler. She was five years old now. Maybe even six.

"Did you know Charlie's thinking about running for mayor next year? People say he's too young, but I think he'd do a brilliant job. No wedding bells for you yet?"

"I'm married to my job, which is how I like it."

"Bet your mother has something to say about that."

Blake cleared her throat and waved the shopping list." Speaking of my mother, if I don't get the shopping done, I'll be the one with a broken leg."

Tina cackled and waved a hand. "I'll tell Judy you're home. I'm sure she'd love to catch up."

Smiling, Blake waved back then wheeled the trolley around to the next aisle. A scowl returned to her face. So now she was not only bordering on jobless but was apparently on the shelf and hopelessly barren. She just loved coming home.

She continued shopping, wrenching tins and packets from shelves and crossing them off the list. Every so often, she would see a familiar face—someone from school or a friend of the family—and duck in the other direction. Finally, with the trolley full, Blake joined a queue at the checkout. A mother and young son were in front of her, the boy slotted into the seat in the trolley. Blake smiled at him. He pulled a face.

And then there was a sudden commotion on her right. Over at the customer service desk, a woman was talking animatedly, her hands gesturing wildly at the young female assistant, who flinched and stepped back.

Pushing her trolley to one side, Blake left the queue and headed towards the customer service desk.

"Christine?" she called. "What's the matter?"

Christine Truscott was the same age as Blake. Like Judy Moon, Blake had gone to school with her and the two had remained friends into adulthood, albeit from a distance. But as Christine stared at her with wild, panicked eyes, Blake barely recognised her.

Christine shook her head, sending tears into the air. "Lucy didn't come home last night. She didn't turn up for work today and she's not answering her phone." She stared at Blake, a frown momentarily pushing through the fear. "I didn't know you were back in town."

Lucy Truscott was eighteen years old; just a year older than when her mother had fallen pregnant. Christine had been in her final year of her A-levels and was planning to go to university to study English. But when she'd found out about the pregnancy, she'd decided to keep the baby and her life had gone in a very different direction. Lucy's father, a blond-haired surfer whose name Blake had long-since forgotten, hadn't stuck around for more than a minute.

"Have you checked with Lucy's friends?" she asked, placing a gentle hand on her shoulder.

"That's what I'm doing right now." Christine shot a glance at the customer service assistant.

"I'm sorry," the teenager said in a small voice. "Like I told you, me and Lucy haven't hung out in ages."

A line was forming behind Blake and Christine. A man at

the front cleared his throat loudly and glared at them. Blake glared back then gently guided Christine to one side.

"No one's seen Lucy except her best friend Jasmine," Christine said. "They were together last night. They went for a drink at the Badger Inn. Jasmine told me they left just before ten and went their separate ways."

"Have you contacted the pub? Maybe someone there knows something."

"They're not answering the phone." Christine trembled and more tears ran down her face. "Lucy knows to call me if she's going to be out late. She knows I'll worry if she doesn't. And it's not like her to miss work. She loves the pet shop." Christine paused, staring at Blake with wide eyes. "Should I call the police? It's not been twenty-four hours yet."

"The twenty-four-hour thing is a myth. If you're worried, you should call them. But are you sure you've tried all of Lucy's friends? What about a boyfriend?"

"No."

"Girlfriend?"

Christine shook her head. "She's in the middle of applying for nursing college next year. She says there's no point in getting involved with anyone."

A memory pulled at Blake's mind; a strange sense of déjà vu that made her feel like she was falling.

"Can you help me, Blake? I mean, you're a private investigator. Can't you help me find her?"

"I've got to get the shopping back to Mum," she said, weakly. "I've left her alone and she's only just back from the hospital."

Over by the checkout, a skinny teenage shop assistant was eyeing Blake's abandoned shopping trolley.

"Please, Blake. I don't know what to do."

"I'm sure Lucy will be home soon. You know how teenagers can be. We weren't exactly angels ourselves at that age, were we?"

Christine flinched. Her jaw went tight and her tears stopped flowing.

"It's easy for you to say that because you're not a mother," she said, her lower lip trembling. "Lucy is all I have. There's this invisible connection between us, and I can always feel it. But it's gone, Blake. I can't feel her anymore."

Blake reached out and took her hand. "Call the police and tell them Lucy didn't come home. Tell them it's extremely out of character. At the very least they'll file a report and hopefully send someone out. But if Lucy hasn't come home by this evening, then you call me. Dad will be home. I'll come over."

Christine nodded and started crying again. Blake gave her hand a soft squeeze then pulled away, heading back to the shopping trolley.

She had an uneasy feeling in her gut, like something was terribly wrong. It was the same sensation she'd felt years ago, back when she and Christine and Judy Moon had all been friends and their futures had lain ahead of them like an open road. Until the night Demelza disappeared.

Blake glanced over her shoulder and saw Christine hurrying through the exit doors. She had been wrong in her hopes back then. She hoped that she wasn't wrong now.

2

By THE TIME the phone call came that evening, Lucy Truscott had been missing for twenty-two hours. The police had sent an investigating officer to take a statement. He asked questions, searched Lucy's bedroom, and took a list of friends' names and numbers, including Jasmine Baker, who was the last person to see Lucy before she vanished. The police officer told Christine to continue calling around and to use social media to ask if anyone had seen her daughter. In the meantime, he would make his own enquiries, assess the level of urgency and report to his superior to receive further instruction. For Christine, who was already starting to fall apart, it wasn't enough.

Blake tried to assure her that the police would do everything in their power to find Lucy. But she also knew that police numbers had been dwindling in Cornwall in recent years, with government budget cuts forcing several stations to close. With a population of half a million people living in remote clusters across almost fourteen hundred square miles of rural terrain, there just weren't enough police officers to go around.

Now, on a chilly, overcast Tuesday morning, Blake was back

in Wheal Marow and sitting at a corner table at the Honey Bee Café, nursing a watery black coffee that was so far failing to wake her up. The single bed she had attempted to sleep in last night was a relic from her teenage years. On her occasional returns to Cornwall, she had begged for a replacement and had even offered to pay for it, but she was always met with the same answer: 'That room's too small for a double. Besides, you're lucky your father hasn't turned it into an office.' Alfie's bedroom had a new double bed—he and a heavily pregnant Violet couldn't possibly sleep in a single—but the room was currently half-painted and covered with plastic sheeting. Ed and Mary's way of welcoming the arrival of their first grandchild.

Straightening up, Blake felt her lower spine pop. It was a little before nine. Tables were filled with regular patrons who drank steaming mugs of tea and breakfasted on toast, muffins and bacon sandwiches. The aroma of sizzling fat made Blake's stomach heave. She was a breakfast skipper, even though it was allegedly the most important meal of the day. Besides, she was sure coffee fell into one of the major food groups.

Most of the customers were elderly, but that was because it was an ageing town. Adults in their twenties and thirties had mostly left to make their fortunes elsewhere. There were still some young families left behind, whose bored-looking teens hung around the town square at weekends and invariably got into trouble. Blake knew that small-town teen life could some-times feel like a life behind bars, so they had her utmost sympa-thy. Of course, what the youth of Wheal Marow had yet to learn was that adulthood came with its own kind of cage.

Blake sipped her coffee and thought about Lucy Truscott. She didn't know her well, only that she was a kind, gentle soul, who loved to help and whom everyone liked. Blake should have known Lucy better. After all, her mother had been one of Blake's closest friends. She had tried to keep in touch with Christine after leaving for university, visiting her and baby Lucy whenever she'd returned home at the end of each semester. But as Blake settled into Manchester life, her visits home grew fewer and shorter. There was only so much time in the day, she would tell herself, when she'd visit her parents but not Christine or Judy Moon. Besides, Christine was always busy with the baby and Judy was always working. And then, of course, there was what happened to Demelza.

A bell tinkled as the door opened and a young woman entered. She stood for a second, scanning the tables. She was tall and thin, with a nest of red curls and a sprinkle of freckles across her pale white skin that gave her an impish look.

"Jasmine?" Blake waved a hand.

The other customers turned in her direction, then towards the young woman who was still standing in the doorway and letting out the heat. Shutting the door, she crossed the floor and nervously glanced at Blake, before slipping into the opposite chair.

"Thanks for agreeing to see me," Blake said, holding out a hand. Jasmine stared at her outstretched fingers, then awkwardly shook them. "You want something to eat?"

"I have to be at work in half an hour," she replied. "Maybe just a coffee?"

Blake signalled to the silver-haired waitress at the counter, then pointed at her coffee cup and held up two fingers. The waitress arched an eyebrow.

"So, this is about Lucy?" Jasmine asked. "She's still missing?"

"Christine, Lucy's mother, she asked me to talk to you. You and Lucy went for a drink at the Badger Inn on Sunday night?"

"That's right. I met her there just after seven. We hadn't seen each other in a while."

"You two are good friends?"

"We've been best friends since school. We haven't seen each other as much since we left college because we're both working now."

"That's why you met for a drink? To catch up?"

Blake noted the worry lines on the young woman's brow and the way she was twisting the silver ring on her left index finger.

"I don't understand," Jasmine said. "We were only out for a few hours. We said goodbye outside the pub just before ten, then I went home. Lucy said she was going home, too. She only lives down the road. How could she have gone missing?"

"You didn't walk home together?"

"We live in opposite directions. I'm on Lavender Street, near the petrol station."

"It's Jasmine Baker, isn't it? Who are your parents?"

"Dan and Melanie."

"Did they grow up here? I don't recognise their names."

"Mum's from Helston. Dad's originally from Coventry. His family moved to Cornwall when he was ten. We moved to Wheal Marow six years ago."

Blake couldn't imagine why anyone would purposely move to Wheal Marow. The waitress brought over two mugs of coffee and set them down on the table along with a small pitcher of milk.

"All right, Jasmine, darlin'?" the woman said. Her name was Elsie, Blake remembered. She was a familiar face, and no doubt related to someone she probably sort of knew.

Jasmine nodded. "Yes, thanks. You?"

"Yeah, not bad." Elsie hovered, smiling at Blake. "How's that mother of yours? Heard she had an accident."

"She had a fall and broke her leg. And she's fine, thank you. At home recovering."

"Well, you tell her Elsie said hello, won't you, darlin'? She must be glad to have you home. Staying long, are you?"

"A few weeks."

Blake smiled politely at the waitress, waiting for her to leave. But Elsie continued to hover.

"I hear Christine Truscott's girl didn't come home. It's a worry, isn't it? You're friends with her, aren't you, Jasmine? No sign of her yet?"

Jasmine silently shook her head.

"Hope nothing terrible's happened. But you never know these days, what with immigrants and unsavouries hanging out on every street corner."

"Do you like history, Elsie?" Blake asked, staring at her.

The waitress leaned in and squinted. "What's that now?"

"I do. It's full of all sorts of surprises. For instance, did you know that, according to a recent study of ancient DNA, the original population of Britain was almost completely wiped out by climate change and disease? It's true. And they were replaced by newcomers from Europe. So I suppose that makes you, me and everyone else in this country descendants of immigrants. Fancy that."

Elsie's smile faded. "Well, can't leave the customers waiting. Wish your mother well, and I hope Christine's girl comes home safe."

They watched the waitress return to the counter. Then Blake said, "If there's anything you can tell me, Jasmine. Anything at all that could tell us where Lucy is."

"I don't know anything apart from what I told you."

"How was Lucy feeling on Sunday evening?"

"She was fine. I mean, she was a little distracted I suppose."

"In what way?"

"She kept losing track of the conversation, like she wasn't really listening at times. I asked her if there was something on her mind, and she said it wasn't important. Just that she was a bit tired."

"She didn't seem upset to you?"

"No, not upset."

"Did she mention anyone else or tell you anything out of the ordinary?"

"We just talked about work. Life. You know, the usual boring stuff."

"Relationships?"

Jasmine glanced down at the ring on her left index finger. "I got engaged recently, so we talked about that."

"Congratulations".

"Thanks."

"Is Lucy seeing anyone right now?"

"She hasn't mentioned anyone. She's never been that interested in relationships."

"Her mum said she's applying for nursing school."

"She mentioned it once, but I think she changed her mind after the hospital job."

"I thought she works at the pet shop."

"She does. She cleaned at the hospital before that."

"Her mum definitely told me Lucy's applying for nursing school. You don't think she is?"

"Maybe she told her mum that just to keep her happy. All I

know is that Lucy said staying in Wheal Marow is not in her future."

Blake picked up her mug and sipped more coffee. "Lucy's planning on leaving . . ."

"Eventually, but not right now. She said she has to save money first, and she still hasn't decided what she wants to do."

Blake frowned. No relationship issues. Big plans for the future, even if they were currently unknown. Lucy didn't sound like she needed to run away from anything except small-town life. And even that didn't sound imminent.

Jasmine stared at her coffee cup, which was still untouched. "I'm worried about Lucy. What if something's happened?"

"Like what?" Blake asked.

"Like something bad. Like someone hurt her. But nothing like that ever happens around here. It just doesn't."

Blake caught her breath. That wasn't true. Bad things had happened in Wheal Marow. Which was why the unease clawing at her stomach was getting harder to ignore.

Jasmine was staring, trying to read the worry on Blake's face.

"You know the police still haven't been to see me yet?" she said.

"I'm sure they will today. Christine only reported Lucy missing last night, and there's a process they have to follow."

Removing her wallet from her jacket pocket, Blake took out a business card and handed it to Jasmine. "Call me if you think of anything else. It doesn't matter the time of day."

Jasmine stared at the card. "An actual private investigator?"

"Believe me, it's not that exciting." Blake put money on the table and they both stood up. "One more question. Who else was in the pub on Sunday night? Anyone you know?"

Jasmine's eyes shifted to the right as she tried to remember.

"It wasn't that busy. There were a few older couples there. Some old men sitting at the bar . . ."

"Anyone else? Maybe someone hanging about on their own?"

"Well, there was that guy. Kenver something. I don't really know him, but I think Lucy does. She said hello to him when we sat down."

Blake stared at her. "Kenver? As in, Kenver Quick?"

"I think so, yeah. I don't know much about him, only that he's come back to live here after a few years away. Sounds like a bit of a loser if you ask me."

"Why would you say that?"

"Because he was already drunk when we got there at seven. And who would want to come back to this dump, anyway? Me and my fiancé, we're moving to Truro as soon as we can."

Blake thanked Jasmine and they both walked to the door. Leaning over the counter, Elsie waved and watched Blake closely.

Outside, pedestrians meandered along the paved street as pasty smells wafted out from Helen's Bakery. Thanking Jasmine again, Blake told her not to worry and that hopefully Lucy would be home soon. She watched the young woman cross the road and enter Birthdays, the gift and card shop where she worked.

Jasmine may not have known who Kenver Quick was, but Blake certainly did. And she knew exactly where to find him.

3

Kenver Quick lived alone in a two-bedroom Victorian terraced cottage on the outskirts of town. Rental prices in Wheal Marow were dirt cheap in comparison to the extortionate sums of money that Blake knew he'd been paying for his one-bedroom studio in East London. She also knew that he'd left urban chaos behind eight months ago for a quiet life in the country, which was highly unusual for an unattached twenty-eight-year-old.

Blake knocked on Kenver's door, and as she waited for him to answer, she thought about her conversation with Jasmine Baker. Two points stood out to her. The first, that Lucy had been distracted that evening and had played down Jasmine's concern. The second, that Lucy had lied to her mother about applying for nursing college. It was possible that the latter was nothing more than Lucy feeling pressured to please Christine, while still trying to figure out what she wanted to do with her life. Whatever it was, it wasn't going to happen in Wheal Marow. As for the former, Blake was hoping that Kenver might be able to shed some light. Only Kenver wasn't answering the door.

Blake knocked again, louder this time. It was 9:17. She knew that Kenver worked from home these days as a freelance data analyst. She also knew he wasn't an early riser.

Pulling her phone from her pocket, she called his number. As the line connected and started to ring, she crouched down and flipped open the letterbox. A tinny ringtone jingled from somewhere inside then fell silent as the call connected to voicemail.

"I know you're in there!" Blake shouted through the letter box. "It's me. Open up!"

Behind her on the road, a car shot past at a dangerous speed, heading in the direction of the bypass.

"Kenver, get that lazy backside of yours out of bed—it's important!"

Blake hammered on the door again.

"All right!" A gravel-filled voice barked from inside then swore loudly.

Bolts were pulled back. Locks were unlocked. The door swung open a crack and Kenver's pallid face peered out.

"I didn't know you were back in town," he muttered, peering at her through half-open dark eyes.

"Surprise," Blake said. "Are you going to let me in or what?"

Kenver peered back into the house. "It's a mess. I don't want a lecture."

"I'm your cousin, not your parent."

He opened the door and stepped to one side, wincing as the daylight rushed in. Blake entered the cottage and wrinkled her nose.

"When did you last open a window? 1842?"

She glanced at Kenver, who had hastily pulled on a pair of black skinny jeans but had left his lean, pasty torso bare. A nest of curly black hair sprang up from his scalp. Tattoos ran up and down his arms in intricate patterns of branches, leaves and large-winged ravens. A small silver ring pierced his septum.

He closed the front door, and the room was plunged into shadows.

"Brace yourself," Blake said, as she pulled back the curtains. Kenver winced and shielded his eyes. "You really have gone full vampire, haven't you?"

Surveying the living room, she took in the carnage. A coffee table was covered in empty beer cans and wine bottles, while junk food wrappers littered the sofa and dirty plates and glasses lay on the floor.

"I thought the whole reason for leaving London was to clean yourself up," Blake said. "Looks like you're making good progress."

Kenver rolled his eyes. "I thought we agreed no lectures."

"I lied. Go and put some clothes on. I'll make coffee."

Sighing, Kenver shuffled from the room as Blake waded through the mess towards the kitchenette in the corner. She filled the electric kettle with cold water, then selected two mugs from the pile of dishes in the sink and gave them a rinse. While she waited for the kettle to boil, her eyes returned to the mess in the living room.

"I'm not cleaning this up," she muttered, a warning to herself more than anyone else. Her hands were already itching, desperate to grab the waste bin and a dustpan and brush.

By the time Kenver returned, he had dressed in a black hoodie and had attempted to neaten his hair. Blake handed him a mug of coffee. She had already removed the debris from the coffee table and cleared a space on the sofa.

"You didn't have to do that," Kenver mumbled.

Blake sat down next to him. "I didn't want to catch tuberculosis. Anyway, this isn't a social call. I take it you've heard about Lucy Truscott?"

Kenver nodded. News travelled fast in towns like Wheal Marow.

"She hasn't turned up yet?"

"No. And it turns out that you were one of the last people to see her."

"Me? When did I see her?"

"Really? Exactly how drunk were you on Sunday night?"

Kenver shrugged a bony shoulder.

"Bloody hell, Kenver. I hear you were drinking alone that night as well."

"So?"

"So, what happened to cleaning up your act?"

"Yeah. Well, it's work in progress."

"I can see that."

They were both quiet, Kenver nursing his coffee and Blake frowning at the carpet.

"How's Aunt Mary?" Kenver asked.

"She's home. Getting bored already. It would be nice if you went to see her."

"I will."

"Good. Maybe have a shower first. You really don't remember anything from Sunday night?"

Kenver narrowed his eyes. "How come you're in private detective mode, anyway?"

"Lucy's mum has asked for my help. And you haven't answered my question."

"Let me have a minute to think."

Blake waited, drumming her fingers on her knees. Her eyes kept wandering over the living room, finding things that needed to be tidied away. She glanced at Kenver, who had lost more weight since she'd last seen him. He didn't look well, or like he'd encountered daylight in a long time. She supposed his pallid appearance suited his neo-punk Goth leanings, or whatever it was he identified as these days. But still, she worried about him.

"Anything?" she asked, growing impatient.

Kenver rubbed his eyes with the back of his hand. "I kind of remember being in the pub. I vaguely remember Lucy being there with someone. Was it Jasmine?"

"Jasmine said Lucy spoke to you. She said hello."

"Oh yeah. I vaguely recall that."

"How do you know her, anyway?"

"I don't. Not really. Just from being out drinking or the odd party. I think she thinks I'm cool."

Blake pulled a face. "You didn't notice anything unusual that night? No one strange hanging around the pub?"

"Only me." Kenver smiled.

Blake leaned back on the sofa. "It doesn't make any sense. Jasmine and Lucy left around ten, and then they both went their separate ways. Which means Lucy disappeared somewhere between leaving the Badger Inn and the seven-minute walk home, which is mostly through the town."

"How long are you back for?" Kenver asked, clearly not listening. He was starting to look a little more awake now, the coffee working its magic.

"I don't know. Until Mum's a bit more able, I suppose."

"I guess Uncle Ed is too busy with his job to help out, right?"

Blake rolled her eyes. "Don't even get me started."

"And Alfie? Haven't seen him in a while."

"Me either. He's apparently too busy being a high-flying London businessman to even visit his injured mother."

"That brother of yours does like to talk about his job."

"Speaking of working, are you right now?"

Kenver glanced at the floor. "I'm between projects. What about you, Miss Private Eye? Can you afford to take the time off to look after your mum?"

Blake looked away. "It's fine. I needed a break anyway."

They were both quiet again, contemplating their misfortune.

"Listen, I don't know about Lucy," Kenver said, at last. "But there's a party tonight, out in the sticks. I'm sure half of the town's young people will be there. If Lucy hasn't turned up by then, maybe you'll find some answers there."

"A party?" Blake said. "On a Tuesday evening? And you're going?"

"It would be rude not to. Besides, I'm still establishing myself in this town. I left all my friends behind. Got to make some new ones, right?"

"You're twenty-eight, Kenver. Maybe you should be making friends with other twenty-eight-year-olds?"

"And I would, except they've all gone away."

Blake couldn't deny it.

"So you want to be my party date?"

The last thing Blake wanted to do was go to a party on a Tuesday night with a bunch of teenagers. But Kenver was right; it was possible that some of Lucy's friends might be there and able to shed some light on her whereabouts.

She stared at Kenver, narrowing her eyes. "I'm not babysitting you tonight. I had enough of babysitting you when you were a kid."

"No one's asking you to."

Sudden movement caught Blake's eye. A figure appeared in the doorway, a woman in her early twenties, wearing nothing more than one of Kenver's oversized T-shirts. Blake gaped at the woman, then at Kenver, who shifted his weight on the sofa.

"Sorry," the young woman said. She disappeared again, heading back upstairs.

Kenver smiled sheepishly. "I told you, I'm making new friends."

Blake got to her feet and headed towards the front door. She stopped and turned on her heels. "If you get wasted tonight, I'm leaving you in a corner to rot."

4

THE HOLLOW FAMILY kitchen was of average size, with white walls, a flagstone floor, and a small breakfast table and chairs pushed up against the left wall. The main cooking area was on the right. It was not a well-lit room. The windows over the sink were too small, and a low, sloping roof made even the sunniest of days seem dark and shadowy. The view was of the back yard, which had been concreted over before the Hollows had bought the place. Ed had been promising for years to transform it into a proper garden for Mary. In the meantime, she'd done her best with potted plants and narrow flower beds that ran alongside both fences.

Blake stood over the cooker, absentmindedly stirring a pot of tomato sauce and vegetables. Her mother sat at the edge of the table, her plastered leg propped up on a chair with plenty of cushions. Blake had insisted she remained in the living room, where she would be more comfortable, but Mary had insisted on keeping her company. The truth, Blake knew, was that her mother didn't like others being in her kitchen. Every pot, pan, and utensil had its own place, and it was exactly how she liked it.

After leaving Kenver, Blake had walked back into town. The weather had taken a turn for the worse, threatening rain, so she returned to her car and drove back to her parents.

By the time evening came around, Lucy had been missing for almost forty-eight hours, yet her disappearance hadn't been mentioned on local radio or the regional TV news, which surprised Blake. Christine had already called twice. The police had started making door-to-door enquiries, but they weren't moving fast enough. She was frantic for news, but all Blake could tell her was that she was still following up leads. Now, as Blake stirred the pot, the nagging feeling in her stomach grew with intensity.

"What is it?" Mary asked. She was good at picking up on Blake's feelings without her having to say a word.

"Nothing."

"Rubbish. Something's bothering you."

Blake glanced over her shoulder and smiled weakly. "I can't stop thinking about Lucy Truscott. It doesn't make sense to me."

"That she disappeared?"

"Where did she go? Lucy sounded happy enough. She had no relationship troubles and she was enjoying her job at the pet shop. There was maybe a little tension about what she wanted to do with her life, but she and Christine seemed to be getting on well. Does that sound like someone who was planning to run away?"

At the table, Mary picked up a pencil and slid it beneath the edge of her plaster cast, scratching at an itch. "You're talking about her in past tense."

Blake stirred the pot and heaved her shoulders.

"I'm sure there's a reasonable explanation, love. You wait; she'll turn up this evening, full of excuses."

"I hope you're right. But it just sounds out of character for her, as far as I can tell. Do you know Lucy well?"

"Not really. I mean, I see her at Sunday service, and I know she helps out with the church foodbank. She seems like a sweet girl. Are you sure she hasn't had a falling out with Christine? Teenagers can be so wilful, you know?"

Mary flashed a wry smile, which Blake ignored.

"Lucy doesn't seem the type of young woman to punish her mum that way. Besides if they'd had a fight, Christine would have told me. She's not going to hide that kind of information right now."

They were both quiet, the only sound the sauce bubbling on the stove. Blake's stomach writhed and twisted.

"There's something else bothering you," Mary said.

"Honestly, it's nothing. Just old memories. Lucy disappearing like this makes me think about Demelza."

Mary continued to scratch at the itch beneath the plaster cast. She kept her eyes on Blake. "That was a long time ago. Lucy will turn up, she will. Bad things don't happen in this town. Not anymore."

"Bad things happen everywhere, Mum. Even in Wheal Marow."

She watched her mother put down the pencil then try to shift on her seat. Mary winced, clenching her teeth.

"Let me get you another cushion."

"I'm fine. Give the pot another stir before it catches."

Blake did as she was told. Her mind returned to Demelza. It had been eighteen years since her best friend had disappeared. Eighteen years in which no one had found a single shred of evidence or had come up with an explanation for what had happened to her. One minute, Blake, Demelza and their friends had been partying in a field, with music blaring and a bonfire roaring. The next, Demelza had vanished. Blake worried now that the same fate might have fallen upon Lucy. She hoped that she was wrong.

The sound of the front door closing made both women look up. Mary smiled as Ed entered the kitchen. His face and clothing were dusty from a hard day's work at the construction site. Returning Mary's smile, he bent down and kissed her cheek. His eyes flicked towards Blake, and he nodded.

Blake gave him a half smile.

"What are you doing in here, maid?" Ed said to Mary. "Can't be very comfortable propped up like that."

"That's what I've been trying to tell her," Blake said. "But she has trust issues when it comes to the kitchen."

Mary laughed. "That's not true. I'm just tired of staring at the dining room walls. The sooner I get on my feet, the better. For all of us." She reached up and stroked her husband's cheek. "Hard day at the office?"

Ed grunted and said that it was.

"And a sweaty one too from the smell. You best get in the shower. Tea's almost ready."

Ed kissed the top of her head. "First let's get you back on the sofa."

"I told you, I'm fine here."

Shrugging, Ed took a step towards Blake, then stopped, as if he'd hit an invisible wall. "What's cooking?"

"Pasta, vegetables, and a tomato sauce."

"No meat?"

"You don't need to be a carnivore every day, Dad. Besides, eating veggie a few times a week means you're doing your part for climate change."

Mary rolled her eyes.

"Climate change indeed," Ed muttered. His eyes wandered to the table where two places had been set. "You're not joining us, Blake?"

"I'm not used to eating so early. Besides, I need to go out."

"Early? It's almost five-thirty. That's teatime."

"Not in my world." Blake removed two bowls from the cupboard and set them on the counter. "If you're getting in the shower, now is the time."

Ed glanced at Mary, who shrugged.

"Where are you going?" he asked.

"Out."

"She's going to a party," Mary said. "On a Tuesday night, if you can believe it."

"A party?" Ed repeated.

Blake crossed her arms over her stomach. Sometimes coming home felt like stepping back in time. "It may have escaped your attention, but I haven't been a teenager for some time now. Anyway, I'm not going to the party to drink or to have fun. I'm going to ask questions about Lucy. She's still missing. Kenver thinks some of her friends will be there. Maybe one of them knows something."

Now Ed folded his arms. "Kenver? You've been hanging out with that waste of space?"

"That waste of space is your nephew," Mary said, giving him a playful slap on his arm. "Just because he's a little bit different doesn't mean he's all bad news."

"I don't care if he's different," Ed said. "That boy has never done a hard day's work in his life. And as for that ring through his nostrils like he's some sort of pig . . ."

"A hard day's work doesn't necessarily mean physical grafting, Ed," Blake said, arching an eyebrow. "Kenver works. It just happens to be on a computer at home."

"Well, you shouldn't be going to a party with him. You know why he came back to Cornwall, don't you? The boy's got a problem with drink. I hope you're not encouraging him."

"You're running out of shower time. Dinner's in five minutes."

Blake turned her back on her father and gave the sauce a violent stir. She thought about Kenver's pigsty of a house, the dark circles under his eyes, his half naked guest standing awkwardly in the doorway. She glanced over her shoulder. Ed had left the room, leaving behind a trail of dust. Mary was staring at her.

"I'm worried about you, Blake."

"Why? I'm not the one who's missing."

"Well, don't be out late tonight. Make sure you eat when you get home. And keep an eye on your cousin. If Hester finds out her boy's still drinking, she'll have another heart attack."

5

THE PARTY WAS inside a barn on a smallholding situated a few miles outside of town. Upon learning that his parents would be away on business until the weekend, the host of the party—an eighteen-year-old called Harry—had immediately picked up his phone and started texting around. Several vehicles were already parked in the wide yard when Blake pulled up. Loud, pulsating music blared from the open barn doors and rattled the car windows. Switching off the engine, she flashed a side look at Kenver, who was sitting in the passenger seat. He was wearing black skinny jeans, a black short-sleeved t-shirt with a giant white skull on the front, and his tattooed arms on full display. He'd flattened his hair down with oil and combed it into a perfect side parting, although the look wouldn't last long with his curls being so robust. It was a family trait that Blake hadn't inherited.

"You're looking very fresh," she said. "Which is a surprise considering this morning you looked like death warmed up."

Kenver shrugged. "I'm a creature of the night."

He had been smoking weed when she'd picked him up. Her

car stank of it, the fumes seeping through his pores. Blake had driven all the way with the windows cranked down. She shifted her gaze to the barn, which was lit up by strings of colourful fairy lights hanging from its external walls. A path of solar lights was staked in the ground, leading from the yard to the barn doors. Blake stared at the multitude of parked cars.

"So, not only am I going to a children's party, the guests are all drunk drivers. *Great.*"

"Or maybe there are other adults here of a certain age acting as chaperones."

"I'm not even ten years older than you. And I'm nobody's chaperone."

Kenver pushed open the passenger door and flashed her a playful smile. "Well, come on then."

At the peripheries of the fairy lights, the evening had already turned impenetrably black. It alarmed Blake how dark it got in the countryside. With no streetlamps or light pollution from nearby towns it was almost primal. As a child returning home from school on dark winter evenings, the race from the family car to the house had been an ordeal filled with terror, one that she'd never fully outgrown. At least in Manchester the night had a tinge of green to it, allowing her to see shapes and shadows. Her eyes flicked back to the barn. Lit up like a Christmas tree, it made her feel safe.

Kenver was already halfway across the yard, no doubt heading straight towards whatever makeshift bar stood inside. Blake watched him disappear through the large open doors. Perhaps her parents were right. Perhaps she shouldn't be going to a party with someone who was clearly fighting a losing battle against alcohol. She would talk to him. Not tonight, but tomorrow. Because tonight was about finding Lucy.

As she entered the barn, a deafening roar of dance music crashed over her like a tidal wave, shaking her bones and making her heart thrum. There had to be at least a hundred young people inside, all drinking, dancing, and laughing. It was only eight-thirty, but there were already sickly looking teens slumped in chairs and an acrid stench of nearby vomit hanging in the air. Blake had been like that once, so eager to impress her friends that she'd been unwilling to pace her drinking. She had quickly realised that no one was impressed by lightweight pukers.

She had already lost Kenver in the crowd. Where had all these young people come from? The same old story, she supposed. Once word had spread that a college friend's parents were away, everyone came looking for a party: friends, friends of friends, even random strangers. She could only imagine the horror if the host's parents suddenly happened to come home early. At least he had wisely chosen the barn instead of the house. But it wasn't the sheer number of people crammed into the barn that alarmed Blake the most. It was how young they all were.

She felt ancient, an old crone turning to dust and blowing away on the breeze. As if reading her thoughts, two teenage girls sauntered past and stared in her direction. One leaned in and shouted to the other: "Who brought their mum?"

Steeling herself, Blake waded into the crowd, sliding between gyrating bodies and groups that were locked in impenetrable circles, the clique still very much alive and well in today's young world. Long picnic tables had been set up along the left side of the barn, with a row of punch bowls on top and piles of empty spirit bottles underneath. Blake thought she saw Kenver standing nearby, chatting to a group of young men, but then the crowd shifted and she lost him again.

She pushed her way in deeper, steering young people out of her way. She didn't know what she was doing, or where she was going. The idea had been to ask questions. Had anyone seen Lucy since Sunday night? Had she called anyone? Had she texted, or whatever young people used to communicate these days? But Blake was fast coming to the conclusion that this party was the wrong place to ask. People were drunk. The music was too loud. But then, in the corner of the room, she saw Jasmine Baker. It was a surprise to see her at a party, considering that her best friend had been missing for two days now.

Blake pushed her way towards Jasmine and the three young women huddling around her.

"Hi," she said, half shouting.

Jasmine flinched. Her friends stared at Blake uncertainly.

"What are you doing here?" Jasmine said, squirming. No one wanted to be seen talking to an adult at a party like this.

Blake smiled. "I was about to ask you the same thing."

Jasmine said nothing as she stared at the plastic cup of alcohol in her hand

"Well, I thought I'd have a look around," Blake said. "Ask questions. See if anyone might know where Lucy is."

Jasmine's friends all stared at each other, then back at Blake.

"Do any of you know Lucy?"

"We all went to school together," Jasmine said.

"Really? When was the last time any of you saw her?"

One of the young women shrugged. Another one said, "A couple of weeks ago? I think."

"You haven't heard from her since Sunday?"

They shook their heads. The music continued to rattle Blake's ribcage. Voices rose and fell. The group of friends shifted on their feet, uncomfortable in her presence.

"The police came," Jasmine said, as if that would somehow satisfy Blake and make her leave.

"You told them everything that you told me?"

"Yes. They said they were making enquiries and checking social media. But that's all. Shouldn't they have a search party out looking for her?"

"I'm sure they're doing everything they can."

"What?" Jasmine said, squinting. The music had grown even louder.

"I said hopefully they'll find her soon." Blake stared at the friends, who all shared the same doubtful expression. "Well, bye then. Call me if you find out anything."

Blake backed away and was absorbed by the crowd. She pushed and shoved her way to the bar area, feeling claustrophobic and hemmed in. Staring down the length of the bar, she spied Kenver, who was clutching a half empty bottle of vodka and laughing with a handsome man in his early twenties. Blake rolled her eyes. She had given him a lift here, but there was no way in hell she was going to wait until the end to drag his drunken backside home. Someone turned the music up again. Blake winced. How could she ask questions about Lucy if she couldn't even hear her own thoughts?

She decided to leave. Kenver would no doubt find a bed for the night. She was heading to tell him so when, above the din, she heard someone call her name.

"Blake? I thought that was you."

A woman in her mid-thirties with short dark hair and dressed in fitted blue jeans and a white blouse was staring at her.

"Judy Moon. Long time, no see. This is the last place I expected to find you."

Judy was carrying a bottle of water in one hand and her

mobile phone in the other. "I know, right? What are you doing here?"

"Trying to find out what I can about Lucy Truscott. Christine asked me to help look for her."

Judy's expression turned grave. "Oh, I know. The poor thing's worried sick. She's convinced something terrible has happened to Lucy."

"You've talked to her?"

"Of course I have. We're friends." Judy smiled, then winced as a round of cheers flew up from the crowd, the cause for the celebration unknown. "Mum said she saw you in the supermarket yesterday. I didn't know you were in town."

"What?"

"I said I didn't know you were in town."

"I've only been back a couple of days. Just helping Mum while she recovers from surgery."

"I heard she'd had a fall."

Blake leaned in. "Sorry, what? It's so loud in here."

Grabbing Blake by the arm, Judy guided her through the jostling crowds and out through the barn doors. The temperature had dropped and darkness had crept in a little closer.

"Anyway, I hope your mum's okay," Judy said. "So, you're back for a while?"

Blake shrugged, not wanting to think about the answer. "Just until Mum's more mobile. Anyway, what are you doing here at the party?"

"Same thing as you. Trying to find out about Lucy."

"For a story?"

Judy tightened her jaw. "No. For Christine."

"Sorry. Of course. How's the job going?"

"You know. Fine for a local rag. And yes, to help Christine,

I'm thinking about writing a piece for the paper about Lucy's disappearance. Maybe it will help to jog people's memories."

"Maybe."

"Have you found out anything?"

"Only what Christine already knows. Lucy went for a drink with Jasmine Baker on Sunday evening, parted ways around ten, and somewhere between the Badger Inn and home, she vanished."

"Strange, isn't it? Of course the CCTV on the high street isn't working. Never is. And so far, according to Detective Constable Angove, there are no eyewitnesses."

Blake looked up. "Rory? He's a DC now?"

Judy nodded and smiled wryly. "Moved over to CID last year. I'm sure he'd love to know you're in town."

Despite the cold, Blake felt her face warm up.

Judy leaned in closer, her expression growing more serious. "It's weird, but ever since Lucy disappeared, I can't stop thinking about Demelza."

"Me too. I just hope that wherever Lucy is, she's safe."

Judy stared back into the barn at the surging crowd of young people. "Look at them all. So young and innocent, without a care in the world. Any one of them could disappear."

"One of them already has," Blake said, following her gaze.

"I mean right now. They're all so oblivious, distracted by hormones and booze. It would be easy for someone to sneak into that barn and drag one of the girls off into the night. Would anyone even notice? Would they be too wasted to care?"

"Jesus, Judy. That's a bit dark, isn't it?"

"But it's true. Do you know how many people are reported missing every year in this country? A hundred and eighty thousand. That's one every ninety seconds. Last year, I looked into all of the women who had disappeared in Cornwall in the last twenty years. There were so many, Blake. Yes, most of them turned up relatively safe and sound. But what about the others? The ones like Demelza? I wrote a feature article all about it. And you know what? My editor refused to run it. He said it was too gloomy, that we're not that kind of paper. All I was trying to do was remind people of their faces."

Blake's stomach turned and twisted. She watched the party goers through the open barn doors, saw all their young faces lit up with smiles and laughter and drunkenness, seemingly oblivious that one of them had been missing for two days. She turned away and stared into the darkness that lurked at the edges of the lit up path.

"Statistics," Judy said, bitterly. "That's what these women become. Just a bunch of numbers."

Blake crossed her arms and shivered. She hoped that Lucy wouldn't become just another statistic in the annals of history. She hoped she would find her way home.

6

CHRISTINE TRUSCOTT LIVED on a modern housing development on the east side of town. In contrast to the terraced brick mining cottages that populated the west side, these new homes were bland and identical looking. But they were big and airy, perfect for young families and those preferring size over character. Blake had arrived at Christine's home just after ten a.m., and had been shown in by Christine's older sister, Leslie. She didn't know why she had been compelled to come here; she had nothing in the way of new information, and she was sure Christine could do without unnecessary visitors right now. But Blake had been up most of the night worrying, and although she didn't see much of Christine these days, she cared very much about one of her oldest friends. Now, she sat in Christine's living room, with its cream carpet and beige sofas, while Christine sat next to her sister, staring coolly at Blake.

"I'm sorry," Blake said. "I wish there was more I could tell you, but if the CCTV wasn't working on the high street that night . . . I'll keep asking around. Someone had to have seen her."

Christine leaned forward and pulled a tissue from a box on the coffee table. Her complexion was deathly pale, accentuating the shadows beneath her bloodshot eyes. She clearly hadn't slept since Lucy had disappeared, but she would need to sleep soon. Hope and desperation could only fuel a body for so long.

"People don't just disappear into thin air," she said, dabbing her wet face.

Blake, who was still wearing her jacket, tried to swallow. "What about the police?"

"They're going door-to-door, making enquiries. They've taken Lucy's laptop to examine, and they're trying to get access to her mobile phone. They're hoping they'll be able to track her location from it, or at least check her messages." Christine crushed the tissue in her fist. Her lower lip quivered. "I've been calling Lucy's phone, over and over. At first it would ring and then go to voicemail. But now it doesn't ring at all. What if I've used up the last of her battery? What if she can't call now because of me?"

The devastation in her voice hit Blake like a fist, punching the air from her lungs.

Christine sobbed. "Why can't anyone find her?"

Her sister Leslie rubbed her back and regarded Blake with disdain. Three years older than Christine, Leslie had never been Blake's biggest fan. She had even accused her of being a bad influence in the past. Which Blake couldn't exactly deny. As teenagers, she had been daring and rebellious while Christine had been quiet and reserved. It was Blake who had persuaded Christine to go to parties with the older kids. It was Blake who had given Christine her first drink of alcohol. At the time, she had seen it as her duty to help her friend come of age. But then Christine had fallen pregnant with Lucy. Ever the high achiever,

Leslie had placed the blame at Blake's feet for leading Christine astray. It seemed that she hadn't changed her mind, even after all these years.

"The police are sending a Family Liaison Officer over later this morning," Leslie said, handing her sister another tissue. "They're talking about organising a press conference for the local news."

That was good. It meant they were taking Lucy's disappearance seriously. Blake forced herself to smile. "Someone, somewhere, has to know something. Maybe they just haven't put two and two together yet. The press conference could jog their memory."

She didn't know what else to say. Did she tell Christine to stay hopeful? Did she promise that Lucy would be home soon? She had been missing for three days now, vanished without a trace. But Blake knew that wasn't true. In the ten years she'd been a private investigator, she had dealt with occasional missing person cases. There was always a trace left behind. Always. Finding it was the difficult, sometimes impossible part. Which was why she couldn't offer Christine false hope right now.

The three women were silent, each lost in thought, when the home telephone on the side table shattered the silence. Startled, Christine's hand flew to her mouth.

"Lucy!" she gasped, and jumped up from the sofa. She crossed the room in one swift movement, snatched up the receiver, and pressed it to her ear. "Lucy, baby? Is that you?"

Blake caught her breath and flashed a look at Leslie, who stood and went over to her sister.

"Hello? Is someone there?"

Christine twisted around, a look of confusion on her face. She stared helplessly at Leslie, who took the receiver from Christine's hand then pressed the speaker phone button so they could all hear.

Blake got to her feet.

More tears squeezed from Christine's eyes. "Lucy? Sweetheart? Tell me that's you."

A long, deep breath filtered through the speaker. And then a man's voice, deep and undulating, began to hum a nursery rhyme.

Leslie stared at the phone, her mouth half open. Christine's eyes were wild and searching.

"Who is that?" she asked.

The man stopped humming. He began to speak in a forced stage whisper that made Christine recoil.

"I saw Lucy," he said, a smile evident in his hushed voice. "She was dancing with the devil."

A sliver of ice slipped between Blake's shoulder blades.

"Hang up," Leslie said. "It's just some sick pervert."

She moved to cut off the call but Christine gripped her wrist.

"You saw my girl?" she said to the man. "You saw Lucy?"

"Yes," the voice whispered. "I saw her dancing with the devil. Dancing like a whore."

"It's a prank call," Leslie said, angry now. "Hang up the phone."

But Christine was frozen, her grip on her sister's wrist like a clamp. "Who is this? Where's Lucy? What have you done to my little girl?"

The man spoke again, his hushed voice like spiders crawling over Blake's spine. "I saw Lucy dancing with the devil. Dancing with the devil at Ding Dong. And now she must be punished."

A terrible, gut-wrenching scream burst from the speaker

phone. Leslie turned white. Christine raked fingers down her own face.

"Mum, please help me!" the voice shrieked. "Oh God, it burns! It burns! Oh, God, it—"

There was a click and the phone line went dead.

Blake stared in horror.

"No," Christine breathed. "Lucy? Lucy, baby? Where are you?"

Beside her, Leslie was motionless.

Christine's face twisted grotesquely. "That wasn't her. It can't be her. It wasn't. It wasn't!"

Blake was paralysed, her mind trying to process what they had all just heard. Leslie began to wince as Christine dug nails into her wrist.

"Call the police," Blake said. Neither of the women moved. "Christine. Leslie. Call the police. Now!"

Leslie managed to free her wrist from her sister's grip. Christine stared into space, her mouth moving silently up and down.

Blake hurried towards the door.

"Where are you going?" Leslie called after her.

Blake peered over her shoulder. Christine was watching her now, the light gone from her eyes.

"To Ding Dong Mine," she said.

Then she was running from the house and racing towards her car.

THE CAR SHOT along the twisty, narrow country road, tyres careering in and out of potholes. Blake was driving too fast and she knew it. But the terror clawing her insides was spreading out of control. The caller's voice still whispered in her ear, cold, taunting, and filled with glee. She told herself it was a prank call. It had to be. But in the darkest part of her heart, she knew it was all true.

As she drove deeper into the countryside the landscape grew more remote. Hamlets and villages gave way to lonely moorland dotted with heather and gorse, which stretched out far into the distance. The road curled sharply and Blake spun the wheel, tyres skidding on the uneven surface. She eased her foot off the accelerator pedal. She would be no good to Lucy or anyone else if she was dead.

Above her the sky was huge and rolling, an endless wash of mottled, grey clouds tinged with black and threatening rain. A silhouette appeared on the horizon, a narrow ruin of a building with a tall, crumbling chimney stack that reached past its flat roof like a finger pointing to the heavens.

I saw Lucy dancing with the devil at Ding Dong.

"Please," Blake whispered. "Please let it be a sick joke."

A working tin mine until its closure in 1877, Ding Dong was situated beneath the moors of West Penwith, in the parish of Madron. An amalgamation of sixteen smaller mines, it was believed to be the oldest tin mine in Cornwall, and almost certainly one of the oldest in the United Kingdom. Legend told of its history dating back to Roman times. But legend also told of the mine being a source of copper for King Solomon's temple, and of Jesus Christ visiting Ding Dong during the Roman occupation. Just as strange as the myths was the mine's name. A commonly held belief was that Ding Dong had been named after the bell that used to ring out from Madron Church, signalling the end of the miners' work shift.

Parking the car on a narrow verge on the roadside, Blake switched off the engine and sat for a short while, trying to get a hold on her fear. Then she climbed out, shut the door, and pulled her coat tightly around her body. It was cold up here on the moor, the moaning wind only adding to the sense of desolation.

The ruined engine house loomed in the near distance. Blake felt the history around her. This was a place filled with ghosts and long dead things. She just hoped that Lucy was not among them. Locking the car, she stepped off the road and onto the moor, quickly finding the thin, stony path that led towards the shell of the engine house. Another ruin stood on her left, no more than a few crumbling walls that had once formed the mine's counting house. Blake's eyes darted to the left then the right, searching for signs of life. Sometimes dog walkers could be found up here, but not today. As far as she could tell, she was alone.

On a clear day at Ding Dong, you could see right across to the coastline and the sandy beach of Mount's Bay, where a tiny coastal island named St Michael's Mount had sat for thousands of years. The 12th century castle at its summit was where the first sighting of the Spanish Armada had been made in 1588, and a beacon had been ignited, starting a chain of fires that would light up the south coast to warn of the pending invasion. To distract herself from creeping dread, Blake tried to locate the coastline, but a fine mist was creeping along the edges of the moor, rolling in from the sea. Sometimes up here, a mist could turn into a thick fog before your eyes, and you'd suddenly find yourself disoriented and stumbling blindly along, which was not ideal for walking on top of long abandoned mine shafts.

Blake quickened her pace, stones crunching and wet mud squelching under the soles of her boots. An icy blast of wind stung her face and whipped her hair into a frenzy.

She was six feet away from the engine house when she slid to a halt. She stared up as it towered above her like a giant. Built from Cornish stone, the engine house had withstood hundreds of years of exposure to rain and wind. With open stone windows and a wrought iron gate blocking the front entrance, it had the appearance of a miniature castle fallen into ruin. Some restoration work had been carried out in recent years, mostly to repair the chimney stack, and the engine house was now protected as a World Heritage Site. Blake wrinkled her nose. An unpleasant smell was hanging in the air, like meat burning on a spit.

She glanced back over her shoulder, half expecting someone to be there. But all she saw was the bleak moorland and the bank of mist slowly creeping towards her. The wind changed direction. The scorched smell grew more intense. Blake stared at the iron gate. She tried to step forward, but her legs refused to cooperate.

"Lucy?" Her voice was small and weak. "Lucy Truscott? Are you here?"

She managed to get her feet working again and stepped towards the engine house. Moisture gleamed on its stonework. Effervescent lichen glowed in the cracks. Reaching the gate, she swallowed hard and peered inside. The interior was empty. She saw pools of rainwater, sludge on the ground, and a cemented up hole where an old steam engine had once sucked up water from the depths of the mine below. And then Blake looked up and across.

"Oh fuck!"

Her hand flew up to her mouth. She staggered back, tripping over her own feet, then hurried around the side of the engine house. Tears stung her eyes and nausea climbed her throat. Rounding the corner, Blake came to a standstill and stared in horror.

There was another entrance into the engine house. Lucy Truscott had been placed in the centre. Her left arm was stretched out horizontally, forming half of a cross, and a thick masonry nail had been hammered through her upturned palm, pinning her to the wall. Her right arm was bent at the elbow, where a second nail had been driven into the stonework, while her forearm reached across her stomach, the palm turned upwards. Her feet were positioned in a T shape, and two further nails had been hammered through them, pinning her to the ground.

But the crucifixion was not what sickened Blake the most. Nor was it Lucy's nakedness, or the terrible patches of burns and blisters that covered her skin, the outer layers peeled back to reveal charred muscle and sinew.

It was her eyes. They were gone. All that remained were two melted black holes in her tipped back head, staring lifelessly across the moor.

Blake slid one foot back, then the other. She fell to her hands and knees across a metal grate that covered the old mine shaft. Sucking in ragged breaths and fighting off sickness, she stared into the inky darkness below.

"I'm sorry," she whispered. "I'm sorry I couldn't get to you in time."

She had to get away from here. To run back to the car and drive as fast as she could all the way back to Manchester.

But she couldn't. Not yet.

Lucy Truscott was dead, crucified and covered in burns, her hopes and dreams turned to ashes. Blake was desperate to pull out the nails and lay her softly on the grass. But this was a crime scene now and Blake was already contaminating it.

Climbing to her feet, Blake forced herself to stare at Lucy. Bile fizzed in the back of her throat. Her gaze dropped from Lucy's eyeless face, down her body, and along the length of her left arm. There was something on her wrist that Blake hadn't noticed before. She took a single step closer and stared at the textile band.

Confusion swarmed her mind. She blinked, telling herself she was imagining things. But the bracelet was still there, its criss-cross rainbow pattern defying the abhorrence of her flesh.

Somewhere at the back of Blake's mind, a memory woke up.

The distant wail of sirens filtered into her ears. The Truscotts had called the police.

Her eyes still fixed on the bracelet, Blake let out a moan. The mist continued to roll in as the sirens grew louder.

_____

8

EVENING DESCENDED OVER THE MOOR. The fog persisted, making it difficult for the Crime Scene Investigation team to do their job. Blake had already been processed, her shoe prints taken along with a DNA swab that would help to eliminate her presence from the murder site. She had then been directed to the police station in Truro, Cornwall's only city—and a cathedral city at that—where she had spent the last few hours answering questions about how she came to discover Lucy Truscott's body at Ding Dong Mine.

Now she sat at a desk in a cramped room, sipping coffee from a plastic cup while a uniformed officer finished writing up her statement. Terrible images flashed in her mind, images that she knew would haunt her later tonight, crawling from the depths of her dreams to wake her screaming.

Poor Lucy Truscott, she thought. Poor Christine.

She imagined her friend at home, a traumatised, hysterical mess, her insides ripped open by a terrible, gaping chasm of grief. At least her sister was with her. Hopefully she'd been given strong sedatives, too.

The uniformed police officer, a young man in his early twenties, looked up from the paperwork and asked Blake if she would like more coffee.

Blake stared numbly. "Let's just get this over with."

All she wanted was to go home to her parents. It was funny how that desperate need didn't fade as an adult when troubled times arose. Lucy wasn't the first dead body Blake had ever seen, but it was the first she'd witnessed with such horrific injuries.

Not injuries, she told herself. Brutal, deliberately inflicted wounds.

Lucy's killer had wanted her to suffer. The way her body had been posed was deliberate too, but Blake had no idea why.

Finished with the statement, the police officer slid it across the table for Blake to read over and sign. But as her eyes skimmed over the words, her mind kept returning to Ding Dong Mine, and she had to go back to the top of the statement and start over. It was all there, everything Blake could remember about what had happened that morning. Everything except for one small detail.

The bracelet on Lucy's wrist.

It looked just like the friendship bracelets Blake and her friends had worn in their final summer together all those years ago, before they went their separate ways. Blake, Judy, Christine, and Demelza. The Forever Four.

Blake had to be mistaken. Perhaps the one Lucy had been wearing was a different design, because kids these days still wore friendship bracelets, didn't they? Or perhaps Christine had kept hers all these years and given it to Lucy as a rite of passage into adulthood, which she would now never reach.

Something else was troubling Blake. Lucy's body was covered in terrible burns, yet the friendship bracelet was intact. A little worn, yes. The colours had faded greatly. But it was clean and undamaged.

She shut her eyes, exhaustion making them sting. When she opened them again, the words on the statement blurred together.

Why hadn't she told the police that she recognised the bracelet? Was it because she was jumping to conclusions? Demelza had disappeared eighteen years ago and hadn't been seen since. Lucy disappeared three days ago, but her body had already been found. And her killer had called to torment her mother.

Was there a connection? Or was shock and horror blurring the boundaries of what was real and imagined?

Nausea swam in Blake's stomach. She glanced at the police officer, who was checking his mobile phone as he waited for Blake. Picking up the pen, she signed the statement and pushed it across the table.

"Done," she said. "Can I go home now?"

———

As she was shown through the offices and back towards the reception area, Blake struggled to remain steady on her feet. Lucy's horribly burned face peered at her from the recesses of her mind. It was a twenty-minute drive home. Twenty minutes too long in her current state. She was debating whether to call a taxi then pick up her car in the morning, when two plainclothes detectives with grave expressions entered the building. Blake recognised one immediately and her shoulders sank.

"Blake?" he said, stopping in front of her.

"Hello, Rory."

Detective Constable Rory Angove was in his mid-thirties. He was of average height with a slim build, and had almond-shaped eyes and small, protruding ears that reminded Blake of a Cornish Piskie. She had told him so once years ago, meaning it as a term of endearment. But comparing Rory to a mythical sprite in front of his fellow police cadets had done little for his ego.

"I heard you were the one to find the body," Rory said, concern creasing his eyes. "Are you all right?"

Blake shook her head. "I honestly don't know how to answer that. Which I suppose means I'm not."

The detective standing next to Rory cleared his throat. He was in his mid-to-late forties, tall and handsome, with broad shoulders and a little grey in his hair.

"You two know each other?" he asked Rory.

Blake detected a trace of a London accent.

"Yes, Sarge. This is Blake Hollow. We . . . grew up together. Blake, this is Detective Sergeant Will Turner."

DS Turner regarded Blake. "Sorry you had to be the one to find the body. I'm assuming someone's taken your statement?"

"Signed and delivered." The friendship bracelet flashed in her mind. "Are you part of the investigation?"

Turner nodded.

"Do you know that he called Christine? We heard Lucy screaming. She was in so much pain. But it had to have been a recording because I got to Ding Dong in under fifteen minutes, and there was no way that Lucy had died just before I found her. Rigor mortis had already set in. Her forearm was bent across her stomach with nothing to hold it in place."

DS Turner's shoulders stiffened as he glanced around the reception area.

"This isn't the place to discuss it," he said in a low voice. "We have officers at Miss Truscott's house trying to gather as much information as we can. Obviously, everything is very raw right now."

Just then, the entrance doors slid open and a gaunt looking woman in her early sixties came rushing in. She swept past the trio, barely registering them as she headed straight for the reception desk.

Blake's heart jumped into her throat. She watched the woman place her hands on the lip of the reception desk and lean in until her face was almost touching the protective glass screen. The duty officer on the other side leaned back a little. The woman spoke quickly and at a low volume. Blake couldn't hear what she was saying, but she could sense the desperation emanating from her in waves.

"Blake?" Rory's voice sounded far away.

The woman glanced over her shoulder. Blake quickly twisted away.

"Who is that?" DS Turner asked quietly, his eyes fixed on the woman, who had now turned back to the duty officer.

Rory shifted on his feet. "Faith Penrose. Her daughter Demelza vanished back when we were teenagers. She still comes in every now and then, wanting to know if we've learned anything. I guess Lucy's murder must be bringing it all back."

Rory and Blake glanced at each other, then awkwardly looked away. Over at the reception desk, the duty officer was shaking his head. Faith Penrose's shoulders drooped. Her chin sank down to her chest. Slowly, she turned, and with her gaze fixed on the floor, she shuffled across the reception area and disappeared through the front doors.

Shame burned in Blake's chest.

"Well, we have your statement, Ms Hollow," Turner said. "In the meantime, if there's anything else you can remember, any small detail . . ."

He fished one of his cards from his wallet and handed it to Blake, who produced her own card in return. Turner raised an eyebrow. "A private investigator?"

The police were never quite sure how to deal with private investigators, particularly when a licence wasn't currently required to practice in the UK. Blake had a licence and she was damn good at her job, too. Which was why she was surprised that she still hadn't mentioned the friendship bracelet

It's because you're mistaken, she thought. You're tired and in shock.

Her eyes were still fixed on the entrance doors through which Demelza's mother had vanished like a ghost.

"Blake's been working as a PI in Manchester for years," Rory said.

DS Turner pocketed Blake's card. "I see. Well, this is a police investigation now, Ms Hollow. Thank you for your help and please get home safely. We'll be in touch if we have further questions."

He smiled at Blake, but there was a hardness to his gaze, as if he didn't trust her. Right now, she was too tired to take offence. Saying goodbye, she watched him nod at the officer at the reception desk, who shrugged, before heading through a door in the far wall.

Rory's dark eyes glistened with worry.

"Are you sure you're okay?" he asked.

"Of course I'm not okay, Rory. Far from it. But thank you for asking."

"Judy Moon told me you're back in town for a while. I didn't know that. Maybe we could go for a drink one evening?"

Blake shot him a look. The last time the two had been alone, they'd drank way too much and ended up in a sweaty tangle of limbs on Rory's living room floor. For Blake, it had been a pleasurable if awkward nod to their former teen relationship. Rory had seen it as an opportunity to start over. Until Blake had made haste back to Manchester.

"So, you're a DC now?" she asked him, avoiding the question. "You're working on Lucy's case, too?"

Rory paled slightly. "It's my first murder case. Never thought it would be someone I knew."

"You were friends with Lucy?"

"No. She's—she was—eighteen. I meant because of Christine. Although me and Chrissie mix in different circles these days."

Me too, Blake thought. Except my circle is three hundred miles away.

"So, about that drink." Rory was staring at her again, seemingly oblivious that he was asking Blake out on the same day she'd discovered the brutalised body of their mutual friend's daughter.

Her stomach churned and she thought she would vomit. But then the main entrance doors were opening again. To Blake's relief it wasn't Faith Penrose returning. It was her father. Ed spotted her immediately and walked over. He muttered hello to Rory, who smiled politely and told Blake he would give her a call in the week, then hurried in the direction of DS Turner.

Alone, Blake stared at her father and felt a sudden urge to throw herself into his arms, but she resisted. "Dad, what are you doing here?"

Ed stood, upright and uncomfortable, his eyes darting around the station interior. "Your mother was worried about you. Everyone's heard the news. It's a terrible thing."

"It really is."

"How was it you that found her?"

Blake rubbed her stiff neck. "It's a long story, Dad. One I don't really want to talk about right now."

"Right on. Well, I'm here to drive you home. Your mother's orders."

"But my car is here."

"Then it's a good job your mother already thought of that and made me take the bus."

They stared at each other, silence thickening the air.

"Thanks, Dad," Blake said. "I mean it."

Ed gave a curt nod towards the door. "Well, if you're done here, we should go. Your mother's on her own."

He paused, opened his mouth to say something, then shut it again.

Tears welled in Blake's eyes, threatening to spill over. The urge to hug her father was slipping out of her control. But Ed was already walking through the swing doors like a man on a desperate mission. Blake followed him, wiping her face with her sleeve. She was glad that he was here, even if it was only because her mother had made him come.

The air was cold, the dark sky clear and filled with countless stars that glittered above the dual carriageway. Blake sat in the passenger seat, feeling displaced that she was not behind the wheel of her own car. She glanced at her father, who was just a silhouette, silent behind the wheel. The road was empty, the evening's traffic long gone. It was just the two of them alone in a dark expanse. Blake focused on the shapes and shadows shooting past the passenger window as the day's terrible events replayed in her mind. Lucy Truscott's eyeless face peered at her from the abyss. Shivering, she stared at her father as he expelled a deep, heavy sigh. She couldn't see his expression, but she sensed the tension in his body.

"Thanks again for coming to get me," she said.

Her father gave a short nod and continued to drive in silence. Was he mad at her? It was hard to tell sometimes. Ed seemed to have two states. Quiet and angry. The anger erupted rarely, and it was usually caused by a problem at work. But the quiet was always present, and it had so many layers that, over the years, Blake had been learning to decrypt her father's body language like a cipher.

She stared through the windscreen, lured by the green glint of cat's eyes in the centre of the road. The more she focused on them, the heavier her eyelids grew.

"Have you eaten anything?" Ed's voice rumbled in the darkness.

"Not since last night. After today, I don't think I'll eat again."

Ed heaved his shoulders and let out a deep sigh. "You got to eat something, maid, or you'll make yourself sick."

The hum of the engine thrummed between them.

"Dad, are you angry?"

Ed's gaze remained fixed on the road, his hands placed perfectly at ten to two on the steering wheel.

"It's a crying shame about Christine's girl," he said. "I hope they catch the monster who did that."

"You didn't answer my question."

Another long, drawn-out sigh. "I don't understand what you were doing up there. You were meant to be at home helping your mother."

"Christine asked for my help," Blake said, instantly regretting that she'd opened the door to this conversation. "My job by its very definition is to help people."

"Except that wasn't your job. Your mum's been at home, struggling and worrying about you. She shouldn't be worrying about anything right now."

Tiredness pressed down on Blake's shoulders, but a spark ignited in her chest. "Lucy was missing. Was I meant to ignore that? Pretend that she wasn't? Christine is my friend, Dad."

"All I'm saying is your mother expected you at home. That's why you came back, wasn't it? To help out while she gets better?"

"And I am," Blake snapped. "Because no one else seems to be. Why is it that I'm having to take time off from work? Why can't you? She's your wife."

There was a brief silence, then Ed forced out a sharp breath. That was another way Blake could decode how her father was feeling: through the length and depth of his sighs.

"From what I hear you don't have any work to take time off from," he said.

"Ouch, Dad." Blake flinched and turned to stare out of the passenger window.

They drove the rest of the distance in muted silence, headlights slicing through the pitch darkness of the countryside. Anger and guilt seethed in Blake's veins. Her neck ached but she refused to turn around. The car exited the A30 onto a two-lane road. Houses appeared. Then they were moving through the high street of Wheal Marow. It was empty, a ghost town punctuated by pools of orange streetlight that fought back against the night. Blake pressed her face to the window as they passed by the Badger's Inn. How easy it would have been for Lucy's killer to take her as she walked home along the empty street, not a soul around to see.

The town disappeared in the rear-view mirror and the car was plunged into darkness again as they drove along the country lane towards home. Ten minutes later, Ed turned onto his sloping drive and parked the car. Blake stared up at her parents' house. A light was on in the downstairs hallway, illuminating the glass partitions of the front door. She clenched her hands together and pressed her fingertips into her palms. Was her father right? Had she let her mother down?

But she had just endured one of the worst days of her life. She had seen horrors no one should ever have to see. And yet, to her father, she was a disappointment. Blake glared at him in the darkness, words fighting to push through her lips. She swallowed them down, along with her anger. Just like she always did when it came to her father.

Ed opened the driver door. His eyes searched her out in the darkness.

"Are you coming in?"

Silently, Blake opened the passenger door and staggered outside. She shut the door and it slammed loudly. Ed locked the car. He handed her the key fob then stood for a moment, swaying back and forth.

"Your mum is already in bed," he said quietly. "She'll want to see you, but best keep it short."

Blake squeezed the key fob in her hand until her fingers hurt.

Swallow it down. Swallow it all down.

"I'll be there in a minute. I need some fresh air."

Ed paused, seemingly reluctant to leave her behind.

Go, Blake thought. Just leave me alone!

Expelling another heavy sigh, he crossed the driveway and went up the front step. Blake watched him disappear inside, saw the way he hesitated before closing the front door. A tear slipped from her eye and she snatched it away. Then, with heavy feet and a troubled mind, she slowly shook her head and followed her father inside.

9

Morning came. Blake had slept badly, tossing and turning on the uncomfortable single mattress as terrible images kept her awake. When she did sleep, Lucy Truscott's horribly burned body was waiting for her. Blake sat up with the blankets pulled up to her neck and the headboard digging into her back. Her body was exhausted. Her mind was thick and heavy like uncooked dough. Her eyes wandered over the cramped room, catching the light that seeped between the curtains. A chill hung in the air, the radiators only now coming to life, knocking and clunking as they filled with hot water. She missed her flat in Manchester with its city views of the River Irwell, and her king-sized bed in which she could sleep with limbs splayed like a starfish. Not that she ever slept much there either.

The radio alarm clock announced it was seven a.m. Her mobile phone lay next to it. She still hadn't contacted Christine Truscott. She wanted to, but what could she say? Besides, she doubted Christine was receiving calls right now.

Somewhere in the house, she heard voices followed by the unmistakable thud of her father's work boots on the stairs. Blake stiffened. Last night, all she'd needed from him was a hug and a few comforting words. Not a lecture. And yet, somehow, she felt as if she'd let *him* down.

The toilet flushed, sending water rushing through the pipes in the walls. A minute later, Ed was on the move again, slowing down outside Blake's bedroom door before returning downstairs. The front door opened and closed. Soon after, she heard the rumble of the garage door opening, then her father's van driving away. Quiet resumed.

Blake sat, feeling wretched. She reached for her phone and tapped out a text message: *I'm so sorry, Chrissie. Call me if you need anything.* She hesitated, added three kisses and pressed send.

What else could she do in such a terrible situation?

Throwing back the sheets, Blake quickly made the bed and left the room. Downstairs was colder, the floorboards numbing her bare feet. Mary was awake and propped up on the sofa bed in the dining room. Her plastered leg was elevated on cushions and her eyes were glued to the television. On the screen was Lucy Truscott's school photograph. She had a kind, innocent face, with warm eyes that were filled with life and possibilities.

Blake shuddered. Those eyes were gone now.

The news report cut to a distant shot of Ding Dong Mine. The solemn voice of the reporter spoke over the images. Few details about the murder had been released so far, but the police would be working around the clock to apprehend Lucy's killer.

Mary glanced up from the sofa.

"Sorry, bird," she said, reaching for the remote.

Blake stepped into the room. "It's fine. Leave it for a minute."

They watched in silence as the camera cut to the news reporter, who was standing in the quiet cul-de-sac where Christine Truscott lived. It was unsettling to see Wheal Marow on television, like waking up in the middle of the night to find a burglar inside your home.

Mary hit the standby button on the remote, and the screen went blank. They were quiet, neither of them knowing what to say. Blake scuffed a foot on the floor, wishing she'd put on some warm clothes instead of staying in her pyjamas.

"Did Dad make you breakfast?" she asked, noticing the tired lines on her mother's face. Blake hadn't been the only one up all night.

"No. I wasn't hungry." Mary tipped her head to one side. "How are you feeling?"

"Awful. And guilty."

"Whatever for?"

"I didn't find Lucy in time."

"It's not your fault, Blake. You didn't do this."

Blake said nothing.

Mary returned to stare at the blank television screen. "That dear, sweet girl. And Christine! How do you come to terms with something like this?"

You don't, Blake thought, and a wave of grief rose up inside her.

It was as if Mary sensed it, because she opened her arms. "Come here."

Blake sank to her knees at the side of the sofa bed and fell into her mother's embrace.

"At least she's not suffering now," Mary whispered in her ear. "And the police will do their job. They'll catch the monster who did this."

Blake pulled back and stared at her mother. "You mean like how they did their job when Demelza disappeared?"

"Oh, Blake." Her mother sighed.

"What?"

"I was worried this business with poor Lucy would bring up all those bad memories again."

"Again? Mum, those memories never really went away."

Mother and daughter stared at each other. Mary's mouth twitched. Blake searched her mother's eyes for an answer that wasn't there.

"How's that leg of yours?" she asked, freeing herself and running fingers along Mary's cast. "Does it hurt?"

"It itches more than anything. Right in the middle of my thigh. I just can't seem to get to it."

Blake got up and looked around. She found a basket of wool and pulled out a long knitting needle. "Here, try this."

She watched Mary's face light up with relief as she slid the needle beneath the plaster and moved it up and down.

"Shall I make breakfast?"

"That would be nice. Just a little fruit and yogurt for me. And a nice, strong cup of tea."

Blake bent down and kissed her mother on the head. She was concerned by how tired and frail she looked. "I'll be right back."

In the kitchen, Blake made breakfast for her mother and a large mug of coffee for herself. She forced down two slices of toast and peanut butter, then returned to the dining room, where she set the breakfast tray on her mother's lap and adjusted the cushions behind her back.

"What are your plans for today?" Mary asked, warming her hands on the tea.

"I don't know. Hang around here, I suppose. I can do the housework."

"You know what you could do for me? You could finally sort out your things in the attic. Me and your father have been wanting to have a clear out for ages."

"Remind me what's up there again."

"You tell me. Things from when you were younger. It's all in boxes. You just need to go through them and decide what you want to take back with you and what you want to throw away."

"Fine, I'll take a look once I've showered and got you set up for the day."

The thought of delving into her past made Blake tense and uneasy.

"Blake, love?"

"Hmm?"

Mary was staring at her, a deep frown accentuating her tiredness. "I know what happened to Lucy is terrible, especially because she's Christine's girl. But I remember when Demelza disappeared and how much it changed you."

"She was my best friend, Mum. What's your point?"

"I don't want to see you go through that again. You get so obsessed with things. Besides, your father says —"

Blake clenched her jaw. "I don't need to know what Dad says right now. And I certainly didn't need the lecture he gave me last night."

"He's worried about you, that's all. We're not used to this kind of thing happening."

"And I am?"

"No, but with your job . . . I suppose sometimes you see the darker side of life."

"I've never seen someone nailed to a wall before, if that's what you mean. Certainly not my friend's daughter."

Mary winced, splashing tea over the edge of the cup and onto the tray.

"Sometimes, I think Dad would be happier if I had a nice husband who went to work while I stayed at home with the children," Blake said.

"There's nothing wrong with staying at home to raise your children. Nothing at all."

"I know that. But it's not who I am, Mum. I like my job. I'm good at it. And we wouldn't even be having this conversation if it was Alfie we were talking about."

Mary was staring at her plaster cast, pulling at a few loose threads of bandage that protruded at the edge.

Blake stared at her bare feet. "I'm sorry. It's been a rough couple of days and I'm tired."

Her mother nodded, but she wouldn't look at her. "Your father cares about you very much. He's just set in his ways."

Doesn't mean I have to accept it, Blake thought.

Reaching over, she kissed her mother's cheek and apologised again. "Do you need anything else?"

Mary shook her head and switched the television back on. The news report had finished and a morning chat show was playing.

Returning to the kitchen, Blake drank more coffee and quietly seethed.

10
———

THE ATTIC SPACE was dark and dusty, with loose planks placed over the ceiling joists as a makeshift gangway. Wind howled outside, disturbing the slates of the roof and making the rafters creak. Shapes and silhouettes wavered in the light flooding out from a battery-powered lamp. Crouched on her haunches, Blake was busy examining the contents of a large cardboard box that had been not-so-subtly labelled by her mother: 'For Blake - to take or throw away.'

Blake's parents had been meaning to convert the attic into another room for some time now, but apparently the entire two boxes she had found of her old belongings were standing in their way. She didn't feel like rooting around in her past right now, but it was better than thinking of Lucy Truscott.

Blowing on her hands then rubbing the palms together, she sifted through the contents of the box, finding old vinyl records and carefully rolled posters of now-defunct rock bands, a couple of stuffed toy animals, and an embarrassing teen romance novel. Why had she insisted on keeping these things when they had remained hidden in boxes for years like forgotten memories? She blew a strand of hair from her eyes. Maybe she'd keep the records; she'd been meaning to purchase a record player again. But the rest could go to charity or into the recycling bin.

Shoving the box to one side, she dragged the second over, sneezing in the dust as she peeled back the lid. A waft of aged paper, not unpleasant, drifted up from inside. The box contained a stack of old notebooks. Removing one, Blake caught her breath and groaned. Not notebooks. Old diaries.

Pressing the first one to her chest, she leaned over and stared through the open attic hatch. If her mother had ever gone through these boxes and found the diaries . . . Blake made a mental note to take them all with her when she returned to Manchester, or to burn them in the back garden later today. Steeling herself, she flipped through the pages of the diary and was immediately assaulted by the angst-ridden ruminations of fourteen-year-old Blake Hollow, who lamented about growing pains and menstruation and stupid boys who didn't know how lucky they were, and how utterly poisonous celery tasted. Wincing, she snapped the diary shut and sifted through the other volumes in the box. There were at least five years of her musings. A therapist's dream, she thought, before an idea came to her.

Removing all the diaries, she organised them into years and volumes, then selected the last diary she'd ever written. Silence settled on her shoulders as she flicked through the pages. She had been eighteen at the time of writing, the final entries recorded during her last summer in Cornwall before heading off to her new life in Manchester as a university student. Skim-reading a few entries, she noted that her thoughts had matured since the age of fourteen. Now she worried greatly about the future, about what her life might be like in Manchester, free and independent of her parents. She'd been more anxious than she remembered, which surprised her because she had always thought of herself as a confident teenager with ego to spare.

Blake continued to flip through the pages, her heart beginning to race uncomfortably, until she neared the end of the diary and that final, fateful summer. Her fingers froze on the page. She sat down on the loose planks, crossed her legs, and began to read.

Dear Diary,

Demelza is still missing. It's been forty-eight hours since she left the party but didn't make it home. It's so weird. I've sent her texts and left voicemails, but she's still not answering her phone. Christine hasn't heard from her and neither has Judy. We were all there at the party, but no one can remember her leaving. Only that she'd been in a bad mood all night and definitely wasn't having a good time. I tried asking her what was wrong, but she kept saying she was fine. I remember seeing her wander off to the side and talking to someone on the phone. That was the last time I saw her. I wonder who she called. I told Demelza's mum about the call, and I told the police when they interviewed me. Something feels wrong. People don't just disappear, and I don't think Demelza would have run away, no matter what everyone else says. We're best friends. But she still couldn't tell me what was wrong. And something WAS wrong. I know it. I can't stop thinking that something really bad has happened to her. It's more than a thought. It's like a feeling, deep in the pit of my stomach. Oh, Demelza, where are you? Please come home soon.

A wave of nausea churned Blake's stomach. But it wasn't Demelza she was thinking about now. It was Lucy and Christine. There were a few more entries in the diary, dated sporadically and detailing her growing fear. She came to the final entry, dated two months after Demelza vanished from the face of the earth. It was a short entry but to the point.

Dear Diary,

Demelza is gone. No one can find her. They all say that she ran away, but I know she didn't—and I know now that she's never coming back. This will be the last time I write. I'm going to Manchester next week. It's time to grow up. At least I still can.

Blake shut the diary and set it aside. Rummaging through the box again, she found a couple of photograph albums. Taking the top one, she flipped it open and turned the pages. There were pictures of her at home with her parents, pictures from her final year of sixth form college, wearing Doctor Martin boots and dresses over jeans, and her hair dyed bright red. Memories flooded her mind, a mixture of pleasure and pain. She turned the page, and there they were: the Forever Four. Blake, Christine, Judy, and Demelza. She had been a pretty thing, Demelza. Tall and graceful like a dancer, with long, dark hair, and world-weary eyes that seemed to penetrate the camera. She had always seemed older than the others, and her eyes reflected that.

Blake removed the photo from the album and held it up to the light. It had been taken at a playing field on a hot summer's day. The four of them were sitting on a blue and red picnic blanket, all smiles for the camera, which was surely nothing to do with the empty bottle of gin lying in the foreground. Christine had taken the picture, holding the Polaroid camera at arm's length: a primitive selfie. Blake's heart ached.

And then she drew in a sharp breath.

Enlarged on Christine's wrist, but blurred and out of focus, was a brightly coloured friendship bracelet. Blake examined the image closely, squinting her eyes. All four friends were wearing them, but the quality of the picture was too grainy to make out the details.

Was it the same bracelet she'd seen on Lucy's wrist? She still couldn't tell.

The wind moaned and whistled outside, unsettling the attic. Blake was unmoving, her mind racing.

A loud buzz made her gasp. She pulled her phone from her pocket and saw that Judy Moon was calling.

Blake wondered if she should answer. She didn't want to talk about the details of finding Lucy, especially if this was a professional call. But she did want to know about Christine.

"Blake?" Judy's voice was taut and upset. "Are you okay? I heard you were the one who found her."

"Someone's been talking, then," Blake said. She flipped the photograph over. There was an inscription written on the back: *26th June. The last time we were all happy.*

"Have you forgotten how small towns work? Everyone knows you found her. It's just awful. Poor Lucy! And Christine . . ."

"Have you spoken to her?"

"No. I tried, but Leslie says Chrissie's heavily sedated right now. Who can blame her? I'd want to stay sedated for the rest of my life." Judy paused, the silence filled with the sound of Blake's breathing. "Did you learn anything from the police?"

"Are you asking as a journalist or as a friend?"

"Jesus, this again? Christine is my friend, Blake. I was Lucy's Godmother." Judy's voice cracked.

Blake winced. She stared at the photograph, at the blurry details of the friendship bracelets. "Sorry. Bad habit. Where are you right now?"

"At work."

"Are you busy? Can I come over? There's something I need to show you."

"I've got my hands full here. Besides, I'm not in the mood." Judy blew her nose and choked back more tears. "What is it, anyway?"

"It's best if I show you," Blake said. "What about this evening?"

"I don't —"

"Please, Judy. It's important. It's to do with Lucy."

There was a brief moment of silence. Then Judy said, "Come over after six-thirty. And Blake?"

"What?"

"No more 'off the record' bullshit."

11

JUDY MOON'S house was modern, warm, and a chaotic mess. The screams of her two young daughters filled the air as they ran about the living room, burning off the last of their energy before bedtime. Blake watched as Judy's husband Charlie chased doggedly behind, imploring them to pick up their toys and games from the evening's activities. Seeing Blake, the girls slowed down and eyed her curiously.

An exhausted-looking Judy winked at Blake. "See what you're missing out on?"

Blake shrugged. At least she wouldn't have to worry about her daughters never coming home again.

"Girls, pick up your toys and get ready for bed. Now." Judy's voice was short and sharp. "Honestly, why am I always the bad cop in this relationship?"

Across the room, Charlie watched in disbelief as the girls dropped to their knees and began tidying up. He waved at Blake, who waved back.

"We'll be in my office," Judy told him. "And girls? I'll be up in ten minutes to say goodnight. If you're not in your own beds, there's going to be trouble."

Blake followed her in silence along the hallway and into a small office on the right. Shutting the door, Judy pointed to a chair in the corner and told Blake to sit. It was a cramped room with enough space for a desk in the corner, an expensive looking chair, and a filing cabinet. Press clippings of Judy's news stories covered the walls, along with family portraits and a glass frame containing Judy's graduation certificate for her journalism degree.

"It's pokey, I know," she said, sweeping a hand around the room. "But it's my sanctuary. Now if only I could get it sound-proofed."

Blake leaned forward on the chair. "How are you doing?"

Judy's expression collapsed into deep loss. "I can't stop thinking about Lucy. She was such a sweetheart with her whole life ahead of her. You know she used to babysit the girls some-times? I can't stop thinking about what I'd do if . . ." She grimaced, picking up a pen from the desk and flipping it between her fingers. "I wish I could talk to Christine. I wish I could make it all better for her. But no one can. Not ever again."

An eruption of laughter and thunderous footsteps broke the quiet as Judy's children raced up the stairs, with Charlie following behind. Judy flinched and, despite the warmth, rubbed her upper arms.

"Have you found out anything about what happened?" Blake asked her gently.

"No. Rod's covering the story. Normally that would piss me off, but it's the right thing to do. I'm too close. Besides, the national press is crawling over the town, which means our little paper won't get a look in. We've had journalists coming in and out of the office all day, asking for archives of this and that, as if we're some sort of reference library. It doesn't seem right for them all to be here. But that's the nature of journalism, I suppose—you go where the story takes you. I just never expected Lucy to be the story." She looked up from the desk, her shoulders braced. "You saw her, didn't you? Did she suffer?"

A flash of crucified limbs, burned flesh and exposed ligaments assaulted Blake's mind. She winced.

"Sorry. You don't have to tell me that," Judy said. "It's just that Wheal Marow has been quiet for so long. Most of the stories I cover are banal and boring at best. But bad things do happen in small towns, don't they?"

"Bad things happen everywhere," Blake said. "The size of the town doesn't matter. It's who's in it."

"You said on the phone you wanted to show me something."

Reaching into her jacket pocket, Blake removed the photograph and turned it over, staring at their four young faces. She passed it to Judy, who took it between both hands and gently touched the surface with her fingertips.

"We all look so young and innocent." A nostalgic smile creased her lips, before quickly fading. "I've been thinking about Demelza a lot the last few days. I'm guessing you have, too."

Blake nodded. "Do you remember the friendship bracelets we're wearing?"

Judy looked closer at the picture, holding it up to the light. "Of course I do. Forever four, forever friends. I still have mine."

"You do? Can I see it?"

"Didn't you keep yours?"

"I . . . I lost it a while ago." Blake avoided Judy's gaze as she tried to still the pounding of her heart. "Do you have it here?"

"It's in my keepsake box. It's silly really, but you never know, maybe one day I'll get dementia and a box filled with memories will come in handy." Judy lowered the photograph, but didn't hand it back. She was staring at Blake, her eyes keen and alert. "Why are you asking about this now?"

Blake wanted to tell her. She did. But what if she was wrong?

"I don't want to cause any unnecessary upset," she said. "I don't want this to turn into a story when I might be wrong."

"This is Christine's daughter, Blake. If you know something that could help . . ."

"Please. Can you just get the bracelet?"

The air in the room grew thick and heavy. Judy got to her feet.

"Give me a minute. It's upstairs at the back of my wardrobe, and I want to say goodnight to the girls."

Giving Blake a long, silent stare, she left the room and shut the door quietly behind her. Blake let out a shuddering breath. Getting up from the chair she paced around the small office, staring at the press cuttings on the wall and trying to keep her breathing steady. The headlines told gentle stories of farming news, lambs birthed in spring, a charity fundraiser for the local care home for the elderly. There was a longer feature story about child poverty in the local area and an increased use of the food-bank. Blake skim-read it. Judy was a talented writer with keen ideas and a sympathetic point of view, who could easily excel in her career beyond the confines of a local newspaper. Yet Judy had chosen to stay and raise her family here in Wheal Marow. It was a compromise Blake didn't think she could make, given the same circumstances.

Her breathing was fluctuating again, one minute quick and shallow, the next struggling to get out. What would she do if her suspicions were confirmed? The immediate step would be to go to the police. And then what? This was an official murder investigation, not one of her cases. And yet it felt like hers. Why was that? Her gaze wandered down to Judy's desk, where a thick folder sat on top. Blake opened it and flipped through the papers. It was her private investigator instincts; you kept looking, even when you weren't searching for anything specific. The folder contained various missing persons reports and printed news clippings detailing women who had disappeared in Cornwall. It was the research Judy had told Blake about. Had she been intending to add Lucy to the pile before her body had been found?

The dull thud of Judy's feet on the stairs vibrated through the wall. Blake closed the folder and moved back to the chair. Judy returned with a cardboard box wedged under her arm.

She stared at Blake, as if she had something to say. Instead, she dumped the box on the desk and removed the lid.

"It should be in here," she said, as she sifted through its contents.

Blake slowly got to her feet, respectfully keeping her distance from Judy's mementos.

"Here it is."

Fishing the bracelet out, Judy held it up between finger and thumb. Her eyes lit up with memories.

Blake came closer, her heart thumping in her chest. It had lost some colour over the years and the thread was frayed and brittle looking, but Blake recognised it instantly. Forgotten memories came rushing back, threatening to knock her off balance. Her vision blurred then pulled into focus. The bracelet contained all the colours of the rainbow, carefully stitched together to form thin zig zags that ran the length of the band.

"Oh God," she said, the breath snatched from her lungs.

Judy frowned. "What is it? Blake, come on, tell me!"

But Blake wasn't listening. Her mind was racing back to Ding Dong Mine and Lucy's mutilated body.

"It's the same one," she gasped. "It's the same damn bracelet."

12

RORY ANGOVE ANSWERED the front door on the third knock. He looked exhausted, and was dressed in pyjama bottoms and an oversized t-shirt with a superhero character printed on the front.

Blake raised a hand. "Hi. Nice outfit."

Rory stared at her. "What are you doing here? It's late."

"It's about Lucy. I found something. Can I come in?"

Scratching his head, Rory stepped to one side. "The kitchen's at the end of the hall. Let's go in there."

"Thanks. By the way, it's only nine. Where I live, the evening's only just getting started."

"We can't all be high-flying city girls."

The kitchen was small and square, but immaculately tidy. Clean dishes sparkled on the dryer. A clean bowl and spoon sat on the breakfast bar next to a box of cereal, ready for the morning. On the cooker, the contents of a small pan were gently bubbling. Blake sniffed the air.

"Warm milk? Cute."

"It helps me sleep." Rory crossed his arms over his chest and let out a heavy sigh. "Blake, it's been a long day of going door-to-door. What have you found?"

He nodded to a small square table in the corner. Blake sat down as Rory removed the pan of milk from the hob then joined her.

"I tried to contact your boss. DS Turner is a hard man to get hold of. So I thought I should come to you." She glanced across the room. "Aren't you going to drink your milk?"

"Blake . . ."

"Sorry. I'm stressed out. You know how I used to get. Nothing much has changed." She leaned forward. "When I found Lucy, she was wearing a friendship bracelet. You saw it?"

Rory said that he did.

"Well . . ." Pulling the envelope from her jacket pocket, Blake took out the photograph she'd shown Judy and slid it across the table. Rory picked up the image and stared at the teenage smiles of Blake, Christine, Judy, and Demelza. "Look at our wrists."

Rory brought the photograph closer. He glanced up, a look of uncertainty in his eyes. "Friendship bracelets?"

"It's the same one, Rory. The same friendship bracelet Lucy was wearing." Holding up her mobile phone, she showed him another photograph. "Judy still has hers. See?"

Rory's gaze moved from the image of Judy's bracelet on the phone to the photograph, then back to the phone again. His tired eyes were suddenly bright and alert.

"You know what this means, don't you?" Blake said.

"Of course, I know what it means. I'm not stupid. Are you sure it's the same bracelet?"

"Positive. Here, I'll send you the picture so you can compare." Blake fiddled with her phone. A second later, Rory's mobile vibrated in his pocket. Rory took it out and swiped the screen. A wrinkle appeared in his brow.

"You took this tonight?"

"About an hour ago."

"Judy doesn't know Lucy was wearing a friendship bracelet, does she?"

Blake pressed her hands flat on the table surface and shrugged.

"Blake?"

She opened her mouth, then shut it again.

"For God's sake, you told her, didn't you?" Rory was glaring at her. Red blotches flashed on his cheeks. "Judy's a journalist. And now she knows key information that we're deliberately trying to keep from the press! Do you realise what you've done?"

"I had to get her to show me the bracelet. What else was I supposed to do? Anyway, Judy is also one of Christine's oldest friends, which means she's not going to tell anything to anyone. And Judy may be a journalist but she's one of the good ones. You know that."

They were both quiet, shoulders hunched as they glared at each other.

"I hope you're right. Because with all the big papers crawling over town right now, the last thing we need is one of them to find out."

Blake shrugged and glanced away. "So I'll talk to Judy. Not that I need to, but if it puts your mind at ease . . ."

Putting down his phone, Rory stretched out his spine and rubbed the back of his neck. "I'm sorry to snap. I'm tired. Really tired. I never thought my first murder investigation would involve someone from this town, never mind someone so young. It's a lot to take in."

Blake's mind was racing, trying to make sense of it all. "Do you remember the party? I've been trying to think back, to go over all the events of that night. Who was there. Demelza's movements. What time she disappeared. It's all fragmented."

"Eighteen years is a long time ago. A lot has happened since. I remember bits and pieces. Mostly you and me arguing about you leaving for Manchester. Me wanting us to continue long distance and you thinking it was a bad idea."

Rory flashed a glance at Blake. There was still hurt in his eyes, even after all this time.

"We were just kids back then with our whole lives ahead of us. Unlike Lucy. Or Demelza."

They were both silent, lost in memories. The smell of warm milk nauseated Blake's stomach.

"What are you going to do about the bracelet?"

"I'll call it in. Let Turner know what you've found."

"I don't think he liked me much."

"He's all right. He's just seen a lot. You remember the murders at Devil's Cove a few years ago?"

"Those crazy cult killings—who could forget?"

"Well, Turner was caught up in all that. Saved a young girl from getting thrown off the top of St Michael's Mount."

"That was him? I remember that. Maybe he isn't such a dick, after all." Blake smiled briefly. Rory, too. "So, there's been no forward movement on the case? What about the phone call to Christine? Were they able to trace it?"

"You know I can't tell you anything about it, so please stop asking."

"Bad habit. Anyway, I should go. Let you get some sleep. Mum and Dad are probably wondering where I am."

"You sound like a teenager."

"Don't get me started." She got to her feet and hovered for a moment, feeling Rory's gaze on her skin. "Don't forget to drink your milk."

They said goodbye on the doorstep. Blake got into her car and drove away, catching Rory's reflection in the rear-view mirror as he watched her leave.

Driving the short journey back to her parents' house, Blake felt the night rush in around her like dark water. There was a connection between Lucy's murder and Demelza's disappearance all those years ago. The most obvious theory was that whoever had killed Lucy had also killed Demelza. But why had Demelza's body never been found when Lucy's had been put on grotesque display for all to see? And why now after all these years?

Trees closed in on both sides of the road, reaching skeletal hands towards her. She could still smell warm milk and it churned her stomach. What was the killer trying to say? The answer was lurking here, somewhere in the darkness. It was calling to Blake, tempting her to step into the shadows.

13

THE SUNDAY CHURCH service began with a hymn: *The Lord's My Shepherd, I'll Not Want.* As the organist played the first few bars, Dennis Stott looked around the half empty church. A deep sadness pulled at his insides. He was standing in the right half of the church, third pew from the back and next to the aisle. No one cared about church anymore. Certainly not the younger generation, who were all so busy with taking selfies and becoming internet influencers, whatever that entailed. Even half of the congregation that was in attendance only came out of habit. At least, that was how he saw it.

As the rich tones of the organ soared high above his head, Dennis shut his eyes and pushed away the dismay. He let the organ music enter his body. It was glorious, like the Holy Spirit. The undulating vibrations reached deep inside his very soul, making his bones rattle and his heart hum. It was a pure sound, perfectly in tune, reverberating around the church interior like the trumpets of angels.

Dennis drew in a deep breath and began to sing, heartily and with passion. His voice rose high above those of the congregation, who, in his eyes, all lacked vigour and enthusiasm. Some barely opened their mouths, while others needed their hymn sheets to follow along. Dennis knew every word. He felt the love and power behind each syllable.

The organ rumbled on, seeping into his very blood, pitch perfect and under-appreciated by the rest of the churchgoers. Opening his eyes again, he glanced around with a sneer. And then his powerful singing voice cracked.

Across the aisle, four rows up, two teenage girls were huddled side by side and pretending to sing along with mock exaggeration. They glanced at each other, attempting to restrain their laughter.

A fire ignited in the pit of Dennis's stomach and burned up to his chest. The girl on the right leaned in to the one on the left and whispered in her ear. They both giggled then glanced around. Where were their parents? Why were they not castigating their daughters for their disrespect? The fire spread from Dennis's chest, down his arms and into his hands. His fingers reached for the hymn sheet on the narrow shelf in front of him and began rolling it into a tight tube.

The girl on the right was blonde and pretty, and she clearly knew it. She was the ringleader of the two. A wolf in sheep's clothing. Her friend was an ignorant fool, easily led into sin. Dennis knew this because he had seen them before, on his previous visit to the church. He had stood and watched in horror as the two of them had danced around the pulpit, giggling like idiots as they'd taken turns pretending to be the vicar delivering mock sermons. They'd thought the church was empty, that they were quite alone. They hadn't seen Dennis crouched in the vestry. But he had seen them. And he'd heard her name. Leanne.

The hymn was drawing to a close. The thunderous tone of the organ shook the church rafters. Dennis sang louder, his eyes fixed on Leanne. The fire inside him blazed like an inferno. The rolled up hymn sheet in his hands suddenly tore in half, making the nearest churchgoers turn their heads. The elderly woman standing next to Dennis cleared her throat and shot him a disapproving glare. Murmuring an apology, Dennis stared at the torn pieces of paper still clutched in his hands. The fire reached his cheeks, making them burn with shame. He willed his fingers to unfurl then took the pieces of the hymn sheet and placed them carefully on the shelf in front. His eyes returned to Leanne. She had made him do that. She had made him destroy the word of God. The inferno inside him burned out of control.

As soon as the service had ended and the vicar had bid them goodbye, Dennis slipped a twenty pound note into the donations box and hurried out of the church. It was cold in the churchyard. Flowers were dying in sodden beds. Lichen-covered headstones stood like crooked teeth on either side of the path, some of them more than two hundred years old, their epitaphs eroded by time and mostly unreadable. As the rest of the churchgoers filed out of the building and swarmed around him, Dennis bowed his head and imagined he was invisible. Stepping off the path, he leaned down to inspect one of the headstones. Leanne and her friend were coming out of the church, practically skipping arm in arm over the threshold. As they passed by, all giggles and chatter, Dennis sniffed the air and recoiled. The stench of sin was seeping from her pores like a toxin, infecting everyone in her radius.

The girls stepped off the path just ahead of him, almost standing on top of one of the graves. They glanced back at the crowd then leaned into each other conspiratorially.

"I don't know that bar," the dark-haired friend said in a hushed voice. "Are you sure it's okay?"

Leanne smiled. "Nancy says it's fine. It's a bit of a dive but the staff don't look too hard at IDs."

"Is she sure?"

"She says she's been there lots of times and she's never been caught. Have you seen her ID? It's such an obvious fake. *And* she looks younger than both of us."

Dennis felt his hands curling into fists again. Forcing his fingers apart, he gripped the top of the headstone and risked a glance at the girls. All of his previous suspicions about Leanne had just been confirmed. She was dangerous. A sinner. Worse still, she was an influencer and a temptress, with the power to lead others into darkness.

"Stop worrying," she complained. "You're parent's already think you're coming to mine to study. Besides, it's just a couple of drinks. Everyone else is doing it, so why shouldn't we?"

"I don't know. If we get caught Mum and Dad will kill me."

"We won't. Anyway, I bet our parents aren't as innocent as they make out to be."

Just then, a woman's voice called out from the crowd. "Leanne? We're leaving now."

Leanne rolled her eyes and gave her friend a playful shove. "See you tonight. Don't have a panic attack before we get there."

She flashed a wicked smile then walked over to a soberly dressed couple in their late forties.

"You don't need to shout. I'm right here," she said to her

mother, who reached over to pluck a piece of lint from the collar of Leanne's jacket.

Crushed against the headstone, Dennis's fingertips were impossibly white. Pain rippled through his wrists and up his arms. He could take her right now. Castigate her in front of the churchgoers as a hard lesson. It was his duty after all. But to do so would force a premature ending to his work, and he couldn't allow that to happen.

Slowly releasing his grip on the headstone, he slipped his hands inside his coat pockets and walked away from the crowd. Passing through the church gates, he crossed the quiet road to where his van was parked. Getting in, he slipped the key into the ignition and turned on the heaters. As he waited for the interior to warm, he blew into his cupped hands and rubbed them vigorously together. Congregation members were leaving through the church gates, all unaware that they were being watched. Then came Leanne, her arms linked with a young boy, and her parents walking by her side. She leaned down and whispered in the child's ear and then they both threw their heads back and laughed.

"Liar," he hissed. "Filthy whore."

Dennis knew the truth about Leanne. She needed to be cleansed.

He watched her and the boy climb into the back of the family's car, while their parents got into the front. A moment later, they pulled away from the curb and began the journey home.

Dennis followed them at a discreet distance.

Leanne's transformation would be glorious. But first she would need to endure great suffering, for it was the only true path back to cleanliness.

14

ONE HOUR earlier and thirteen miles southwest of Dennis Stott, Blake shivered in the cold as she pushed her mother's wheelchair through the churchyard. She had spent Saturday at home, feeling restless and frustrated. To distract herself, she had cleaned the house from top to bottom and prepared meals for the next few days, which she put into containers and stored in the freezer. Rory hadn't called. Neither had DS Turner. And why would they? Blake wasn't part of the investigation.

Frustration turned to drinking, then retiring to her bedroom for an early night. But she hadn't slept well, instead staying up half the night as she thought and theorised about Lucy Truscott's killer and the connection to Demelza. Now, she was tired and grouchy. She had still barely said a word to her father, who walked silently beside mother and daughter, looking uncomfortable in the crisp blue shirt he wore beneath his coat. More than once she felt his eyes on her, but she refused to meet his gaze.

Mary hadn't wanted to miss Sunday service, despite the awkwardness of getting her in and out of the eight-seater taxi. Blake was not a churchgoer, but she needed respite from her relentless brain. Besides, Sunday service was an opportunity to observe the townsfolk.

Dating from the seventeenth century, the church was small and ornate. Organ music floated out through the open door as churchgoers drifted in. A few slowed to greet the Hollows and enquire after Mary's health.

"Don't you worry about me, I'm fine," she told them, tapping the plaster cast of her outstretched leg. "But the quicker I'm out of this bloomin' thing the better."

Blake appeared to be invisible to the well-wishers. A small town like Wheal Marow could be unforgiving once you'd left it behind. Sometimes Blake wondered if the locals thought she was a snob, living her fancy city life and occasionally coming home to look down at them. Whenever she was stopped in the street by a familiar face, the same question was asked over and over again: "Don't you ever think about coming back home?"

Her answer was always a resolute no. Why come back to a place where she'd never really fitted in?

Reverend Thompson was a new face to Blake. The vicar had taken residency at the church last year after transferring from somewhere in Devon. She was a kind-faced woman, with a shock of grey hair and soft-looking skin. She smiled broadly as the Hollows approached.

"Hello, Mary," she said, leaning down a little. "I wasn't expecting to see you, what with the accident and all. What a nice surprise. And Ed, how are you?"

Blake brought the wheelchair to a halt. Mary repeated the same answer she'd given the others, to which Reverend Thompson smiled and nodded.

"Well, I wish you good health and a swift recovery. I remember when I broke my ankle a couple of years ago. It was a skiing accident. Wasn't quite prepared for the slalom." She winked at Mary, then peered up at Blake. "And who do we have here?"

"My daughter, Blake. She's come home to help take care of me."

Blake smiled uncomfortably and gave the Reverend a polite nod.

"Well, it's lovely to meet you, Blake. And nice to see another younger face at the service today."

Blake shot a glance at her father, who was tugging at his shirt collar.

"The organ's sounding lovely today, Reverend," Mary said. She twisted around in the chair to peer up at Blake. "It's been a little out of tune lately."

"Ah yes, Bertha's recently had her annual tuning. She's sounding glorious, isn't she? It goes to show even old instruments like us can clean up nicely with a bit of spit and polish." The Reverend smiled warmly, then took on a serious tone. "Anyway, must get in. It's going to be a different kind of service today, in memory of dear Lucy. I'm hoping it will provide some warmth and comfort until a funeral can be arranged."

"Bless that girl," Mary said.

Blake got the wheelchair going again, pushing her mother towards the arched doorway as she followed Reverend Thompson. The front wheels caught on the stone threshold. Blake grunted, pushing harder.

Ed leaned over. "Here, let me."

"It's fine, I've got it." Blake pushed again, shoving her mother over the threshold with a bump.

Inside, the organ music was loud and ethereal, soaring up to the rafters. The church was full, with only a few spaces left on the back pew. Parking Mary at the end, Blake slid in next to Craig Butcher, the local green grocer, who gave her a solemn nod. Ed came next, wedging himself into the space between Blake and the end of the pew. He leaned over and whispered in Mary's ear, then gave Craig a nod.

The organ music ended and the service began. As Reverend Thompson welcomed everyone, Blake switched off and stared around the congregation. It was mostly older folk, with a few younger families scattered in between. Somewhere to the left, young whispers rose up from one of the pews, followed by a hissed parental warning. Reverend Thompson asked everyone to stand and sing *Morning Has Broken*. As the organ rumbled to life again, the congregation stood and began to sing.

Blake remained silent, examining the backs of people's heads. She was not in the best position to observe any unusual behaviour. Not that she knew what she was looking for. Next to her, Ed sang softly, his lips barely moving. Blake was glad to see he was feeling just as awkward about singing in public as she was.

The song ended. The congregation took their seats again. Reverend Thompson returned to the lectern and let out a heavy sigh. "As most of you will know, last Sunday young Lucy Truscott was taken from us in the most terrible of ways. I understand this is a tragic, difficult time for the people of our humble town, one that triggers strong feelings of shock, grief, and intense anger. But we must place our trust in the authorities to find the culprit and bring him to justice. We must also place our trust in God, that He has removed Lucy from harm's way and enveloped her with His gracious love. Lucy is at peace now, and while we comfort each other in our grief and loss, I would like to ask you to join me in prayer for dear Lucy, taken from us too soon, and for her mother, Christine, who will need this community's love and support more than ever. Perhaps we can begin with an old classic: *the Lord's Prayer*."

The congregation lowered their heads as Reverend Thompson led the prayer. Blake looked around, a maelstrom of emotions swirling up from the pews. Ahead of her at the front, a small group of young women were sobbing quietly and dabbing their eyes with tissues. Jasmine Baker sat in profile, her head turned away from the large crucifix hanging at the front. Blake's heart ached for her. She knew only too well how it felt to lose your best friend. A pain that was indescribably raw and unforgiving, and thorny with guilt. Blake shifted her gaze from the grieving friends and fixed it on the left side of the congregation. All heads were bowed except for one, like a boat floating on still water.

Blake recognised the woman instantly. Faith Penrose was staring straight ahead, her tight bun of black hair streaked with silver, her shoulders slumped from almost two decades of grief and loss. Until a few nights ago at the police station, Blake hadn't seen Faith in years. In fact, she'd purposely avoided her. It was the emptiness in Faith's eyes that she couldn't stand. It was infinite and paralysing, like staring into the eyes of Medusa. Every time she saw Faith, guilt would knife Blake in the stomach. Because she had come back home that night and Demelza had not.

Faith suddenly twisted around in her seat. Blake was frozen, her breath caught in her throat. She forced her head downward, until she was staring at her shoes.

The prayer came to an end and the service continued, with Reverend Thompson announcing another hymn: *How Great Thou Art.*

Blake's head was spinning. Her cheeks burned with shame. As the congregation stood and the organist began to play, she sprang up and squeezed past her father into the aisle, where Mary looked up.

"What's wrong, bird?" she asked.

Faith's eyes burned into Blake's back, searing the flesh. "Nothing. I need some fresh air."

She hurried past her mother, throwing open the church door and letting in the light. Heads turned in her direction. The door slammed shut.

Outside, the cold slapped Blake's skin. Dragging in a breath, she pulled her phone from her pocket and called Rory. When he didn't answer, she swore under her breath and considered calling Detective Sergeant Turner. She hated that this wasn't her case. She hated not knowing what the friendship bracelet meant. She peered back at the church, imagining Lucy's burned body crucified on the cross. She took out her phone and called Kenver.

"What time is it?" he asked in a voice like sandpaper.

"Almost midday. Put some clothes on and make some coffee. I'm coming over."

15

KENVER'S LIVING room was a chaotic mess and the heating was turned up so high that Blake immediately began stripping off layers until she was just in her jeans and t-shirt. Kenver handed her a mug of coffee then pushed a pile of clothing off the sofa so she could sit down.

"So, what's up?" he asked, rubbing his eyes. He was awake, but clearly hadn't been for long. "Shouldn't you be at home with Auntie Mary and Uncle Ed? It is Sunday, you know, and Sunday in Wheal Marow is family day."

Blake flashed him a side-eyed look. "Aren't you family? Anyway, I've just been with them at church."

"They let you inside a church and you didn't burst into fire?"

"Funny." Blake stared at the mug of coffee in her hands. She searched the table for a clear space and set it down. "How do you live like this?"

Kenver surveyed the room, a genuine look of confusion on his face. "It's not that bad."

Blake leaned forward, resting her elbows on her knees and her chin in her hands. "The church was full with people coming to pay their respects. The Reverend was talking about Lucy, about what happened to her, and then I glanced over and saw Faith Penrose. I've seen her twice this week and both times I just looked away. Everything that's happened with Lucy must be bringing up bad memories for Faith, forcing her to relive it all again, and I don't even have the decency to look her in the eye."

Blake winced, feeling a stab of guilt in her gut. Kenver stared at her and shifted on the sofa.

"I was just sitting there at the back of the church, thinking about Demelza, trying to stop all of the horrible images of Lucy that I keep seeing in my head, and . . . it all just got on top of me. I ran out of the church. Left Mum and Dad there. Mum will be worried."

She stared into space. Hopelessness weighed her down.

Kenver brought his feet up on the sofa and crossed his legs. "You shouldn't be so hard on yourself. You found Lucy's body, which would traumatise anyone. Auntie Mary will understand that. As for Uncle Ed, who knows?"

"He's not exactly one for emotions, is he?"

"Or anything outside of being the manliest man of all men. God knows what he thinks of me."

"To be honest I don't think he thinks much of anyone."

"Aren't we full of joy today?"

"Sorry. I don't even know why I came here. I just wanted to be away from that church and all the sadness." Blake curled her hands into fists and placed them down by her sides. "I hate that this isn't my investigation. That I have to sit back and wait to find out what happened. I need to know what the connection between Lucy and Demelza means."

"What connection?"

"I . . . I can't tell you that right now."

Kenver leaned forward, picking up a half-eaten chocolate bar from the table. "Can't trust the family drunk?"

"It's not that. It's information that can't be leaked to the public without compromising the investigation. Besides, I promised Rory that I wouldn't tell anyone."

"Rory? You're not sleeping with him again, are you?"

Blake narrowed her eyes. "No. Are you?"

"I don't think I'm his type." Kenver chewed noisily on the chocolate bar, smacking his lips together. "I suggest you let the police get on with doing their job. You can't be a private investigator all the time."

"Tell that to my brain. Besides, the way things are going back in Manchester, being a private investigator might not be in my future at all."

"Is that why you came home?"

"You know why I came home. To take care of my mum."

"That's as good an excuse as any, I suppose."

"It's not an excuse, or did you miss the giant plaster cast and wheelchair? Anyway, what about you? The last I heard you were living the high life in London, with your well-paid tech job and swanky flat. What happened?"

The remains of the chocolate bar wavered in Kenver's hand. He set it down on the table and wiped a crumb from the corner of his mouth. "You already know what. I got a little too much into the partying lifestyle, so I came down here to take a break."

Blake looked at the empty bottles on the coffee table that were lined up like the headstones of an alcoholic's graveyard.

"And how's that going?"

"About as well as your career."

"Ouch." Blake snatched up her coffee mug and took a sip, wincing at the bitter taste. She thought about her life in

Manchester, about what it had become. Friends had fallen by the wayside. There had been a few romantic relationships, but nothing significant to speak of. It was the hours she kept. They made it difficult to hold down any kind of relationship. When you were a night owl, flitting from hiding place to hiding place, snapping covert photographs of illicit affairs or spending endless hours hunkered down in a driver's seat, limbs aching, bladder bursting, waiting for something, anything to happen that would close a case, solitude became your only companion.

It wasn't that Blake felt lonely. She spoke to her mother on the phone once a week, and enjoyed her solitude. But lately, with work drying up, minutes were turning to hours, hours to days, time into an endless, sprawling expanse with no end and nothing to fill it. She had thought about getting a dog, but she was afraid she might neglect it and it would starve to death.

What did she have in Manchester that kept her anchored? There was her rented flat by the riverside, which was airy and modern with comfortable furnishings and landscape prints on the walls. There was her pokey little office, again rented, where she welcomed clients and apologised for the lack of space. And there was her ten-year-old car. All material things. Nothing of worth. At least she had breath in her body.

Blake glanced over at Kenver, who had also fallen into a miserable stupor, his eyes dark and glistening as he stared into the half distance.

"What a fine pair we are," he said.

Eighteen-year-old Lucy had been tortured and brutalised, her life stolen away. Demelza, also eighteen, had vanished from the face of the earth. Blake tried to picture them together, but all she saw was Lucy's savaged remains. She tried to imagine the pain and suffering she must have endured in her final hours.

Blake set the mug down again, this time pushing it far away from her.

"It's been exactly a week since Lucy Truscott disappeared," she said. "A week that feels like a month."

Kenver looked up. "Aren't you glad you came back home?"

"I wonder if he feels guilty. Or if he feels anything at all."

"Who?"

"Lucy's killer." Blake shut her eyes, the frustration of not knowing pressing down on her chest. "I wonder where he is right now. What he's doing at this exact moment."

"Something sick and psychopathic I expect."

"Without a shred of remorse."

16

THE PIRATE'S Hook was a rundown pub with dirty red carpets, beer-stained tables made of dark wood, and an old jukebox in the corner. What set it apart from other pubs were the nautical dressings. Old fishing nets hung from the ceiling, a ship's wheel and painted crab pots were pinned over the bar, and various prints of old pirate ships hung from the walls. It being Sunday evening, the bar was quiet, with just a few patrons sitting at tables.

Wedged in a corner booth and watching the room, Leanne Curnow and Heather Hargreaves sat side by side, a collection of empty glasses on the table in front of them. Despite Leanne's earlier bravado, she had grown nervous as the two had walked through the doors. Her fake ID, freshly made by Jed at college, had felt heavy and conspicuous in her pocket. This was not her first time drinking alcohol, but it was her first time drinking alcohol at a bar.

Her best friend Heather had been equally anxious, but when their IDs had been accepted without more than a glance, they had both bloomed with excitement. Neither of the teenagers had known what to order from the bar. So far, they had tried Pernod, rum and coke, and something called a White Russian. The alcohol had worked quickly on Heather, and she was already slurring her words, while her eyes had taken on a glazed sheen. Leanne felt resolutely sober and underwhelmed. She shifted in the booth, uncrossing her legs and pulling at the material of her skinny denim jeans. Music played from a nearby jukebox, something ancient from the eighties that her dad had played a million times while driving. Behind the bar, a young man in his early twenties polished glasses in between checking his phone.

At the end of the bar, two older men were drinking pints of beer and talking loudly. They had spotted Leanne and Heather a while ago, and had been leering at them ever since.

"Gross," Leanne said quietly. "They're staring again."

Heather picked up her empty glass and gave it a disappointed look. "Dirty perverts. I swear they're older than my dad. Should we get another drink?"

She wiped her mouth with the back of her hand.

Leanne produced a tissue and handed it to her. "Here, you smudged your lipstick."

"Who cares?"

Leanne cared. They were sixteen years old, two years below the legal drinking age. While their fake IDs had appeared to work and a little make up had helped to age them, she was still very much aware that they were breaking the law. Perhaps it was the paranoia that was keeping her sober.

The men were still staring. The one on the left, whose beer belly hung over his trousers, blew Leanne a kiss. She grimaced and stared at the table.

"I think we should go."

"Why? Aren't you having fun?"

"I'm bored. We should have come on a Saturday when there would have been more people."

"No way. I told you, my sister would have been here. If she'd seen me, she would have gone straight home and told my parents. Besides, what if I'd embarrassed myself by throwing up or something?"

"You're embarrassing yourself now." Leanne took the tissue from Heather's hand and wiped the smeared lipstick from the corner of her mouth. "You're not going to throw up, are you?"

"I'm not drunk," Heather said, batting Leanne's hand away.

"It's almost nine thirty. We have college tomorrow and I still need to finish that philosophy essay."

Heather leaned back against the booth, pursed her lips and blew out a stream of air. "I suppose it *is* really boring here. Maybe we should try a different pub next time. Somewhere my witch of a sister doesn't go."

"I suppose." Maybe it was the guilt, or maybe it was the sharp taste of alcohol, but Leanne had already decided that underage drinking was not as exciting as she'd been led to believe. Still, Heather could be right and a different pub might have a more ambient atmosphere. After all, everyone she knew went underage drinking. She bet her parents had done it too a long time ago, not that they'd ever admit it.

"Come on then," she said.

"Fine. Those pervs are making me sick anyway."

As they readied to leave, one of the men at the bar nudged the other. Beer glasses in hand, they got to their feet and made their way over.

"Oh, shit." Leanne's heart started to race. She could smell the alcohol on their breath before they'd even reached the table.

The one with the huge beer belly swayed on his feet. His

friend was thin and wiry, with a stringy comb over plastered to his pate. He stared intensely at Leanne's breasts. "Going so soon?"

She quickly zipped up her jacket and nudged Heather. "Come on."

"Oh, don't be like that," the man with the beer belly said. "My friend's only saying hello. You should stay a bit longer. We'll get you both a drink."

Heather was struggling to slip her arm into the sleeve of her jacket. Moving quickly, Leanne grabbed her by the elbow and tugged her from the booth. The balding man blocked their escape.

"Wait a minute, what do you think you're doing? Me and my friend here, we've offered to buy you drinks. The least you can do is say thank you."

Leanne stared at him. Her heart crashed against her chest.

"We have to go now," she said quietly, but the man made no move to get out of their way

"What's the matter? Can't you give us a smile? A pretty maid like you shouldn't look so serious."

The man with the beer belly leaned forward, beer sloshing from his glass as he grinned at Heather. "You're gorgeous. Bet you're not as frigid as your friend."

Leanne felt Heather's hand squeeze hers tightly.

"Oi! You two!" The barman's voice boomed across the room. "Leave those girls alone or I'll bar you for life."

The balding man froze, his teeth mashing together as he turned towards the bar. "All right, Dan. Calm down. We're only saying hello."

"No crime in that, is there?" his friend called after him, then muttered under his breath. "Dick."

Grabbing Heather, Leanne bolted forward, pushing the man out of the way and spilling his beer on the sticky carpet.

"Fucking dykes!" the bald man shouted after them.

They reached the entrance door and Leanne shouldered it open. Then they were running out into the cold night air.

———

Neither friend spoke as they rounded the corner and hurried away from the pub. Truro was a cathedral city, no bigger than a large town, which meant on Sunday nights the streets were empty and quiet. Leanne's heart was still thumping. Her shoes slapped on the cobblestones as she pulled Heather along. Reaching the end of the street, she glanced over her shoulder and was relieved to see that they hadn't been followed. She stared at Heather in the darkness, who promptly snorted and collapsed into peals of laughter.

"It's not funny!" Leanne said, shoving Heather's shoulder.

"I know, but what dirty bastards. I bet they were older than my grandparents."

They continued to walk at a brisk pace, passing through umbrellas of orange streetlight and passing shops and restaurants that had closed for the night. Now that she was breathing in cold air, Leanne felt the alcohol in her bloodstream begin to fizz.

"Honestly, if that's what's going to happen every time we go to a pub, you can count me out."

"I thought it was fun. Well, apart from those dickheads."

"You think everything is fun."

"That's because I'm an optimist."

"Well, I prefer to be a realist."

They walked along, chatting about college and their week

ahead. Occasionally, Leanne peered into the street behind, searching for signs of the men. A white van drove past them and turned right at the crossroad up ahead. The friends ground to a halt.

Leanne tried to read Heather's face in the shadows. "How drunk are you?"

"I don't know," Heather said, her words slurring together. "Not that drunk, I suppose. Why?"

"Because I don't feel comfortable leaving you to walk home alone."

"God, you sound like my mother. It's only five minutes, Leanne."

"I know, but still." She glanced over her shoulder again.

"They're not coming. Anyway, how drunk are *you*?"

"Not much at all, I think." Leanne checked the time on her phone. It was 9:45 p.m. She had fifteen minutes to get home, sneak past her parents so they didn't smell the alcohol, and get upstairs to finish off the essay.

Heather was swaying slightly on her feet. "How about this? We walk home by ourselves, but we keep each other company on the phone."

It seemed like an acceptable compromise. Not the best, but if it meant not getting a lecture from her parents . . .

"Okay, fine. Get your phone out. I'm calling you now."

They hugged quickly and parted ways. Leanne called Heather's number, then turned right at the crossroad. She glanced over her shoulder and saw Heather heading left.

"The things we women have to do to stay safe," Heather said in Leanne's ear.

"It's better than being raped and murdered."

Leanne walked quickly, spinning around again to check on

Heather, who had done the same. They both waved at each other. Heather wasn't swaying as much and she was managing not to wander into the road.

"If you keep walking backwards like that, you'll fall over," Leanne said, smiling.

She heard Heather giggle. They both turned around again.

"Honestly, those men were so gross," Heather said. "I bet they've got daughters older than us, the sickos."

"It wouldn't surprise me."

"Hey, what are you doing on Friday night? There's that new Marvel film coming out. Do you want to go and see it?"

"Sure."

"You want me to invite Hannah and the others?"

"I suppose."

Leanne was heading down a residential street, lined with parked vehicles and three-storey townhouses. As Heather chatted in her ear, a cat sprang from under a car and dashed across the road.

The rumble of an engine filled the air, growing louder. A white van was coming towards Leanne at a steady pace. The hairs on the back of her neck stood up. Hadn't she just seen that van a minute ago at the crossroad? It had driven past them and turned right, in the same direction Leanne was now walking. So, why was it coming back?

She watched it sail past her. The driver was a silhouette at the wheel and difficult to make out.

Heather was still talking in her ear. Leanne twisted around, watching the van as it headed back towards the crossroad. But then the van was slowing to a halt and slowly turning around.

"Hello?" Heather said. "Are you even listening to me?"

Now, the van was heading up the street again, back towards

Leanne. Her heart began to beat hard in her chest. She turned and quickened her pace.

"Leanne? What's wrong?"

"Sorry," she said. "There's a van. It's driving behind me."

"What do you mean?"

"I think it's following me."

Leanne glanced back again, her heart in her throat. The van was still chugging along, staying just behind her.

Heather had quickly sobered up. "How far are you from home?"

"A few minutes."

Leanne walked faster. The van revved its engine.

"Is it still there?"

"Yes. I'm scared."

"I'm coming back."

"No, don't."

"Stay on the phone, I'll be two minutes."

"Heather, don't."

But she could already hear Heather running along the street, her shoes hammering on tarmac.

And then there was a dazzle of headlights and a loud roar as the van sped past her. It swerved off the road and onto the path, blocking Leanne's way.

She froze. Blood rushed in her ears. She tried to step back, but her feet were paralysed.

The driver door flew open. A hulking shadow sprang out and lunged towards her.

"No!"

Leanne turned and ran. She made it three steps before powerful hands gripped her shoulders and spun her around.

Fingers wrapped around her throat. They squeezed tightly, choking the air from her lungs.

She couldn't scream, couldn't breathe. The man pulled her forward, then slammed her against the side of the van.

Leanne's vision turned white. Chemicals invaded her nose as a cloth was pressed into her face.

The world went red. Then yellow.

As she slipped down the van, the man caught her by her jacket. Dragging the side door open, he threw her roughly inside. Leanne's head slammed into the van floor. Her body twisted like a rag doll. She lay on her side, falling into unconsciousness.

She heard someone running. Then screaming. Through the open door she saw Heather racing straight towards her with outstretched arms. She saw the man's heavy frame twist around.

Then everything went dark.

17

BLAKE SAT at an empty desk in a cramped interview room, nursing a plastic cup of coffee. Her head was throbbing painfully and the hard plastic chair wasn't helping. She had remained at Kenver's for the rest of the day. She'd got drunk with him—so drunk that she'd been forced to stay the night. Waking early with a blistering hangover, she'd taken the bus to her parents' house, where she'd showered and made coffee, and instantly regretted her actions. Enabling a burgeoning alcoholic just so that she could indulge her own self-pity had not been one of her finest moments, even if the alcohol had numbed her frantic mind. Had she known that DS Turner would call, she would have opted for chocolate instead.

Turner had asked her to come to the station in Truro. He hadn't said why, but he had sounded on edge. Now, as the detective sergeant entered the room, Blake noticed that his suit was crumpled and the left point of his shirt collar had folded in on itself. She could also see that his agitation had multiplied. Shutting the door, Turner gave a quick nod and sat down. He placed a notebook on the desk, followed by a mug of coffee. He removed a ballpoint pen from the breast pocket of his jacket, opened the notebook to a clean page, clicked the top of the pen, and looked up.

Blake continued to observe him. Turner's shoulders were stiff. His eyes were dry and a little puffy. A day's growth of stubble shadowed his chin. Someone didn't sleep much last night, she thought.

"Thank you for coming in, Ms Hollow," Turner said. "I know it was short notice."

"I think you can call me Blake. Ms Hollow sounds like an old maid."

The detective cleared his throat. "I wanted to ask you about the friendship bracelets. How many of you had them? Who made them? What was their point?"

Straight down to business. And there was a definite urgency to his tone. "As far as I can remember, it was the four of us who had them. Me, Judy, Christine, and Demelza. Judy says Demelza made them. It was eighteen years ago, I don't really remember. But what I do know is that we all wore them in our last summer together. Judy, Demelza and I were leaving Cornwall to go to university. Christine was already heavily pregnant with Lucy by then."

"You all went to the same university?"

"No. I went to Manchester, Judy to Middlesex. Demelza was meant to go to Warwick. As for the purpose of the bracelets, the clue is in the name. They were a way to remember each other as we went off on our own paths. I don't know what else to tell you."

Turner nodded as he took notes.

Blake watched him write, saw that he was holding the pen

too tightly. "Is it a match? Judy's friendship bracelet and the one on Lucy's wrist?"

"Tell me about Demelza's disappearance."

"What do you want to know?"

"Anything you can remember. What kind of party was it? Who was there? Did anything out of the ordinary happen that night? You know the drill."

"I do," Blake said, holding his stare. "Like I said, it was our final summer together. We'd all taken our exams and college was officially over. The party was a big send-off for everyone, before we all had to start growing up."

"You organised it with your friends?"

"I've no idea who organised it. But everyone was there, including Detective Constable Angove. It was held in a field, a few miles outside of town. It wasn't exactly permitted, shall we say. We were all probably trespassing, but it was far enough away from people so the noise wouldn't bother anyone."

"How many people?"

"Honestly, I don't remember. A lot. Maybe a hundred?"

"And Demelza?"

"She'd been in a strange mood all night but was trying to keep up appearances. But I'd noticed something wasn't right with her. She seemed upset, so I got her alone and asked if she was okay. She said she was fine. When I pressed her about it, she told me to drop it, and that there was nothing to worry about. Which was clearly a lie."

"How do you know?"

"Because I'm good at reading people and we were best friends. She always came to me when she had a problem. Just not that night."

"What kind of problems?"

"The usual teenage angst. College, relationships, family stuff."

"Family stuff?"

"Demelza and her mum clashed a lot."

"Faith Penrose? The woman who was here the other night?"

Blake shifted uncomfortably and nodded.

"What did they fight about?"

"The usual teenage stuff. It's a rite of passage, isn't it? To fight with your parents when you're a teenager? Didn't you?"

Turner looked up. "No. Did you?"

Blake lifted the plastic cup to her lips and shrugged. She didn't like this. Usually, she was the one asking questions.

"What time did Demelza leave the party that night?"

"It was eighteen years ago, Detective Sergeant. Besides, I may have been a little drunk that night. All I know is that one minute she was there, the next she wasn't. Not a single person remembered seeing her leave. But what I do remember vividly is that there was a bonfire, and Demelza was standing next to it, staring hard into the flames. She looked so sad. The saddest person you ever saw. You'd never think that she was about to head off for a new and exciting life. It broke my heart a little bit. Not just because she was sad, but because she wouldn't tell me why. It's stuck with me all this time. The not knowing."

Memories assaulted Blake's mind. She put down the coffee cup and shifted again on the uncomfortable seat.

"Demelza's parents reported her missing the next day. There was a search party, but of course they found nothing. Some people thought she'd run off, but that didn't make sense to me, not with university just a couple of months away. Besides, none of her belongings were missing and the money in her bank account was untouched. The only anomaly from that night came after the police searched Demelza's phone records. She'd made a phone call to an unregistered mobile number at 9:13 p.m. The call had lasted exactly one minute and fifty-three seconds. I saw her make that phone call at the party, but I have no idea who she was talking to. Nothing ever came of it. Demelza disappeared. Along with all traces of her."

The scratch of Turner's pen was the only sound in the room. Blake was momentarily lost in the past, a great sadness pushing down on her. She blinked it away and leaned forward. "The friendship bracelet found on Lucy's wrist—was it Demelza's? Please, I need to know."

Turner peered up at her. Amid all the exhaustion and worry in his eyes, Blake saw great empathy. "We're waiting on the test results. They're being fast-tracked so we should have them soon. There are samples of Demelza's DNA still on record, so if there is a match, we'll know about it soon."

"What about the burns on Lucy's skin? It looked to me like she'd been tortured."

"You know I can't tell you anything about that. What else do you remember?"

Blake smiled. She liked Turner, but there was something he wasn't telling her. It was hidden in the way his knee jigged up and down beneath the table. In the haunted look in his eyes. And it seeped from his pores to hang in the air, a deep cloud of anxiety that smothered the room.

"Something's happened," Blake said, instantly knowing she was right. "If you're waiting on the test results for the friendship bracelet, it's something else. That's why all these questions now. So, what is it?"

Turner arched an eyebrow but said nothing.

"I may not be a police detective, DS Turner, but I've been

watching people for years, seeing through the different masks they wear. Yours is slipping."

"Why *aren't* you a police detective?" Turner asked, straightening his spine.

"You're dodging the question."

Turner's knee moved up and down furiously, sending tremors through the desk. He glanced down at the pen shivering on top of the notebook, and brought his leg to a standstill. He stared grimly at Blake. "It will be hitting the press later today, so I suppose I can tell you this now. Another two teenage girls have gone missing. They disappeared last night."

Blake stared at him, her mouth wide open. "From where?"

"Truro. They played one of the oldest tricks in the book, each girl telling her parents she was studying at the other's. As we learned from a friend of theirs just this morning, they'd gone to a pub to enjoy a spot of underage drinking. As far as we can tell, they left around nine-thirty. A call came in not long after. A civilian reported hearing screams coming from the street. When they looked outside, a white van was speeding away. They didn't manage to catch the number plate."

"What about ANPR?"

"We're working on it."

ANPR - Automatic Number Plate Recognition. The technology allowed police to track and identify vehicles of interest through a network of cameras placed on roads all over the country. The white van's number plate would have been captured by any ANPR camera that it passed, thereby allowing detectives to trace its journey, and to identify who the van was registered to. It could work wonders, so long as the vehicle's plates were genuine.

Blake felt sick. "And you think these girls are connected to Lucy's murder?"

"Not yet," Turner said. "All I know is that Lucy Truscott disappeared last Sunday, while walking home from the Badger Inn. Last night, Leanne Curnow and Heather Hargreaves vanished from the face of the earth after leaving The Pirate's Hook. Also on a Sunday."

Blake trembled in her seat. Her mind was screaming at her, trying to tell her something she already knew.

Turner leaned forward. "What day did Demelza disappear from the party?"

Blake looked up. Suddenly, she couldn't breathe.

"It was the twenty-eighth of July," she said. "A Sunday."

18

BY THE TIME EVENING FELL, news of the missing girls had spread like wildfire. Blake had returned to her parents' house and spent the rest of the day taking care of her mother. She had cleaned the house again and prepared further meals, while her mind raced frantically. Her father returned home at a quarter past five. The three of them ate dinner together in the living room, trays of food balanced on their knees and a television game show filling the silence. Blake and her father washed the dishes and put them away, with barely a word spoken between them. Then they returned to Mary and watched the evening news.

The young, smiling faces of Leanne Curnow and Heather Hargreaves peered out from the screen. Those smiles will be gone now, Blake thought. She wondered where they had been taken.

"I can't stop thinking about their parents," Mary said, her leg propped up in front of her, one hand squeezing Ed's. "They must be worried sick, especially after what happened with . . . Oh, I hate to even think about it. You think they're still alive?"

"I doubt it," Blake said. "If they are, it won't be for long."

Mary tutted. "Don't be so morbid. You have to have hope, for their sake."

Blake wanted to believe her mother, but hope hadn't kept Lucy alive. She was thankful that she wouldn't be the one to find those girls. Finding Lucy had scarred her forever.

"Did that detective tell you anything?"

Ed looked up from the television. "What detective?"

"Blake had to go up to Truro today. She's helping with the investigation."

"I'm not helping, Mum."

"Why is this the first time I'm hearing about it?" Ed said.

Because I'm not a child. And I don't have to tell you anything. "It was nothing. Just some follow up questions."

"About what?"

"Come on, Dad. You know I'm not allowed to say."

It was the longest conversation father and daughter had had in days.

"Well, I just hope they find those dear girls," Mary said, reaching for the TV remote. "Blake, have you called Christine yet?"

"No."

"Why ever not?"

It was a good question. "She won't want to hear from me."

"Rubbish. That poor woman needs all of her friends right now. You should call her."

"Maybe."

Should she call? On the one hand, Blake knew it was the

right thing to do, because even if Christine couldn't bring herself to talk on the phone, she would at least know Blake was there for her. On the other hand, Blake was scared Christine would ask her to describe in detail the state in which she'd found Lucy. And Christine would ask, whether she wanted to hear the answer or not.

Blake squirmed. She didn't want to have that conversation with Christine right now, if ever. So, she would go on avoiding her, just like she'd been avoiding Faith Penrose for years.

"Anyway, let's not talk about it anymore," Mary said, changing the channel. "EastEnders is about to start."

Ed was staring hard at the television, a deep line creasing his forehead. It suddenly occurred to Blake how old her parents were getting. It was more noticeable in her father. He had once been strong and powerful, towering over a wide-eyed young Blake like a giant blotting out the sun. He still had strength, but his muscles were no longer as defined. More than that, there was a weariness in his eyes that went beyond the realms of tiredness.

Blake was hit by the sudden terror of losing her parents. Even if her relationship with her father had always been strained, the idea of his death was inconceivable. But wasn't losing your parents just part of the circle of life? The inevitability didn't make it any less terrifying.

"Those girls shouldn't have been out drinking in the first place," Ed said to the television screen. "They were underage. If they'd stayed home, this would never have happened."

Like a candle flame, the fear flickered and died. "So, you're saying that because they decided to chance having an underage drink, they deserved to be abducted and murdered?"

"Oh Blake," Mary said, waving a hand. "Don't start."

Ed glanced away. "No, not at all. I'm just saying that —"

"Because every teenager on this planet goes underage drinking at some point, Dad. I certainly did. And don't try to sit there and say that you didn't. You want to blame someone? Blame the psychopath who's taken them. Because those girls did nothing wrong."

The sound of the television filled the room. Blake turned stiffly towards the screen and tried to calm her breathing. She shot a glance back at Ed, who sucked in a deep breath and blew it out through his nose.

Mary squeezed his hand. "I wonder if they knew each other. Those girls and Lucy."

It was a question that Blake had already asked. It had led to a much bigger question. How were Lucy Truscott and the missing teenagers connected to Demelza? Eighteen years lay between them. None of the girls had been born when Demelza had vanished. And yet a thread connected them together through time.

Four young women had been taken on a Sunday. Only Lucy had been returned. Why was that?

Blake watched her parents, who in turn watched the lives of fictional characters play out on the screen. She couldn't sit around anymore, waiting for the police to find out. She had to do something.

Excusing herself, she went upstairs to make a phone call. Judy picked up almost immediately.

"Did you see the news?" she asked, sounding out of breath.

"Yes. It's bad. Really bad. Can I come over?"

"No, I've just put the girls down. Tomorrow?"

"Okay, fine. Tomorrow."

Blake hung up and sat down heavily on the edge of the bed. She felt sick to her stomach.

"Why Sundays?" she said out loud.

She was determined to find out.

19

IT WAS JUST BEFORE eight when Blake arrived at Judy's house and was ushered into her office.

"I can only give you two minutes," Judy told her, clutching a mug of coffee. "Charlie usually takes the girls to school but he had to go into the office early."

The children thundered overhead, making Blake wince as she glanced at the ceiling.

"Mornings in the Moon household aren't exactly peaceful. I've been up half the night with Lola."

"I hope she's not sick?"

"No, she's scared. She overheard some of the older children at school talking about Lucy. She woke up screaming in the night. Bad dreams. She wanted to know if someone would take her away, too. She's nine years old. She shouldn't be worrying about things like that."

Blake's eyes moved around the office space, then back to Judy, who looked like she needed a vat of coffee rather than a mug. "Have you heard anything about the investigation?"

"The police are keeping a very tight lid on what they know.

They're micromanaging the press even more than usual, barely giving us anything. Which means either they don't know much yet, or they're trying to prevent what they do know from leaking to the public. I have a feeling it's the latter."

"That's pretty standard in a murder case, isn't it? Withholding information to root out suspects from false confessors?"

"True. But it's more than that. They're not telling us anything."

"It's still early days in the case."

"It's more than that, and you know it." She locked eyes with Blake, a flash of accusation there. "In the space of a week, Lucy vanishes and is found murdered. Now we have two teenage girls apparently abducted from the street. Two days ago, Rory came by to collect my friendship bracelet for analysis. He wouldn't tell me why or anything about it, just that it was to do with the case. The other night, you said it was the same bracelet. The same one Lucy was wearing when you found her. Are you saying that Lucy's murder is connected to what happened to Demelza?"

"I don't know. It's not my case."

"Come on, Blake. Don't treat me like I'm stupid. If Lucy was wearing the same bracelet then of course there's a connection. Even without the bracelet, she's Christine's daughter. Are you telling me that's just a coincidence?"

Blake felt a tightness in her chest. "How is Christine?"

"As you'd expect. She's out of it most of the time and just wants her daughter back. The police still haven't released the body."

Judy's children thundered down the stairs, shouting and laughing. "What about those girls? Is that a coincidence, too? Or are they just two more names to add to my file?"

Blake crossed her arms and leaned against the desk.

"I hate this," Judy said. "Honestly, never have children. It will save you a world of worry."

"Just because I don't have kids doesn't mean I'm incapable of worrying," Blake said quietly. "I'm sorry you're stressed, but I don't know what to tell you. Yes, Lucy was wearing the same bracelet. Maybe the missing girls are just a coincidence. But I don't think so. Demelza, Lucy, now Heather and Leanne, all disappeared on a Sunday. I don't know what that means, but I do know it means something. And maybe there's a way to find out more."

Judy's face was lined with worry. "How?"

"Your case file of missing women. I'd like to borrow it. Maybe we can uncover something that will help the police investigation."

"Why would there —"

"Look at the facts. Demelza disappeared eighteen years ago. Now Lucy has been murdered and two other teenagers are missing. What if we assume that whoever killed Lucy also killed Demelza. Because after all this time she has to be dead. Isn't that what the friendship bracelet is telling us? It's hers, Judy. So if the same person murdered Demelza and Lucy eighteen years apart . . ."

"There could be other victims in between."

Judy retrieved the file from a shelf and held it in her hands. "You're talking about a possible serial killer."

"Maybe. I've no idea. That's why we need to check the file and look for anyone else who disappeared on a Sunday."

"A serial killer," Judy repeated, staring at Blake. "That would explain why the police aren't releasing any details. They don't want to cause a panic when they're not sure what they're dealing with. Especially when there's only one body."

"So far."

Serial killer. The word seeped into Blake's brain like poison. It was all speculation and guesswork, but the feeling in her gut told her it was true.

The office door suddenly flew open and Judy's eldest daughter marched in.

"Mum, Stacey's got my pencil case and she won't give it back!"

Judy hugged the file to her chest and sighed. "Why do you even have your pencil case out when it should be in your school bag?"

"It was in my bag. She took it out to use my colouring pens!"

"Well, you tell Stacey if it's not back in thirty seconds, she'll be dealing with her mother who has yet to finish her morning coffee. And put your coat on, we're leaving in one minute."

Lola hovered in the doorway, tired shadows under her eyes. She glanced curiously at Blake, who winked.

"Now we're leaving in fifty seconds. Go!"

Lola shut the door. They heard her bellowing at her sister as she stomped down the hall.

Blake turned back to Judy, who nodded stiffly and held out the file.

"Fine, take it. But be careful; that's months of hard work. If you find any kind of pattern or connection, anything at all, I'm the first to know about it, okay? You're not the only one with a vested interest."

Blake felt the weight of the file in her hands. Slowly, she nodded. "If there's anything in here, we'll take it to the police together."

20

BLAKE DROVE the short distance to Wheal Marow Library, which stood nearby to the high street. It was walking distance from Judy's house, but after years of stakeouts and following clients, Blake's car had replaced her legs when travelling even the shortest of distances. She had to do something about that.

Judy's case file sat on the passenger seat. Blake hadn't looked at it yet. She needed a quiet space and uninterrupted, intimate time with it. She wasn't going to get that at her parents' house because Mary was having friends over for coffee. She'd told Blake to have time to herself. Blake hadn't needed any encouragement.

The library was surprisingly large for a small town, with shelves of fiction on the lower floor, and a study space and reference books on the upper. It was a quaint old building from the Georgian era, with high ceilings and once elegant cornice that had cracked and crumbled over time. With the library's limited funds and annual threats of closure, restoration wasn't exactly a priority.

As Blake entered, a rush of warmth and nostalgia enveloped

her. She had spent much of her early teenage years browsing the shelves for adventure and escape, or sitting in a corner chair with her head lost in a book. As she grew into her late teens, she had little time for reading, but she still visited the library on occasion when in need of solitude. She had always thought of the library as a warm nest, like a gentle arm around the shoulder.

The library had been open just fifteen minutes, with two elderly patrons returning borrowed books. The librarian, Margaret Pascoe, stared at Blake in surprise. She was an older woman, around Mary's age, and had been working at the library for as long as Blake could remember. Blake greeted the librarian with a smile, who nodded respectfully and gazed at the case file pressed against her chest.

Climbing the stairs, Blake entered the study area. Four large mahogany desks took up most of the space. A shelf of reference books stood in rows on the right, while a noticeboard was pinned to the wall advertising long-expired community events. No one else was there, giving Blake plenty of room to untangle her knotted thoughts.

Sitting down in the farthest corner, she placed the case file on the desk and pulled out a notebook and pen from her bag. A large, yellowed sign taped to the wall read: No Mobile Phones. Setting her phone to silent mode, Blake slipped it beneath the cover of her notebook and looked guiltily towards the stairs. She drew in a long breath and opened Judy's case file.

A cursory flip through the pages revealed photographs, names and dates, brief descriptions spanning a period of twenty years. There were many more women than Blake had antici-pated. Women who had been here one moment and vanished the next, apparently into the ether. Cornwall had a population of half a million people, which paled in comparison to most other counties. But the land here was remote, with towns, villages and hamlets scattered like seeds in the wind. There were plenty of places to get lost. Moors, mine shafts, woodlands, and countryside. Coastline, cliffs, and sea caves, many of which were known suicide spots, such as the infamous Hell's Mouth found at the North Cliffs, or Desperation Point at Devil's Cove.

Glancing through the pages, Blake didn't doubt that some of these women had met accidental deaths, their bodies lost in the wilderness and slowly returned to nature. Others would have had mental health or addiction issues, which could often end in tragedy, again by accident or by their own hands. But Blake also knew that among these missing women there were those who were still very much alive. They had chosen to disappear, perhaps to escape an abusive spouse or family member, or because they had nothing and no one to anchor them here, and the promise of a new life with a new name in a new place was their only chance at survival.

But what about the other missing women? The ones who hadn't disappeared, but had been taken?

During her decade as a private investigator, Blake had dealt with missing person cases, many of them cold and their families unable to let go of their absent loved ones. Out of all the cases she had investigated, the only missing people she'd found were those who'd deliberately chosen to run away.

Blake turned back to the beginning of the case file and began to read. Soon, she was lost in the details of each missing woman. They were of different ages, social statuses and classes, and they had disappeared from a variety of spots all over the county. The first entries were the earliest, from twenty years ago. Blake stared into the eyes of each woman, trying to read them. But pictures were pictures, not eyes, and she could only go so deep.

The women who were still alive would look very different now. Their hair would be whiter, their skin loose and lined. She read each name: Martha, Sadie, Eleonora, Carolyn. She acknowledged that each picture was a person, each person a woman who had once lived a life with breath and thoughts and feelings. Blake turned the pages, imagining their pain, anguish and fear. Soon, an hour had passed and Blake hadn't written down a word. She closed the case file, then her eyes. She drew in a breath and centred herself. She wasn't here to read the women's stories. She was here to look for connections. Facts and figures. Dates and numbers. To think methodically, not with her emotions.

She opened her eyes and the case file. She began again, this time avoiding the faces and focusing on the text. Judy had been thorough with the details, noting down dates, times and places of the disappearances, but there was one thing she hadn't noted —which day of the week. Blake removed her phone from its hiding place and opened the search browser. This was going to be slow work.

Starting with the first profiles, she noted the dates, typed them into Google, and found online calendars for the corre- sponding years. Martha Tallack, 32, had vanished on a Monday. Brenda Tonkin had disappeared on a Friday. Blake discarded them both, ignoring the guilty feeling in her chest. Susan Heller vanished on a Thursday. So did Gracie Hale. And then, twenty- five minutes later, she turned the page and found Henriette Bolitho. She had been eighty-two when she disappeared from a garden party in Fowey, seven years ago on the eighth of January.

A Sunday.

Blake stared at the elderly woman's face. She had kind eyes that glittered with wisdom. At eighty-two, she didn't match

Blake's criteria. Nevertheless, she removed Henriette from the case file and set her to one side. Right now was about searching for Sundays. The profiles could be whittled down later.

She continued turning the pages, writing down dates, consulting Google, and separating profiles. Two hours later, twenty-three missing person profiles sat in a tidy pile on the desk. Blake's spine was aching. Her bladder pressed uncomfortably against her jeans.

Twenty-three names. More than she'd anticipated. Hidden among them were possible secrets waiting to be revealed. Information that might help identify Lucy's killer and find the missing teenagers. But these twenty-three women needed further research, analysis and elimination.

Blake stared at the wall clock. "Damn it!"

It was almost two in the afternoon. She'd promised Mary to be home by one-thirty. Packing up her things, she slipped the profiles inside her notebook and made her way to the lower floor, where she quickly used the bathroom and waved goodbye to Margaret, the librarian.

Outside, the day was muted by clouds and a cold breeze stung her face. Blake headed for her car, then stopped as a voice called her name.

"Blake, darlin'? Yoo-hoo!"

Tina Moon, Judy's mother, was marching up the street, heading straight for her. When Blake had bumped into Tina at the supermarket last week, she had been full of smiles. Today, a frown troubled her brow.

"Hello Tina. Everything all right?"

"I'm not sure," she said. "I just had a call from Alice about Brett."

Alice was Tina's sister-in-law and Judy's aunt. Her son Brett worked for Blake's father as a bricklayer.

"Brett? What about him?" Blake asked.

Tina peered cautiously over her shoulder then leaned in closer. "He phoned Alice. Said the police are down at the site. Rory's there looking all serious, along with that other detective I've seen around town. The one who never smiles."

Turner, Blake thought. "What do they want?"

"Don't know exactly. But Brett said they wanted to speak to your father in private. It must be about poor Lucy."

"Why would you think that?"

"What else would it be about? Anyway, Brett said there were two more police snooping around. One was taking samples of the building materials. It's strange, isn't it?"

An unsettled feeling was churning Blake's stomach. She searched Tina's face. "How long ago was this?"

"Well, Alice called me ten minutes ago and she'd just got off the phone with him. They were still there then." Tina frowned and shook her head. "I'm sure it's nothing to worry about, darlin'. Probably just following up a lead or something, like they do on the television. Anyway, I'm sure your father will tell you all about it when he gets home. You seen Judy yet?"

"This morning."

"Ooh, lovely. Right on, I better get back. Those potatoes for tea won't peel themselves. Give my love to your mum, won't you? Hope she's back on her feet soon."

Tina waved a hand and continued on her journey. Blake watched her go, the missing girls temporarily forgotten. What did the police want with her father?

The construction site was a new housing development just outside of town. She could drive there in five minutes. But she was already late for her mother, who would be alone unless one of her friends had stayed behind.

Heading to her car, Blake placed the case file carefully on the passenger seat. She started the engine and pulled away. Her father would have some questions to answer when he returned home that evening.

21

Ed Hollow returned home at his usual time of a quarter past five. Blake was waiting for him in the kitchen, where she was busy cooking dinner. He greeted her with a nod as he carried his lunch box and flask over to the kitchen sink. He looked lost, as if he wasn't sure what to do with them. Then he began washing them up in silence. Blake stared at him, ready to hear all about what the police had been doing at the building site. But Ed dried his hands and excused himself to greet Mary before heading upstairs to remove his dusty work clothes and take a shower.

They ate dinner together in front of the television. Mary was tired, her leg aching and uncomfortable, but she asked her usual questions of Ed's day: 'Was it busy? How were the boys?' Ed responded with his usual answers: 'Busy enough. Oh you know, lazy as dogs but they're good boys, really.'

Blake watched her father closely but resisted speaking up. With dinner over, she collected her mother's plate and headed for the door. "Dad, can you give me a hand with the dishes?"

Ed looked up, perplexed.

"Your father's had a long day," Mary said.

"Me too. Come on, Dad. We can have father-daughter time."

Ed let out a deep sigh and got to his feet.

"I'll make you a cup of tea, love," he told Mary. He stroked her hair as he passed.

In the kitchen, Blake filled the sink with soapy water. For years, her mother had resisted purchasing a dishwasher, insisting that a machine couldn't clean as well as a pair of hands. Her father had remained indifferent; he wasn't exactly in the habit of washing dishes. Now father and daughter stood next to each other, Blake scrubbing at dirty plates, Ed gently towelling them dry and placing them on the counter, as if he wasn't quite sure where to put them away. They made idle talk about the weather and Mary's recovery time. Until Blake couldn't hold her impatience any longer.

"I heard the police came down to the site today," she said, staring at him.

Ed froze. Panic flickered in his eyes.

"Who told you that?" He got moving again, picking up a plate from the rack and drying it methodically.

"Small town grapevine. What were they doing there?"

"Nothing. Whoever told you should have minded their own business."

"I'm glad they didn't. I heard Rory was there, along with D.S. Turner."

Ed set the plate on the counter and grabbed a handful of cutlery. His frown grew deeper. "They were asking questions, that's all."

"About Lucy? Or those missing Truro girls?"

"They asked if any of our materials had gone missing from

the site. They took a few cement samples and asked for a list of employees. Like I said, it was nothing."

Blake stopped scrubbing. "That doesn't sound like nothing, Dad. What do they need the samples for?"

"Didn't ask. Not my business."

"Of course it's your business. Quite literally. If police were snooping around *my* business, taking things and wanting a list of employees, I'd be deeply concerned. Why aren't you?"

"The Angove boy said it was nothing to worry about. They're just following up on information, looking for clues, that's all. It's what the police do, isn't it? The boys are good lads. Despite what I say, they're hard workers. There's not a bad seed among them."

"I'm sure the Yorkshire Ripper's boss thought he was a good worker, too."

Ed wiped his hands on the towel and hung it up to dry, then filled the kettle with water at the sink. He glanced back at the kitchen door. "It would be better if you didn't tell your mother about the police coming by. She's got enough on her plate with her leg."

"Mum is going to find out sooner or later. You know what Wheal Marow is like. News travels fast."

A sudden sense of urgency was making Blake's pulse race. Why did the police want cement samples? It certainly was a strange request.

Scratching the stubble on his jaw, Ed let out a long sigh. "All the same. For now, your mother doesn't need to know."

"Okay, fine. My lips are sealed."

Her father stood, staring into space with the weight of the world pressing down on his shoulders. He's worried, Blake thought. Only he's too damn pig-headed to admit it.

"I'll make the tea," she said. "Go and keep Mum company."

Ed turned to leave, wavered again, and turned back to Blake. "The other night in the car, I was hard on you. You probably didn't need that after seeing what you saw."

"It doesn't matter now. Forget it."

Her father lingered, his eyes fixed on the floor. Then he left the room and carefully shut the kitchen door.

Emptying the sink of dirty water, Blake dried her hands and leaned against the counter. She was shaking and she didn't know why.

Why cement?

The kettle boiled and clicked off, but Blake didn't hear it. She was back at Ding Dong Mine, staring at Lucy Truscott's crucified, eyeless body and her horribly charred flesh.

Blake's breath caught in her throat. Suddenly she knew why the police were so interested in cement, and the knowledge filled her with horror.

22

Leanne lay on the cold ground with her knees pulled up and her thumb tucked in her mouth. As she slowly drifted back to consciousness, she felt the heaviness of her head and limbs, and the stiffness of her muscles. She tried to swallow but her throat was dry. There was a taste on her tongue, sharp and chemical. Pushing herself up on her hands, Leanne slowly opened her eyes. Darkness swarmed around her. She blinked and panicked, convinced she'd gone blind. Memories returned to her like shards of ice piercing her brain. Terror rose up from the pit of her stomach. There had been a white van. A large figure springing towards her. Powerful hands gripping her throat.

The memory was a match thrown on a petrol-drenched bonfire. Her synapses lit up. Adrenaline shot through her veins.

Leanne jumped up. She stumbled forward and immediately slammed into an invisible wall. The breath was punched from her lungs. She was on her back again, red and white fireworks filling her vision as pain assaulted her body.

Gasping for air, she pushed up on her elbows and scrambled

backwards. The back of her head slammed into another wall. Rolling into a crouch, she backed away until she hit a corner.

Her entire body was trembling as if in seizure. She waved a hand in front of her eyes, but the darkness remained.

Another memory came to her.

"Heather?" she whispered. She swallowed and tried again, louder this time. "Heather, are you here?"

Leanne waited in the dark, listening intently as terror gnawed at her bones. She sucked in a breath and shrieked. "Heather! For God's sake, where are you?"

Silence.

Getting to her feet again, she stretched her hands out in front. She took three steps forward and her palms collided with the wall. It was cold and smooth against her skin, like glass rather than brick or cement. Taking small side steps, she followed the length of the wall, reached a corner, and continued along. Three more steps and she found another corner.

Her heart thumped painfully. Tears slipped down her face. She came to yet another corner then felt the outline of a door. Her fingers searched for the handle, but there was only a keyhole and a small shelf at waist height with a sealed flap above it.

Leanne raised her hands over her head. Her fingertips touched the ceiling.

"Oh no," she whispered. "No, no, no."

She was trapped inside a box that was approximately five feet wide, three feet deep, and six feet high. A prison cell made of plastic glass.

Leanne lowered her hands and wrapped them around her ribs. Her lungs were on fire, making it hard to breathe. She slid one foot back then the other, until she was pressed up against the rear wall.

Why was this happening?

She and Heather were good and kind. Yes, they'd been underage drinking, but they hadn't hurt anyone. Hot tears splashed her face. A strange, guttural moan climbed her throat.

"Heather!" she cried. "Can you hear me?"

Where had she been taken? Was she still in Truro or somewhere else? It was still night-time judging by the darkness, but she couldn't hear anything except for her own pitiful sobs.

She pressed her back into the wall and slid down it. She wanted her mum and dad and her little brother, Tony. She wanted to be far away from here, bathed in daylight and surrounded by safety. Uncurling her arms, she checked her pockets for her phone, then got on her hands and knees to search the ground. Cold metal bit her fingers. She gripped the object with both hands and let out a shocked gasp.

It was a bucket. She was trapped in a cell with only a bucket to piss in. No water. No food. No escape.

Tears came. Great, undulating sobs that shook her body. The scream that had been climbing her throat broke free, erupting as a tortured, desperate wail.

"Please! Someone help me!"

She couldn't stay inside this box. She felt the walls pressing down on her. The air being sucked from her lungs.

Leanne sprang to her feet again and threw herself in the direction of the door. The small shelf slammed into her stomach.

"Let me out! I'm begging you, let me out!"

She drew back and launched herself at the door again. This time the shelf slammed painfully into her ribs. Leanne spun, rolling against the glass wall. She slapped her hands against the surface, making the cell shake. And then she stopped breathing.

Someone was here. In the dark.

She couldn't see them, but she could sense the shifting air particles and feel their energy pulsating outwards like heat waves on a summer's day.

Leanne backed away from the door. Her voice was a whisper. "Heather? Is that you?"

Footsteps moved towards her, heavy and deliberate, with a slight echo.

Leanne strained her eyes and clutched her hands against her throat. The footsteps stopped on the other side of the glass.

Was there a silhouette there? It was still so dark that she couldn't see.

But she could feel it. Feel *him*.

"Please," she whispered. "Please, I won't say anything."

Now she thought she could see a shape. Darkness on top of darkness. A black hole tearing open in space.

And she heard breathing, slow and steady like the pulse of a reptile.

"If I did something wrong, I'm sorry. Please. I'm only sixteen. Won't you let me go?"

Trembling in the darkness, terror igniting her blood, Leanne stared at the shape. And then the shape spoke, and its voice was like a knife hacking through flesh and bone.

"Sin when it is fully grown brings forth death," it said. "And you, my corrupted child, are the worst kind of sinner of all."

23

BLAKE ARRIVED at Kenver's house just before nine, armed with two cups of takeaway coffee and a paper bag of pastries. She hammered awkwardly on the door, spilling coffee on her coat. When Kenver didn't answer, she grumbled under her breath and knocked harder. She had stayed up much of the night, wading through medical journals and documents, and analysing images of shocking burns. She learned that cement was a binder, used to mix other materials together to form concrete and mortar. It was less caustic in its powder form, but once mixed with water a chemical reaction occurred that sent its pH level soaring. If it got on human skin, the effects could be devastating. It could easily burn through flesh and eyes. Left untreated long enough, it could eat through muscle and even bone. Years ago, Blake's father had slipped and fallen on a freshly concreted floor. The cement had seeped through his trousers and stripped the skin from his knees. He still had the scars to this day.

At 3 a.m., Blake had come to the nauseating conclusion that the chemical burns she'd seen on Lucy's body matched the images on her laptop screen.

Anyone could buy cement from the nearest hardware store, so it didn't necessarily mean the killer was a construction worker. Even if they were, her father's company wasn't the only one in Cornwall. But it was the most local. Was one of Ed's employees Lucy's killer? The idea sent shivers through Blake's body.

Hammering on the door with renewed fervour, she called Kenver's name. When he still didn't answer, she tried the door handle. The door swung open.

Stepping inside, she sniffed the stale air and wrinkled her nose.

"Kenver? It's your favourite cousin."

She closed the door and went to the living room, where the curtains were still drawn and detritus littered the room. What was Kenver doing with his life? More to the point, where was he?

Returning to the hallway, she climbed the stairs. Kenver's bedroom was the first door on the right. It was wide open. Blake slid forward and hovered on the threshold. The curtains were closed in here too, but she could make out two forms slumped in the bed. She watched them for a moment before sucking in a deep breath.

"Fire!" she yelled. "Quick, get up! The house is burning!"

Immediately, the body on the left sat bolt upright, threw back the sheets, and sprang out of bed.

Blake arched an eyebrow. It was the young man she'd seen Kenver with at the barn party last week. He stood, naked and tense, and thoroughly confused. Spotting Blake, he covered his crotch with one hand, then tore off the top sheet from the bed and wrapped it around his waist.

On the right side of the bed, Kenver's eyes opened and blinked twice.

"Sorry," Blake said. "If I'd known you had a guest, I would have brought more coffee."

Kenver let out an exasperated sigh. "What do you want, Blake?"

"You know you really shouldn't go to bed with the door unlocked. Anyone could break in. In fact, judging by the state of the house, it looks like someone already did."

The young man was still hovering, one hand clutching the tightly wrapped sheet.

"Get up, Kenver," Blake said. "I need to talk to you."

Ten minutes later, Kenver's guest had made a hasty exit and Blake had opened the living room curtains. She looked at the debris, resisting the urge to tidy. Now dressed but barefoot, Kenver sat on the sofa. His hair was a mess and he was still waking up. He sipped the coffee Blake had given him. The pastry had been unceremoniously dumped on the coffee table next to several empty bottles of wine.

"So, what is it?" he grumbled.

Blake pulled a folder from her bag and handed it to him, then started to pace in front of the window. "Inside you'll find missing person reports on twenty-three women. They all disappeared from various places around Cornwall over the last couple of decades. None of them have ever been found. On the surface they appear to have little in common—except for one thing."

"Which is?"

"They all disappeared on a Sunday. Just like Lucy Truscott. Just like my friend Demelza eighteen years ago."

Kenver put the file down on the sofa. "Can you sit still? You're making me nauseous."

Blake slipped her hands inside her jeans pockets. Nervous energy thrummed through her body and a deep-seated fear coiled in her stomach. Lucy. Demelza. Now these two young women. They all called to her, asking for help. It was too late for Lucy. Too late for Demelza. But for Leanne Curnow and Heather Hargreaves, there was still perhaps a chance.

She knew it was the police force's job to find them. But she could still help.

Blake turned back to Kenver. "You're a data analyst, which means you're good at spotting patterns. So I need you to go through all twenty-three files and find out what connects these women."

"What makes you think there's a connection?"

"A feeling."

"No evidence?"

"Not yet. That's why I need you to look. Did any of these women know each other? Did they have similar jobs? Did they move in similar circles, social or otherwise? Collate the ones that have any kind of similarity. Remove the ones that don't."

"That sounds like a lot of work. Why can't you do it?"

"Because you'll be faster at this kind of thing, and I've been neglecting Mum."

Kenver eyed the file. "What do I get in return? I assume I'm not getting paid."

Blake smiled. "I'll tell you what you won't get. You won't get a lecture from me about whatever it is you're doing with your life right now, which from where I'm standing, looks a lot like self-sabotage."

"Exactly how is this not a lecture?"

"You're right, fair enough. But I also won't tell your Auntie Mary about the things I've seen, which means she won't call your mother."

Kenver put down his coffee cup and stared squarely at Blake. "News flash. I'm twenty-eight years old. A fully grown adult. My choices, whether you like them or not, are mine to make. Neither you or Auntie Mary, or my mother, come to that, get to tell me what to do with my life. Which means if I want to fuck it up, it's my absolute right. Besides, when did you get to be so judgemental? You're not exactly the Virgin Mary."

"I'm not talking about your bedroom activities, Kenver. I'm talking about this." Blake swept a hand towards the littered coffee table. "It smells like a bar in here. One of those really nasty ones with sticky carpets."

"Oh, so I'm an alcoholic now, as well as a slut."

"I'm worried, that's all. Aren't I allowed to worry about my little cousin?"

"Your cousin isn't so little anymore. And you haven't been my babysitter for years." Snatching up the folder, Kenver thumbed through the first few pages. He was quiet for a minute, his expression intense. He looked up. "Fine, I'll help. But stop pushing me around. If I want to live like a pig, I'll live like a pig. Whether you like it or not."

"I don't. But fine. Thank you, little cuz."

"Don't ever call me that again."

Blake's phone began to ring in her coat pocket. Retrieving it, she saw that the caller ID read: Private Number.

"Blake Hollow," she answered.

She sensed anger before the caller had spoken a word.

"It's Detective Sergeant Will Turner. I need you to come to Truro station as soon as possible. Now, in fact."

"Is everything all right?" Blake glanced worriedly at Kenver. "You sound agitated."

"No, I'm not all right, Ms Hollow. In fact, I'm bloody livid. So please, get here as soon as you can because you've got some explaining to do."

Aware that her cheeks were flushed, Blake turned away and dropped her voice. "Explaining to do about what?"

But D.S. Turner had already hung up.

Blake slipped her phone back inside her coat pocket. What on earth was he talking about? She thought back over the previous few days but couldn't think of a single action she'd taken to incense the detective.

"Well, well," Kenver said, with a wry smile. "Looks like I'm not the only one making bad choices today."

Blake glared at him as she headed for the front door.

24

BLAKE WAS BACK inside the interview room. But there was no coffee this time, and no friendly faces. DS Turner entered and sat down on the other side of the desk. DC Angove came next, his eyes fixed to the floor.

"Hello Rory," Blake said.

Angove only nodded.

"Thank you for coming in," DS Turner said, staring directly at Blake. "I don't have time to waste, so I'll get straight to the point. We'd like to know why you tampered with Lucy Truscott's body before the authorities arrived at the scene."

Blake's jaw fell open. Her eyes shifted from Turner to Rory. It took her a moment to find her voice.

"I have no idea what you're talking about."

Turner leaned forward. "Ms Hollow."

"It's Blake."

"We have two missing young women, and a teenager's horribly mutilated body in the morgue. I need you to be honest with me."

"I didn't touch her. I'm not stupid, Detective Sergeant. I know better than that."

"I'm not stupid, either. And I'm *very* close to charging you with spoliation of evidence. You need to explain to me right now in clear detail exactly what you did, and whether you removed anything from the body."

"Whatever this is, you've made a mistake." The room seemed to shrink around Blake as a shocked smile involuntarily spread across her face. She stared at DC Angove. "Come on, Rory. You know me. I wouldn't do something as reckless as interfere with a crime scene. It's against my code of conduct."

Rory's gaze remained fixed on the table.

"I didn't realise codes of conduct were taught at private investigator school," Turner said. "I'm deadly serious, Ms Hollow. If there is evidence missing from the crime scene, now is the time to speak up."

Blake leaned back in her chair, staring from one detective to the other. "I swear I didn't touch Lucy. I stayed at least five feet away from her at all times."

Her gaze shifted back to DS Turner, whose complexion had turned a shade of red. "Then, please enlighten me. If you didn't touch the body, why is your DNA all over the friendship bracelet?"

Blake caught her breath. "What are you talking about?"

"The forensic test results came back," Turner said. "The bracelet that Lucy was wearing, the one you tried to convince me belonged to your friend Demelza, the DNA we found on it matches the sample swab we took from you last week."

"There has to be a mistake," she whispered. Her mind was racing, along with her heart. None of this made sense.

"Newsflash. DNA doesn't lie. If you didn't touch the bracelet then explain to me why you're all over it."

Blake couldn't, and she was quickly realising the position she was in. "What about the rest of the body? Did you find my DNA anywhere else?"

"Just the bracelet. Did you place it on Lucy Truscott's wrist? What else have you been lying about?"

"Nothing!"

She hadn't touched the bracelet. She stared squarely at Turner as she struggled for breath.

"There are two possibilities," he said, "The DNA is new, which means you tampered with the body. Or the DNA is old, which means the bracelet isn't Demelza's. It's yours."

The realisation struck Blake like a punch to the gut. "That's impossible. That bracelet is eighteen years old. How could my DNA still be on it?"

"Quite easily. All you'd have to do is store it in an airtight container at a cool temperature and out of direct sunlight, and your DNA would last for years. More and more cold cases are being solved with DNA testing every year, some with evidence that's a lot older than the bracelet."

The room was spinning. She had lost her bracelet years ago. She didn't know where or how. All she knew was that it had gone missing around the same time as Demelza. The thing was always making her skin itch, so she'd frequently taken it off. Maybe she'd put it down somewhere one day and forgotten to pick it up. All she knew was that she'd done a good job of hiding its loss from Judy and Christine.

Turner was staring at her. "So which is it, Ms Hollow? Old DNA or new?"

Blake swallowed. She shook her head and stared back at him, creeping dread climbing up her throat.

25

DENNIS STOTT STOOD in the darkness of the warehouse, spine upright, shoulders broad and his eyes shut, as he listened to the girl's gentle sobbing. She had shrieked hysterically for five long minutes, begging for release and wailing uncontrollably as she hammered against the walls. She would not be able to break them. The cell was made of polycarbonate, the same near-indestructible material that police riot shields were made from. It had been easy to get hold of; he'd simply ordered the sheets from a hardware store. They had even cut each sheet to his requested measurements. The cell had withstood many beatings and escape attempts over the years, but it was still standing as strongly as the day he'd built it.

The girl had told Dennis she'd done nothing wrong, but she was a liar. He had seen her with his own eyes. She was a sinner. A vile hypocrite basking in God's love at Sunday church, then committing sacrilege by drinking in dilapidated bars like Satan's whore. Liars had to be punished. Hypocrites too. For hypocrites were the worst kind of liar, self-righteously preaching what is good and right, then wallowing in sin like pigs in mud. Dennis could not stand hypocrites, especially those that snivelled in the dark, claiming innocence.

Opening his eyes, he stared through the shadows towards the cell. He couldn't see her, but he could still hear her quiet weeping and he could sense her fear. It made his skin prickle. She would soon join the others. She would be cleansed and brought back to righteousness. Such was the will of God.

Dennis turned his back to face the wide, open space of the warehouse. He could feel the others in the darkness. All of his beauties, cleansed and transformed.

"Exquisite," he whispered.

She would join them soon, but first there was an urgent problem needing his attention. Because instead of taking one, he had taken two. Leanne was in the tank. The other was in the basement of his home. She had not been part of his plan, but all the noise she'd made in the street had drawn unwanted attention, and he'd been forced to take her. Now that unwanted attention was mutating dangerously.

The girls' faces were all over the television news bulletins and the front pages of the newspapers. The police knew about his white van, but the number plate would not lead them to him. As for the girls' mobile phones, he had tossed them from the window before escaping, so they couldn't find him that way either. Dennis was thoughtful and intelligent. He had spent years designing and executing his plan. It was fool proof.

And yet his elation was quickly deflating. All these years, he had moved around like a ghost, undetected and unrealised. Now the unwanted media attention was threatening his anonymity and shrinking his window of opportunity.

He would not be stopped now. Not when he was so close to completion.

What should he do with the girl in the basement? She had no purpose and nothing to offer. Although Lucy Truscott had not been part of his plan either, he had found a use for her. But the girl in the basement? She was simply a problem that needed to be erased.

He crossed the warehouse floor, work boots echoing in the air. Behind him, Leanne's whimpers grew louder and more desperate. Dennis squeezed his powerful hands into fists and counted his steps through the darkness, until he reached a steel security door.

Anxiety was to be expected this close to completion, but he didn't like the way it squeezed his heart and pressed down on his chest. Leanne would be cleansed in four days. Then there would be just one more to take and his work would be complete. Perhaps he would need to advance his plan, before the search for the girls brought further unwanted attention. Or worse, identification.

Or perhaps there was a way to divert the police detectives' focus elsewhere.

An idea came to him. It meant the plan would have to be amended slightly, but he could permit that if it allowed him to complete his work in peace, and without the risk of discovery.

Dennis slipped the key into the lock. His heart pounded in the darkness like a timpani drum. He stared over his shoulder at the inky blackness of the warehouse, sensing his girls all around him. He heard their whispers, soothing his mind, telling him all would be well soon. Silvery daylight seeped in as he opened the door and slipped outside. As he shut the door again, he caught sight of what lay inside.

"Beautiful," he whispered. "Beautiful and pure."

A fog had crept up from the ocean to descend upon the

coastline. It swarmed around him, cold and wet against his skin as he crossed the yard. The deep drone of a ship's horn broke through the thick blanket. Salt hung heavy in the air and tasted sharp on his tongue. A building emerged from the fog, a quaint oceanside cottage that was in need of a fresh coat of paint. Rounding the corner, he unfastened a padlock on the side door and entered a small workshop. He slid two deadbolts across, passed through the workshop and into the kitchen. Warmth enveloped him. Dewy drops of moisture began to evaporate on his skin.

A diversion, then. But first he needed to take care of the girl in the basement. She would be awake soon. She would not be joining the others, but she still needed to be cleansed.

Filling a kettle with water, he placed it on the range, lit a match, and watched blue petals of flame flicker from the hob. He spooned loose tea into a teapot, then fetched a packet of digestive biscuits from the cupboard and shook a few out onto a plate. His reward for doing good work.

As the kettle began to heat, he removed a meat tenderiser from one of the drawers and flipped it over in his hand. Too light. Even with his strength it would be a long, drawn out task.

Returning the tenderiser to the drawer, he got on his knees and pulled out an old toolbox from a cupboard beneath the sink. Inside, he found a claw hammer. The handle was worn, the metal chipped and rusted, but the weight felt good in his hand.

Dennis paused to remove strands of hair caught between the claws, then got to his feet once more. He crossed the room and opened the basement door. Humming under his breath, he descended the steps into darkness. Dennis took no pleasure in his work. It was a necessary evil to rid the world of sin.

26

Darkness came early, bringing heavy rain. Blake returned to Kenver's house. She was accompanied by Judy, who had left Charlie in charge of the girls. To their surprise, Kenver had tidied up and made dinner. Blake wasn't hungry. She was quiet and distracted, deeply troubled by the bracelet found on Lucy Truscott. How could it be hers? But as DS Turner had stated, DNA didn't lie. How the bracelet had ended up on Lucy's wrist was another mystery. One she was reluctant to solve.

Blake had spent most of the afternoon at the police station. After removing Rory from the interview room, Turner continued to grill Blake about the night of Demelza's disappearance. Who was there? What happened? Did anyone have reason to hurt Demelza or end her life? Blake answered as succinctly as she could, even though he'd asked the same questions just days before. She even suggested he dig out the old case file and take a look for himself, which didn't go down well.

Turner then circled back to Blake's discovery of Lucy's body. He asked why she thought her friendship bracelet had ended up on Lucy's wrist. He quizzed her until she wanted to lean over and punch him in the face.

Frustrated and tired, Blake finally interrupted the detective to share the findings from her own investigation: twenty-three other missing women had all disappeared on a Sunday from all over Cornwall in the past twenty years. Confusion and unease swept over Turner's face. He demanded she hand over the files at the first available opportunity, then he warned her not to interfere any further with police business.

Now, huddled on the sofa with Kenver in the middle and Judy on his right, Blake struggled to focus.

"Here's what I found so far," Kenver said, as he stared at the laptop on the freshly polished coffee table. There was a difference in him, Blake noted, a brightness in his eyes and an energy that straightened his entire posture. "I've managed to eliminate seven of the women from the list. They'd either already been found alive, were too old, or didn't match the connection I discovered."

Judy leaned forward, staring at the screen. "What connection?"

"As we know, the sixteen remaining women all disappeared on a Sunday. What we didn't know until now is that all sixteen vanished after leaving a bar or nightclub. If you add Lucy to the list, that makes seventeen."

"Demelza makes eighteen," Blake said. "She disappeared from a party, which is close enough."

Kenver tapped the table excitedly. "There's more. These women disappeared one per year, every year, starting with your friend Demelza."

"Eighteen years. Eighteen women," Judy said. "That has to be more than just a coincidence."

They fell silent, the glare from the laptop screen bleaching their faces.

"Sunday is the Sabbath," Blake mused. "Is drinking on the Sabbath considered a sin?"

Kenver snorted. "If it is, I'm going straight to hell."

"Drinking alcohol isn't considered a sin as far as I know," Judy said. "Getting drunk, maybe. But the blood of Christ, water into wine et cetera . . ."

Blake stared at the laptop and drummed her fingers on her knees. "Were these women churchgoers?"

"Lucy was," Judy said. "Did Demelza go to church? I can't remember."

"She did. Mostly to keep her parents happy. Kenver, what about the others?"

"Unknown."

"All these women are disappearing from pubs or clubs on a Sunday; it has to mean something. And once a year is significant. Did they vanish the same time each year?"

Kenver scanned his notes on the screen. "No, they didn't."

"Where are the bodies?" Blake asked. "Most serial killers dump their victims once they've served their purpose. They might hold onto body parts as a keepsake, but the rest usually get thrown away like rubbish. So where are all these women? And what about Lucy? She was splayed out for all the world to see. Why was she returned when the others weren't?"

Judy clasped her hands in a steeple and tucked them under her chin. "Don't forget the two missing students. One woman, once a year. But Lucy, Heather Hargreaves and Leanne Curnow make three. Heather and Leanne were taken together, which doesn't fit either."

"Maybe it's not a serial killer," Kenver said. "Maybe we've got it wrong, and this is all just coincidence."

"It's not," Blake said.

"How can you be sure?"

Because of the friendship bracelet, she thought. Because it's mine.

Whoever left it on Lucy's wrist was sending her a message. Telling her to look to the past.

She stared at Kenver, then at Judy, who were both waiting for an answer. But she couldn't tell them, not only because Turner would have her head on a plate, but because she didn't want to scare them.

Blake looked away again. "I just am, that's all."

She stood up and stretched her spine, then moved over to the window. The curtains were still open, and rain spattered the glass. It was dark outside, a single streetlamp casting a weak pool of light across the road.

"You both should continue digging into these missing women's lives, including Heather Hargreaves and Leanne Curnow. Find out if they were churchgoers. See if there are any other connections."

Kenver shook his head. "Look, I was happy to help out, but I need to be looking for work."

"Come on, Kenver."

"I can handle it myself," Judy said. "What about you, Blake? What are you going to do?"

"I need to talk to Christine."

"Are you sure that's a good idea? She's a mess right now."

"I know, but I have to try. Lucy is different to all the others. She's the only one whose body has been found. I need to find out why. Sooner rather than later."

Judy was staring intensely at Blake, her eyes half narrowed. "What do you know that you're not telling us?"

"Nothing."

"Bollocks. I've known you long enough to know when you're lying."

Kenver was staring now too, his dark eyes glittering with curiosity.

"I can't tell you," Blake said. "Not yet. Not until I've spoken to Christine."

"That hardly seems fair. I thought we were in this together."

"Please, Judy. Trust me on this."

The two women stared at each other, tension growing between them.

At last, Judy relented. "Fine. But you've got some explaining to do when we next meet."

"I will. I promise." Blake sucked in a breath and let it out in a shudder. "So, let's get to work."

27

BLAKE WAS UP EARLY the next morning, preparing breakfast for her mother and sorting out her needs for the day. She felt guilty that she was leaving again, but she had arranged for one of Mary's friends to visit so that she wouldn't be alone. Blake's father had already left for work. There had been no further mention of the police visit to the construction site. Yesterday, Blake had been so shocked by the revelation of the friendship bracelet that she had entirely forgotten to ask DS Turner about it. Not that he would have told her anything.

Now Blake stood on the front doorstep of Christine Truscott's home, the cheerful tone of the doorbell resonating in her ears. Her heart raced. Anxiety made her fingers twitch.

Leslie opened the door and greeted Blake with a cutting glare.

"Christine isn't seeing anyone right now," she said.

She went to close the door, but Blake held up a hand. "Please. It's important."

Leslie glowered at her. "You're supposed to be one of Christine's oldest friends. Judy's called repeatedly. Too much, if you ask me. And yet all you've done is send a pathetic text message telling *her* to call you."

Blake stared at the doorstep. She couldn't deny it, yet at the same time she couldn't explain why she'd kept her distance. She had never been comfortable around death, not that most people were. It was the grief, she supposed. It cascaded from those in pain like water from a broken dam, and the only way she knew how not to drown in it was to stay far away.

Leslie had a hand on her hip and was staring at Blake like an old school headmistress. "Just as I thought. No answer."

A tired, blunt voice called out from the hall behind. "For goodness sake, Leslie. Just let her in."

Leslie peered over her shoulder, then back at Blake. She puffed out her cheeks, shot another glare at Blake, then opened the door wider to reveal Christine. She was deathly pale and exhausted-looking.

"Suit yourself," Leslie muttered. She stomped past her sister and down the hall until she reached the stairs, where she continued on without looking back.

Christine and Blake stared at each other in silence.

"She doesn't mean anything," Christine said, her voice slow and unsteady. "She's just being the protective older sister."

She stepped aside to let Blake in, then shut the door. Keeping her coat on, Blake followed Christine into the living room, which was clean and tidy as always. A pot of tea sat on the table, wisps of steam curling from the spout.

"You want some?" Christine asked, as they sat down.

Blake politely declined. Her gaze shifted around the room until she forced it back to Christine.

"I'm sorry," she said. "For not being in touch sooner. I'm not very good at this kind of thing."

Christine picked up the teapot and poured tea into a cup. "You've always shied away from other people's feelings. Besides, I can't imagine anyone being very good at handling a time like this. You're here now. How is your mother?"

Another pinch of guilt in Blake's chest. "She's fine. Recovering well. She's not a fan of being dependent on others and thinks she can still do everything. But you know Mary. Stubborn as a mule."

"Must run in the family."

"How are you holding up?" Blake winced, instantly regretting the question.

Christine shook her head. "I seem to veer between wanting people around me and wanting to be alone. Mostly it's the latter. Between you and me, I think Leslie is scared of what I'd do if I was left on my own for more than a minute." She added milk to her cup then lifted it to her lips, where it hung frozen in time. The cup trembled in Christine's hand. Her eyes were red and filled with tears. She put the cup down again, spilling droplets on the saucer.

"Just when I think I've run out of tears. Where do they all come from?"

Blake picked up a box of tissues from the table and handed it over.

"I'm surprised my body isn't a dried up husk," Christine said. She dabbed her eyes then carefully rolled the tissue into a ball and tucked it beneath the sleeve of her cardigan. Troubled, she stared at Blake. "Did you hear about those two missing girls?"

"Yes."

"I keep thinking about their poor parents. They're younger

than Lucy, you know. People are saying they've been taken by the same monster who took . . . who took my little girl. I hope it isn't true. I hope it's all a misunderstanding and they come home soon."

"Have the police told you anything?"

"No. The family liaison officer is here most days, but she can only tell me what she's allowed to. She's very kind. She stayed with me until late last night. I expect she'll be back again soon." Christine was still staring at Blake, searching her eyes. "Someone told me the police were at your father's site."

"It's true. But it's just routine. They're going door to door, appealing for information."

"I suppose that makes sense."

Blake leaned forward. "Christine, I wanted to ask you something."

"Go ahead."

"Did you ever talk to Lucy about Demelza?"

The question surprised Christine. She was quiet for a minute, a small, blue vein throbbing at her left temple. "Yes, I did. Lucy came to me one day and asked about her. Some of her college friends had been talking about Demelza's disappearance, about how she'd never been found. You know what college kids are like—they love an urban legend. Lucy is . . . was . . . a curious soul. Always has been. She was fascinated by Demelza. I'm not sure why. Maybe she felt some sort of connection."

"Like what?"

"I don't know. Maybe because all of her friends were leaving to go to university and she was being left behind. Just like Demelza. Just like her mother."

Blake felt terrible but she needed to know. "What did you tell her?"

"Everything. Lucy kept asking lots of questions. Was Demelza happy? Had she ever been in love? I even found her going through boxes of my old photographs. In a way, Lucy was like you. She liked to solve puzzles and she hated questions that didn't have answers."

"What about church? I hear Lucy was a regular attendee."

"Another one of her curiosities. She found it fascinating . . . the congregation and the community. She was a good girl, my Lucy. Kind and generous. Did you know she volunteered at the church's foodbank as well? She was like that, always wanting to help." Christine let out a trembling breath and placed her hands on her knees. "What's this all about, Blake? I know you're not here just to see how I am. What do you know?"

"I need to ask you another question."

"Blake —"

"I'm sorry, but please, Christine. It's important and it might help. Do you remember the friendship bracelets the four of us used to wear? Did you give yours to Lucy?"

"No. I've kept it for years in my jewellery box. I still have it. In fact . . ." Pulling up her right sleeve, Christine revealed the old, tattered friendship bracelet tied loosely around her wrist. "I don't know why, but these last few days I've felt a sudden need to wear it. Like it's a protective circle." Christine leaned forward, her face deadly serious. "Now, tell me. What do you know about my daughter?"

Blake knew that she couldn't tell Christine everything, not without jeopardising the police investigation and getting herself arrested. Nor could she tell Christine about the other missing women. Not yet.

"I'm trying to help," Blake said. "That's all."

"You're working with the police?"

"Not exactly. In fact, I think they'd prefer it if I went back to Manchester. But I want to help. I'm *trying* to help."

"I don't want you to get in their way."

"I won't, I promise. I'll hand anything I find straight to the detectives." Blake hesitated before asking her next question. "Do you think I could see Lucy's room?"

"What? No! Why would you ask that?"

"I'm sorry. I thought maybe there would be something that could help."

Christine pulled another tissue from the box. "The police already took everything away, including Lucy's diaries. Right now, there are police detectives poring over my little girl's innermost thoughts. Hasn't she been violated enough?"

Blake sat, helpless and guilty. She reached a hand across the table. Christine took it and squeezed gently.

"The police wouldn't let me identify her. Did you know that? They said it would be too distressing and that they could identify her with dental records instead. You saw my little girl. You found her. Tell me, what did she look like?"

Blake was instantly back at Ding Dong Mine, staring into Lucy's eyeless sockets. "I don't think it's a good idea for you to —"

"Please, tell me. Did she look like she was in pain?"

Blake opened her mouth and shut it again. Tears stung her eyes.

Christine released her hand and leaned back on the chair. Grief slipped from her face and was replaced by cold steel.

"I envy you," she said. "You'll never know the pain of losing a child."

Leslie appeared in the doorway. She crossed her arms and stared at Blake.

"You need to leave now," she said. "My sister needs to rest."

Ignoring her, Blake leaned forward and stared directly into Christine's eyes.

"I'm going to help find who did this," she whispered. "Whether the police like it or not."

28

THE CHURCH HALL was a hive of activity. Tables of dried and canned goods were set up in one half of the room, where patrons could collect donations of food to take home to their families. A seating and refreshment area dominated the other half, giving away free teas and coffees, and juices for the children. Most of the patrons' eyes were pointed at the ground. It couldn't be easy to accept charity when you had no other choice, but in Cornwall it was a growing phenomenon. Despite its outward beauty and pockets of abundant wealth, Cornwall was one of the poorest regions in the United Kingdom. Annual salaries were far below the national average, and there was an over-dependence on tourism to help make ends meet. Years of austerity had also taken a toll, resulting in foodbanks springing up over the county to help feed both the unemployed and those working families who didn't earn enough to cover the bills.

Blake felt guilty for being here, as if she were prying into other people's personal secrets. But for Heather Hargreaves and Leanne Curnow, time was running out. Scanning through the small crowd, she noticed Iris Babcock, a friend of her mother's, who was stationed at the refreshments table.

Blake headed towards her, waving a hand.

"Blake!" The older woman greeted her with a warm smile. "This is a nice surprise. Whatever are you doing here?"

"Just passing through," Blake said.

"How's Mary? Her leg healing?"

"You know Mum. She's desperate to get back to her routines and doesn't like sitting on her backside. But she'll get there. She just needs a bit more patience."

Iris laughed. "Whenever has patience been a virtue of your mother's?"

"True."

Two young children ran up to the table, their eyes fixed on a plate of chocolate chip cookies. Their mother quickly followed. She apologised to Iris, who waved a hand through the air.

"Don't be daft. Here you go, my flowers," she said, handing them each a cookie then pouring hot water into a mug. "And a nice cup of tea for Mum."

The family thanked her and walked away.

"I wondered if I could talk to you," Blake said, now that she and Iris were alone.

"Oh? About what? I'm a bit busy right now."

"I'll be quick. It's about Lucy Truscott."

The smile on Iris's face vanished. "Oh, that dear girl. I still can't believe she's not with us anymore."

"Did you know her well?"

"Only through volunteering here. She was just lovely. A ray of sunshine. Poor Christine must be devastated. I can't imagine what she's going through right now. Have you seen her?"

"I just came from Christine. It's why I'm here. I've promised to find out as much as I can about Lucy's activities in the days leading up to . . . Well, you know."

Iris stared at her. "Playing detective, are you? Isn't that a job for the police?"

"Of course. But I'm a private investigator, Iris. As you well know."

"It's such a funny job, isn't it? Doesn't sound real."

"Well, it is. Anyway, I'm here as a friend of Christine's."

Iris frowned as she refilled a plate with chocolate biscuits. "I don't know what I can tell you. Other than Lucy was here most Tuesday mornings to help out. She was well liked, very helpful, and always treated our patrons with respect. Although she could be a little too curious sometimes."

There was that word again.

"In what way?"

"She could get a little too personal with the patrons, asking questions about their situation. She didn't mean anything by it, she was just trying to help. But Reverend Thompson did ask her to be a little more respectful. Anyway, it was nice to have a young face here instead of just us old folk. It was good for some of the young mums, too."

Blake looked around the room, careful to avoid making eye contact. The other volunteers were indeed older. Retirement age and most likely church members. She recognised some as friends and acquaintances of her mother's, others as faces from around town.

"Are these all of the usual volunteers?"

"More or less. Most of us cover both days the foodbank is open. It's something nice to do, isn't it? Reverend Thompson drops in from time to time to show a friendly face, but this is pretty much our motley crew."

"So, no other younger volunteers like Lucy?"

"You know what teenagers are like these days. Too busy burying their faces in phone screens."

"Not just teenagers," Blake muttered. "Was Lucy friendly with anyone in particular?"

"She got on with everyone, I suppose. But she did show an interest in Faith. Not that Faith volunteers here anymore."

Blake looked up. "Faith Penrose?"

"That's right. She volunteered here for a long while. When Lucy found out who she was, she made a beeline straight for her. They used to talk a lot. I think Lucy reminded Faith of her daughter. That's another tragic story. You were friends with Demelza, weren't you?"

"What do you mean Lucy made a beeline for Faith?"

"As soon as she heard Faith was Demelza's mother, she was all over her. She couldn't stop asking questions about Demelza, to the point I had to pull her to one side and tell her to stop. I suppose it was just her curious nature. And I suppose she was the same age as when Demelza disappeared. Anyway, it turned out Faith didn't seem to mind the twenty questions. In fact, the two got on like a house on fire. Faith even invited Lucy home for dinner on occasion. But then about a month ago, Faith called to say she had to stop volunteering. Said she didn't have time anymore, which I thought was strange. It's not like she's doing anything else, is it? But even stranger was Lucy's reaction. She was utterly miserable for a week after." Iris leaned in and dropped her voice to a whisper. "If you ask me, it seemed like the two of them had a falling out."

"About what?"

"No idea. I haven't seen Faith since she gave up volunteering. She comes to Sunday service once in a while, but mostly she keeps to herself. To be honest, I was surprised when she started helping out at the foodbank. But I suppose even hermits get lonely sometimes, especially ones who've lost everything the way she did."

Above the hum of chattering voices, a deep rumble of organ music began to play, causing heads to look up.

"That'll be Margaret," Iris said, nodding towards the double doors that connected the hall to the church. "She likes to get some practice in before Sunday service. Good thing too, if you ask me."

The rumble turned into an undulating tune that made the plates on the table rattle. Two more families entered the hall through the front doors. They nervously glanced around, then shuffled towards the nearest volunteer.

Iris gave Blake a sad smile. "Well, I best get on. Say hello to that mother of yours. I'll pop around to see her next week."

Blake said goodbye and went to leave, but Iris grabbed her gently by the arm.

"Tell Christine I'm sorry," she said. "That daughter of hers had a good heart. I hope the police catch the monster who took her, and string him up for the world to see."

As Blake headed towards the exit, her thoughts tripped over themselves. Lucy Truscott and Faith Penrose. An unlikely friendship with all sorts of implications. She needed to talk to Demelza's mother. The only trouble was Blake hadn't spoken to Faith in almost eighteen years.

29

HUDDLED on her haunches in the far corner of the cell, Leanne shuddered uncontrollably. The cold glass pressed against her spine. The concrete floor had numbed her feet to the point that she could barely feel them. How long had she been kept in darkness? Hours? Days? The deprivation of her senses had rendered time unmeasurable. If she remained like this for much longer, utterly paralysed by fear, she was going to die. She knew it, deep down in her core.

She needed to get her mind moving. Now.

She leaned forward then slammed the back of her head against the glass. It wasn't hard enough to cause damage, but enough to make her vision glitter like stars in outer space. She gasped, sucking in an icy breath. Her mind cleared a little.

Her captor had visited twice now. The last time, he'd remained silent as he watched her from the darkness. She hadn't even known he'd been there until he'd stepped closer. He hadn't responded to her pleas either, or told her where he'd put Heather. She was not here inside this cavernous room. She would have answered Leanne's calls by now. But something else was in here with her. Leanne had caught a glimpse of it.

At first she'd been captivated by the blinding rectangle of light from the open door. But as her captor had closed it again, she'd seen something at the centre of the room before being plunged back into darkness. Her mind couldn't make sense of it. Now, as she tried to picture it, all she saw was a blank space.

She was in the void again. No patterns or lines or shapes. Only blindness. The only sounds she could hear were of her own making. She had been taken somewhere remote, where no one could hear her screams. She knew that because she had screamed for hours, until her throat burned and her voice was hoarse and she tasted coppery blood. No one had come to her rescue.

Why had he taken her and Heather? What had they done to anger him so much?

Leanne looked up. It wasn't *them*. It was *her*. Because Heather wouldn't even be here right now if Leanne hadn't called her.

Leanne was the target. Heather had got in the way.

Her stomach cramped, then began to churn. She hadn't eaten since yesterday afternoon, or however long ago it had been since she'd sat down with her family for Sunday lunch.

The thought of her parents and her brother Tony made her heart ache and a hopeless moan escape her lips. Her mum and dad would be looking for her. They would have called the police by now. Maybe there was even a search party hunting for her. She hoped they would find her and Heather. They didn't deserve to be taken.

What had she done to be punished like this? An underage drink in a bar? That deserved nothing more than a stern word and a lecture about the dangers of alcohol. What else then? What else had she done?

Leanne could think of nothing.

She was sixteen years old. Sixteen-year-olds could shout and scream and throw tantrums, and tell their parents how much they hated them. But she wasn't that type of teenager. She was kind and thoughtful, preferring to detail her angst and frustrations in her journal rather than go to war with her parents, no matter how annoying they could be. Yes, she'd done the wrong thing by flashing a fake ID and sneaking into a pub, but that really was the worst of it.

She sobbed again, pulling her knees up to her chest and resting her chin on top of them. The cold found a way through her numbness. If only she had a blanket and something to drink, but there was nothing inside the cell except for the bucket. She had used it once, feeling humiliated and ashamed. He expected her to go to the toilet like some animal. Well, she would show him. Next time, she would go on the floor.

What was it the man had whispered in the dark when he had first visited? Leanne had been so shocked that she hadn't fully listened. Something about sin and death. About her being the worst kind of sinner.

Why? How? Surely the worst kind of sinner was someone who killed. Or someone who abducted teenage girls and kept them in glass tanks in the darkness.

Her body shook convulsively. There was only one clear explanation for why she'd been taken. To be tortured and played with, the subject of her abductor's sick fantasies, until he grew bored and killed her, then dismembered her body, just like all those sickos and serial killers from true crime documentaries.

"Please," she whispered to the dark. "Please, someone help me."

But no one could help her because no one knew where she was. Which meant the only person who could help her right now was trapped inside this glass tank with no way out.

Leanne wiped tears and snot from her face with a frozen hand. She could either accept that she was going to die here, or she could try to find a way out. Even if she couldn't do it for herself, she needed to do it for Heather.

Pushing her back up against the glass, she slowly got to her feet. Her body was weak and unsteady, and she thought she would fall again. She pressed harder into the glass and sucked in three long breaths. She lifted one foot, stretched out the toes, then set it down on the ground and lifted the other, repeating the action. The cold had seeped into her bones, but some life began to return to her digits. Next, she stretched out her fingers, then tensed her shoulders and relaxed them.

If she remained crouched in the corner like prey, prey was what she would become.

Keep moving or turn to stone. Leanne got moving.

Turning to face the wall, she spread out her arms and pressed her palms against its surface. She began to sidestep while slowly moving her hands up and down the glass.

She had found nothing last time, but she had been in the grip of terror. She was afraid now, but there was a glimmer of determination waking up inside her. Because if she didn't try to live, Heather would die. And so would she.

No matter how scared she was, Leanne refused to die at sixteen years old. She still had so many life goals to achieve, and being dismembered by a serial killer was not one of them. Sucking in another calming breath, she continued moving.

30

THE WHEAL MAROW Valley Park was situated on the south-west outskirts of town. It was a long strip of nature reserve made up of twisting paths and old chimneys left over from the mining days. A shallow river split the reserve in two from end to end. The park was a perfect place for dog walking, yet as Blake met Jasmine at the gates and they crossed a small wooden bridge over a stagnant pond, they seemed to be the only two people in the world. Yesterday, Blake had tried to muster the courage to call Faith Penrose, but had failed miserably. She knew she had to talk to her, but every time she'd attempted to hit the call button, it was as if an invisible barrier made up of eighteen-year-old guilt had slipped in between her finger and the phone screen. Instead, she'd called Jasmine. If anyone would know about Lucy's obsession with Demelza, it would be her best friend.

Jasmine was silent as they walked. The brutal murder of her best friend was clearly taking its toll. She had lost weight, her body lost inside a long black coat. Dark shadows circled her eyes and her complexion was the colour of sour milk.

"Thank you for agreeing to see me again," Blake said softly, as they stepped off the bridge and onto a winding concrete path that was bordered by tall hedgerows of bramble and gorse. A bank of trees climbed up on the left, twisted branches reaching for the sickly sky. "You're not at college today?"

Jasmine kept her gaze fixed on the path ahead. "I'm taking a week off. My parents think I need time to process what happened to Lucy."

"You should take as much time as you need. Maybe think about seeing the college counsellor. Something as terrible as this doesn't go away after a week."

They walked in silence for a short while. The temperature was colder in the valley, which seemed to act like a wind tunnel. An icy breeze forced Blake to button her winter coat up to her neck.

Jasmine looked up. "Is it true that you were the one who found her?"

Blake nodded.

"Was she already dead?"

Digging her hands deeper into her pockets, she nodded again.

"I still can't believe it. It doesn't make any sense."

"Death never does."

Jasmine looked up again. "Do you know when the funeral will be?"

"I wouldn't know anything about that. Lucy's family will have to wait until —"

Blake cut herself off, suddenly aware of who she was talking to.

"Until what?" Jasmine pressed.

Until the police release the body, Blake thought. To Jasmine, she shrugged and shook her head. The path turned, and they followed it around in a loop. A tall brick chimney shaft rose up from the ground on the left and reached for the treetops. To the right of the path, the ground sloped down to the bank of a narrow river. Another old chimney stack stood on a tiny island in the centre, remnants of a once thriving mining industry now dead in the water.

"If you're up to it, I'd like to ask you a few more questions," Blake said.

"Fine."

"Did Lucy ever talk about a young woman who disappeared a long time ago?"

To her surprise, Jasmine rolled her eyes. "You mean Demelza? Only all the time."

"Really?"

"I mean, well, not lately, but earlier in the year, Lucy was obsessed."

"With Demelza?"

"We were in the common room one lunch hour. People were talking about urban legends and all of that stupid stuff, and then someone mentioned Demelza and how she disappeared. I'd never heard of her before, but some people seemed to know the story. Anyway, everyone started coming up with theories about what happened to her, and wondering if she was dead or alive."

"How long ago was this?"

"A couple of months before we left college, so April or May. Lucy got all excited about the town having an unsolved mystery. Especially because it turned out that Demelza was a friend of her mum's. She drove me mad about it. She had this stupid idea that we could find out what happened to Demelza. She thought it could make us famous or something." Jasmine smiled sadly. "I told her it was a lame idea. I thought it was childish, to be honest. It's the type of thing you watch on TV, isn't it? It's not something that happens in real life, normal people playing detectives."

Blake shrugged. "Sometimes truth is stranger than fiction."

"Well, either way, I told her I wasn't interested. I mean, if the police couldn't find Demelza, how were we supposed to? We were just two teenage girls."

"To be honest, the police didn't try very hard back then. Yes, there was a brief search, but that was it. Eventually they decided she must have run away, and dropped the case."

Jasmine slowed to a halt. The river snaked past them, its trickling water making winter music. "Did you know Demelza?"

"She was one of my best friends. There were four of us. Me, Demelza, Judy, and Lucy's mum, Christine. We were a team. We called ourselves the Forever Four. Inseparable and indestructible, until the day Demelza vanished. I know how it feels to lose your best friend, Jasmine." Blake paused. "So maybe you can tell me more about Lucy's obsession with Demelza."

They got walking again, the path curving away from the river to meander through a copse of barren trees.

"I don't know what to tell you. Demelza was all Lucy could talk about for a while. She was determined to find out what happened to her, even without my help. I know she'd been harassing her mum. She told me she got caught in the attic going through Christine's old photos. She even showed me some of the pictures. Maybe you were in them. Then Lucy told me she'd made friends with Demelza's mum at the foodbank, and that she was going to try to find out what she could. I thought she'd gone mad. I told her so, too. I told her it wasn't healthy and that I didn't want to hear anymore about it. I honestly thought that was the end of it. Until I met Lucy one Saturday for coffee. She'd been crying. When I asked her what was wrong, she told me she'd been fired from her cleaning job at the hospital."

Now it was Blake's turn to grind to a halt, stopping beneath a tall oak tree. "Fired?"

"Don't tell Christine," Jasmine said, worriedly. "Lucy told her she got bored of cleaning and wanted to work at the pet shop instead. I was the only person who knew the truth and Lucy made me promise not to tell anyone else."

Blake's phone started ringing in her coat pocket. She pulled it out and saw that Mary was calling. She wondered if she should answer, but instead hit the ignore button.

"What did Lucy do to get fired?"

"She got caught snooping around the hospital's archive of old medical files. Being a cleaner, she had access to places other staff didn't. But someone walked in and caught her red-handed."

"Why was Lucy risking her job to look at old medical files?"

"She said that she'd found something out about Demelza, and she needed to know if it was true. That's when I realised she hadn't given up playing detective at all. She'd just been hiding it from me. I told her that she'd gone too far and she was lucky the hospital hadn't called the police. But the whole episode frightened her, and she promised that was the end of it. This time, she really was giving up. She didn't mention Demelza again. Today is the first time I've heard that name since."

Blake's phone rang again. She ended the call without even looking at the screen. "She didn't tell you what she'd found in Demelza's medical records?"

"No. I didn't ask either."

"How long ago was this?"

"Mid-September. I'd not long started work at the gift shop."

"Why didn't you say anything about this before?"

"You never asked about Demelza," Jasmine said, with a frown.

Blake's mind was racing. For whatever reason, Lucy had been conducting her own investigation into Demelza's disappearance. Had she found something incriminating? Was that why she had been killed?

Blake's phone started ringing yet again. Swearing under her breath, she apologised to Jasmine and pulled the phone from her pocket.

"What is it, Mum? I'm busy here."

"Blake?" Her mother was sobbing and struggling for breath. "You need to come home. Now."

"Why? What's wrong? Are you hurt?"

"Come home, Blake. Please! The police are here and I don't know what to do."

Jasmine glanced up, her sad eyes suddenly filled with curiosity. Blake turned away from her and dropped her voice to a whisper. "What do you mean the police are here?"

"Come home, Blake," Mary said, her voice high and desperate. "They're arresting your father!"

Blake's heart stopped beating.

"I'll be there in five minutes. Don't let them take him before I get there."

"What is it?" Jasmine asked.

The ground shifted beneath Blake's feet. She spun around, feeling dizzy and faint.

"I have to go," she told Jasmine. "Thanks for your help."

Then she was running along the path and towards the exit.

31

BLAKE DROVE AT A DANGEROUS SPEED, trees and fields reduced to streaks of browns and greens as she raced towards her parents' home. Although her eyes were fixed on the road, her mind was trapped inside a maelstrom of panic and confusion. None of what her mother had told her made sense. But as she drove around the final bend and killed her speed, reality snatched her breath away.

Two police cars and a silver Nissan were blocking the entrance to her parents' driveway. Pulling up behind them, Blake climbed out on unsteady feet and hurried towards the vehicles. The house swung into view on her right. Both the front door and garage door were open. Uniformed police officers were posted at each entrance, while two others stood in the driveway next to a police van, their eyes fixed on one of the patrol cars as they conversed in hushed voices. Blake turned and followed their gaze. Her heart hammered in her chest.

Her father was sitting in the back seat of the patrol car. He was leaning forward slightly with his head bowed and his shoulders slumped. A male police officer sat in the driver's seat, staring at Blake. Ignoring him, she knocked on the rear passenger window. The uniformed officers in the driveway started towards her.

"Miss? Please step away from the vehicle," one called out.

In the back seat, Ed looked up.

Blake's eyes watered. "Dad? What's happening?"

"Miss, I need you to step away from the car."

Blake felt a hand on her shoulder. She shrugged it off as Ed glanced sadly at her, then slowly lowered his head.

"I won't ask you again," the officer said, his tone sharp with warning.

Blake stepped back from the car and glared at him. "What's going on? Why has my father been arrested?"

A crash pulled her attention to the open garage, where gloved officers were conducting a search. One of them stooped to pick up an old paint tin filled with screws then replaced it on a shelf. The others swarmed around Ed's white van. Panic climbing her throat, Blake didn't wait for an answer. She marched towards the front door of the house, desperate to find her mother.

"You can't go in there," the officer called from behind.

She heard footsteps hurrying towards her. On her right, a female uniformed officer rushed to block her path. Blake sped up, dashing through the open front door and into the hallway.

"Mum?" she yelled. "Where are you?"

All of the doors were open. Sounds filled her ears. Murmured voices. Radio crackles. Things being picked up and put down. A shadow filled the doorway as one of the police officers stepped inside.

"Blake?"

Her mother's frightened voice called out from the living room. Blake hurried towards it. Mary was on the sofa, her leg propped up on the ottoman. Her face was worryingly pale and streaked with tears. A female uniformed officer sat beside her. As Blake entered, she jumped to her feet.

"Oh, Blake!" her mother cried.

"It's okay, Mum." The officer tried to step in her way. Blake thrust a finger in her face. "Tell me I shouldn't be here and I won't be responsible for my actions."

The officer opened her mouth to say something, but Blake was already dropping to her knees in front of her mother and reaching for her hand. "What's going on, Mum? Why have they arrested Dad?"

Fresh tears ran down Mary's face. "They think he, well, that he . . . Oh, Blake, I can't even say it!"

But she didn't have to. Blake already knew the answer. She didn't understand. She could hardly believe it. But she knew.

Mary shuddered as she broke down into desperate sobs. Blake squeezed her hand. You weren't supposed to see your parents in such despair. They were supposed to take care of *you*.

"It's going to be all right," she told her mother, hating how weak and filled with lies she sounded. "There's obviously been some sort of misunderstanding. Dad wouldn't hurt anyone. You know that. I know that. It's just a terrible mistake, that's all."

She shot a glance at the female officer, who was watching her closely, and then twisted around to peer at the open living room door.

DS Turner was standing there, watching mother and daughter.

Blake was on her feet and crossing the room in one fluid movement.

"You honestly think my father is some sort of depraved psychopath?" Anger was raging inside her at an alarming rate, like an inferno burning out of control. "You think he's capable of murder? You're wrong. Do you hear me? You've got the wrong person."

She glanced over Turner's shoulder and spied Rory, who was hanging back in the hall with his eyes glued to the floor.

Turner cleared his throat. "I understand this comes as a shock to you. But I need to tell you that we've arrested your father on suspicion of murdering Lucy Truscott, and abducting Leanne Curnow and Heather Hargreaves. He'll now be taken to Truro station for questioning. We're also conducting a search of your parents' premises and grounds, and any relevant evidence will be logged and removed for further examination. This includes any vehicles on the premises, such as your father's van."

The room was spinning. Her breaths were coming thin and fast, and growing harder to expel. "What grounds do you have for arresting him? What evidence do you have?"

Turner's face softened a little. "You know I can't disclose that, Blake. The best you can do now is —"

"You haven't charged him yet, so that tells me that whatever evidence you think you have isn't enough. What is this, Turner? Pressure from the top to make an arrest? The media interest getting to your bosses?" She leaned in towards him, her teeth clenching together. "I'm telling you, you've made a mistake."

Turner stared at her, then over at Mary, who was still crying and wringing her hands together. He let out a small sigh. "I'm sorry, Blake. I know this is hard to understand, but —"

"Tell him, Rory," Blake said, staring at DC Angove, who was

still hovering awkwardly in the hallway. "You've known my father all your life. You know Ed didn't do this. You *know* that he could never hurt anyone!"

Rory only shook his head and murmured an apology.

"Please, Detective," Mary wailed from the sofa. "My Ed wouldn't hurt a fly."

"I'm sorry," Turner repeated, a pained look on his face. "I have to return to the station now. PC Harris here will stay with you until the search has been completed. There will be some paperwork for you to sign." He turned to leave, then leaned in towards Blake. "I know this is a lot to take in right now, but I'm asking you not to come down to the station and cause a scene. It won't help your father. Stay here with your mother. She needs you right now."

Blake glared at him, rage and terror rendering her speechless. She watched him whisper to Rory in the hallway, then vanish from sight. Rory managed a sorry glance at Blake, before following Turner outside.

Mary sobbed loudly. PC Harris reached for a tissue and handed it to her.

Shutting out her mother's cries, Blake stared at the empty space Rory had left behind. Then she bolted forward.

She heard her mother calling out from behind, but Blake kept moving, through the hall and out the front door. Rory was talking to a uniformed officer in the middle of the driveway with his back turned to Blake. She marched towards him with her fists clenched.

"Hey! Rory!"

Heads turned. A few of the officers smirked.

"Rory, I'm talking to you!"

At the end of the driveway, DS Turner was climbing into the

driver's seat of the silver Nissan. Rory pulled away from the officer and met Blake halfway.

"What have you got on him?" Blake demanded. "You must have something or you wouldn't have made an arrest."

Rory shot a nervous glance at Turner's car. "You know I can't tell you anything."

"It's me," Blake said, hating the desperation in her voice. "Come on, Rory. This is my family we're talking about."

"I know and I'm sorry. But I can't lose my job."

Turner honked the horn. Out on the road, a tow truck had pulled up, ready to remove Ed's van.

"Please, I'm begging you." Tears were running down Blake's face. "Do you really believe my dad could kill Lucy? Come on, Rory. You know him! He used to fix your car."

Rory clenched his jaw. His eyes flicked to the silver Nissan again. Turner had the engine running.

"Fuck!" He leaned in and dropped his voice to a whisper. "There was something about him in Lucy's diary. Something incriminating. That's all I can tell you. Don't ask me for anymore and you didn't hear it from me."

Shaking his head, Rory turned away from Blake.

"Make sure you get him a good lawyer," he said. Then he was jogging down the sloping driveway towards Turner's car. He climbed into the passenger seat and slammed the door. Turner and Rory left first, followed by the patrol car carrying her father. He didn't look up as he was driven past, but kept his face forward and his eyes down.

Now only the police van remained, along with one other patrol car and the newly arrived tow truck, which began reversing into the driveway. Blake turned her back on it and stared up at the house. She couldn't breathe. Her heart was beating hard in her chest. And then her phone was ringing in her pocket. She numbly took it out and saw Judy was calling. Blake stared at the screen until the phone stopped ringing and connected to voicemail. She put it away again. Slow and unsteady on her feet, she returned inside and went to her mother.

32

Evening came, bringing rain that hammered on the gravel driveway and the windows of the house, and wind that made the trees tremble and moan. The police had finished their search two hours ago, and while they had left the house in a tidier state than Blake had expected, all of the furniture seemed slightly out of place, as if the Manson family had sneaked into her parents' home to play psychological mind games. She had done her best to return the house to normal. But of course things were far from normal. Her father had been arrested on suspicion of murder and abduction. The police had taken half of his office, including his computer. They had cleared out his garage and confiscated his van.

Choices for a good criminal defence lawyer had been slim, but Blake had picked out a woman called Ivy Trevara. She had been in practice for ten years and had promising testimonials on her website. Blake had to trust that the lawyer would be skilled enough to help her father, but so far, there had been no word from either of them.

Blake had heeded DS Turner's warning and stayed away

from the police station. Her mother had been a wreck ever since Ed's arrest, one minute gripped by panic, the next by confusion. She had asked Blake, over and over again, how it was possible that the police could make such a monumental mistake. But Blake had no idea. Unable to stand her mother's questioning, she had retreated into the kitchen, where she had spent the last twenty minutes asking herself the same question. But now, a quiet voice whispered in her ear, asking its own questions: "Have the police really made a mistake? Or is your father capable of murder?"

Her mother was currently in the living room, speaking on the phone to Blake's brother Alfie. She could hear the tremble in Mary's voice as she told Alfie the bad news.

Blake leaned against the kitchen counter, her arms folded tightly across her stomach. She watched the rain drops slide down the window and stared at the darkness beyond. It was unbearably hot in the house. The air was thick and cloying, making it hard to breathe.

Her mind kept returning to what Rory had told her. Lucy had written about Ed in her diary. Whatever it was, it had been incriminating enough for the police to make an arrest. She wanted to call Rory now and ask him to elaborate. But Rory had already crossed professional boundaries and risked his job just to tell her the barest of facts.

Blake knew enough about the law to know that a diary entry was not enough for her father to be charged. The police would need harder evidence that proved his guilt. She closed her eyes, shutting out her mother's voice and trying to clear her mind. They had taken Ed's van. It was a white transit van, the same type caught on CCTV on the night of the girls' abductions. If it had been Ed's van, the police would have traced him down via his number plate registration and arrested him days ago. Which meant that the van used in the abduction either had falsified plates that couldn't be traced or no plates at all.

In any case, her father had been home last Sunday night, hadn't he?

Blake had been busy drowning her sorrows with Kenver, so she couldn't be certain. But surely her father wouldn't have left her mother alone at night to fend for herself.

Leanne Curnow and Heather Hargreaves had been abducted around nine-thirty. Truro was just a fifteen-minute drive from Wheal Marow. And what about the night Lucy disappeared?

Blake hadn't come down to Cornwall until the next morning. Her mother had spent her last night in hospital. Ed had been alone at home . . .

Feeling sick, Blake opened her eyes again. She went to the sink and splashed cold water on her face.

"You're being ridiculous," she whispered. "This is your father you're talking about."

Guilt crashed down on her in a heavy wave, followed by crippling fear. Her father wasn't a killer. The police had made a terrible mistake.

But even now doubt was still creeping in. It's just a coincidence, she thought. What motive would Ed possibly have?

Except Lucy had written something incriminating about him in her diary.

The kitchen closed in on her, pushing the air from the room. Blake sucked in a breath and struggled to push it out again. Her heart was pounding, sending palpitations quivering through her chest.

What was happening to her father right now? What questions were they asking?

When the police made an arrest, they could hold a suspect for twenty-four hours without being charged, but in more serious cases such as murder, they could apply to hold the suspect for up to ninety-six hours.

Her mind flicked from thought to thought, replaying the events of the day. The police had confiscated Ed's van. They would be searching it for forensic evidence. DNA samples could take months to be returned from the forensic lab, mostly because of the backlog. But this was a high-profile murder and abduction case that was being covered by national press. Devon and Cornwall police had already paid for the forensic results from Lucy's murder to be fast-tracked. Why wouldn't they do the same for Ed's van?

Blake stared through the open kitchen door into the shadows of the hallway. The friendship bracelet. Had her father taken it all those years ago?

Don't be ridiculous, she told herself.

The police were desperate because the girls were still missing, and even though they were wrong about her father, the van was their only lead.

So why was her gut twisting with unease?

Her phone was ringing. Judy was calling yet again. Blake let it go to voicemail, just like she had the others.

Leaving the kitchen, she padded through the shadows and into the living room, where her mother had finished the call with Alfie. Their eyes met, and she saw the worry lining Mary's face, ageing her.

"So, what did Alfie have to say?" she asked. "When is he coming down?"

Mary wrung her hands together. "He says he can't come. He can't leave Violet like that. Besides, Ed will probably be home tomorrow, won't he? There's no point making Alfie come all this way when the police will let your father go. They will let him go tomorrow, won't they?"

"Mum?"

"Yes, bird?"

"Did Dad go out last Sunday night?"

"Last Sunday night?"

"I stayed over at Kenver's. Do you remember?"

Mary frowned and rubbed her face. She heaved her shoulders. "I didn't want to tell you because I knew you'd get mad."

The room stretched out and snapped right back. "Tell me what?"

"Ed had to go out for a little while. He said he'd got a call that someone was down at the site, prowling around. He was worried it was kids coming to vandalise the place or steal materials. He was only gone for an hour or two. Then he came straight back. I was fine."

"Did you hear him take the call?"

"What? No, I don't think so. He was upstairs at the time. Blake, what is this all about?"

Dizziness took hold of Blake's head and spun her around. She needed to get out of the house. She needed fresh air and time to think. Mary was staring at her with desperation and hope, as if she had the power to correct all the wrongs in the world and to bring her father back.

Blake turned away from her and staggered out of the room.

"Blake, love? Where are you going?"

Back in the kitchen, she called Kenver and waited for him to pick up.

"I was wondering when I'd hear from you," he said, when he answered a few seconds later. "I take it you've heard from Judy?"

Blake frowned. "What? Haven't you heard about Dad? Your Uncle Ed?"

"Should I have? What's wrong?"

Good, Blake thought. The one benefit of her parents living outside of town meant the police presence and her father's arrest would have largely gone unnoticed. But it was only a matter of time before the news reached Wheal Marow, travelling from gossip to gossip.

"Have you been drinking tonight?" she asked.

"What? No, I haven't. Are you going to tell me what's —"

"I need you to come over and take care of your Aunt Mary for a while."

"Now? I'm in the middle of something."

"Just get here now, Kenver. Dad's been arrested. Please, I need you here."

Kenver was silent for a long moment, absorbing the news.

"Shit," he said. "Arrested for what?"

"Aunt Mary will fill you in."

"I'll grab my bike. I'll be there in ten minutes."

"Good. Pedal as fast as you can. I'll leave a key under the mat and I'll be back in a couple of hours."

"It's a motorbike, you twa—"

She hung up and slipped the phone back inside her jeans pocket. Her chest was tight and heavy. Sweat trickled down her brow.

She marched back to the living room, where Mary was pale and stricken.

"Kenver's coming over," Blake said, her voice sounding far away. "I need to go out."

Mary stared at her in shock. "Go out where? What about your father? I need you here, Blake!"

"Kenver will stay with you. I'll be back soon."

"What if the lawyer calls? You can't just —"

"Please, Mum!" Blake snapped. She shut her eyes and caught her breath. When she spoke again, her voice was calmer. "Kenver will be ten minutes. He'll let himself in. I won't be long, I promise."

"But Blake!"

She hurried out of the room and grabbed her car key from a bowl on the hallway side table. Throwing open the front door, she slipped her house key under the mat then ran outside. Rain splattered her skin. Trees swayed in the wind. Breathing in an icy lungful of air, Blake raced across the gravel and down the sloping driveway. A chill was already taking hold of her body as she headed for her car, which was still parked on the roadside. She hated leaving her mother alone. But she had to leave because tears were coming, and the voice of suspicion was growing louder in her ear.

Was her father a killer? Now, she honestly didn't know.

33

THE RAIN PERSISTED as Blake drove into town and stopped at the local off-licence on the high street to pick up a pack of beers. The only person in the off-licence was the shopkeeper, who tried to make conversation while Blake tried to make a quick escape. As she hurried back to her car, she glanced over her shoulder, wondering how long it would take for news of her father's arrest to make it to town. But she was alone in the dark street.

With the beers nestled on the passenger seat, she got driving again, heading away from Wheal Marow and onto the A30. She had no destination in mind, only a desperate need to be alone. As the windscreen wipers struggled against the rain, Blake fought with her emotions. Hers was the only vehicle on the dual carriageway, so she sped up, passing the parish of Hayle, then through the hamlets of Canon's Town and White Cross. Slowing at Crowlas, she turned right onto the B3309 and drove along the narrow two-lane road, passing darkened villages, moving deeper and deeper into the countryside, where the only artificial light came from her headlights, cutting through the inky night. And then after a short while, Blake found herself parked on the side of a ribbon of a country lane, with the rain lashing against the car windows and the wind moaning through the vents.

In the rear-view mirror she saw soft yellow light illuminating from a single house far back on the roadside. Blake had often wondered why anyone would choose to live such a remote, solitary life, but now she could see the attraction. Grabbing a beer from the passenger seat, she climbed out of the car and was immediately blasted by the wind and rain. She shut the door then stumbled from the road and onto moorland. Activating the light on her phone, she located a stony path and began to follow it. She was already shivering and her joints were numb from the cold, but she pressed on. Suddenly, at the periphery of the phone light, she saw the shell of the old engine house.

The police had finished their forensic investigation a few days ago and had released the grounds back to the public. Blake doubted that people would come here now. Not when it had been stained with the blood of a young woman.

She reached the engine house. Rain careered down from the dark expanse of sky and stung her face. Keeping close to the wall, Blake veered around the ruin until she came to the stone doorway. She paused, picturing the misty morning when she'd turned the corner and found Lucy's body. Now all she saw was an open black rectangle illuminated by her phone. She stepped through it. But inside the guts of the engine house there was no respite from the rain. Blake huddled in the doorway, conscious that she was standing in the exact spot where Lucy had been nailed to the walls.

Pocketing her phone, she opened the beer and took a deep draft. All she could think about was her father. Blake had spent most of her adult life looking to him for acknowledgement, desperate to hear him say he was proud of her achievements. To tell her even once that he loved her. All that time and energy she had spent wondering what she had done to deserve his indifference. And now he had been arrested on suspicion of murder and abduction.

As a child, her father had called her the apple of his eye. She had been a daddy's girl who could do no wrong, who could light up his face just by entering the room. But that all changed when Demelza vanished.

Blake had turned inward, growing cold and distant. When she'd left for Manchester Metropolitan University that September, it was as if her tether to her parents had been severed. She came home less and less. Her daily calls dropped to once a week, then once a fortnight. She partied all the time, drowning her loss in alcohol and pills. She barely scraped through her first year.

By the time her second year came around, she had expelled much of her grief and learned to repress what remained. Yet her relationship with her father continued to crumble. Ed barely stayed on the phone for more than a minute when Blake called. When she came home for the holidays, her father was always needed at work. Even when they spent time together as a family, Ed never had much to say to Blake. Worse still, he avoided her gaze, as if he was too disappointed to even look at her.

Blake had never known what she'd done to upset him, and she had never asked. Eventually, desperation and confusion gave way to resentment. She began to pick at her father's ways, finding faults in everything he did or didn't do, pointing out his weaknesses, and criticising his treatment of her mother. She hated herself for it. And yet she couldn't stop. This was what she had been driven to, because somewhere along the way, for some unfathomable reason, her father had stopped loving her.

Now, as Blake stared into the pitch darkness, she came to a sudden realisation. She hadn't been the only one to change that night. Her father had changed, too. Why was that?

Her mind started to assemble all that she knew into a clear picture, starting with Lucy Truscott. Lucy, who had conducted her own investigation into Demelza's disappearance, who had been fired from her cleaning job at the hospital for sneaking a look at Demelza's old medical records, who had written incriminating words about Blake's father in her diary, who had been taken one Sunday night to be tortured and killed and nailed to the wall.

Then Blake's mind was travelling back in time, back to the night of the party, back to when Demelza had vanished. Demelza, who had been one of the Forever Four—Demelza, Christine, Blake, and Judy—but who had always been Christine's best friend, the two of them inseparable like twins, even when the four of them were together. Demelza, who, out of the blue, decided the Forever Four should become the Terrific Two. Not with Christine, who she inexplicably dropped like a hot coal, but with Blake. How had that happened? And why? Suddenly Blake was Demelza's best friend. Suddenly Demelza was spending most evenings at Blake's house, and hadn't she always turned a perfect shade of red whenever Blake's father had returned from work and smiled at her and said, "Uh oh. Here comes Trouble with a capital T"?

Blake stared out at the rain, a sick feeling churning her stomach. On the night of the party, she had found Demelza alone and crying, and when she had asked her what was wrong, Demelza had shook her head and smiled sadly, and then said something that had always puzzled Blake. "It's nothing to worry your head about. Just trouble with a small 't'."

Demelza. Lucy. Blake's father, Ed. Medical records. Incriminating diary entries. Trouble with a capital 'T'. Trouble with a small 't'.

Blake threw her head back and swallowed the rest of the beer, not caring that it was only making her colder. She was determined to drown the realisation that was crawling in her gut like maggots.

What should she do? Did she accept her father was guilty of murdering Lucy? Of killing Demelza, who was surely dead after all these years? Of abducting Leanne Curnow and Heather Hargreaves, who had nothing to do with any of them? And what about those other women, who had disappeared, one after the other, year after year, all taken on a Sunday? Was that her father, too?

It was a ridiculous idea. Impossible. Or was it?

There was a certain type of serial killer who could pull the wool over everyone's eyes, who could go to church and pretend to praise Jesus, or who could marry a woman and give her two children and a seemingly everyday life, while underneath his skin there was a sickness that was seething and spreading. An uncontrolled desire to torture and to maim, to rape and to kill. Like Peter Sutcliffe, the Yorkshire Ripper, who murdered thirteen women with hammers and knives, and who attacked several more, all while sustaining the pretence of a happy marriage, before and after his conviction. Like Ted Bundy, who was outwardly handsome and oh so charming, and who confessed to the murder of at least thirty women, not to mention the repeated defilement of their corpses. Was that who her father really was? Was that dear old Ed?

Blake fell against the wall. Nausea rippled through her.

"Tell me what to do," she whispered to Lucy. "Tell me what to do," she whispered to Demelza.

But they were both gone from the world. Dust floating in the ether. And it didn't matter whether Ed was innocent or guilty, because Blake's father was not the man she thought he was, and the last eighteen years had all been a lie. The question now was: what should she do about it?

She had no answer. None at all. But she knew someone who might. Someone who had carried a world of grief and loss on her back for eighteen long years.

Stumbling back to her car, Blake started the engine and sped away. Thirty minutes later, she was back in Wheal Marow and pulling up in front of a detached white house with a front garden surrounded by a low stone wall. A downstairs light was on. Blake got out of the car and stood on the pavement, paralysed by indecision and getting soaked by the heavy rain. Steeling herself, she walked on unsteady feet to the garden gate and unclasped the latch. Before she could change her mind, she opened the gate and walked up the path to the front door. She pressed the doorbell with a trembling finger and stepped back. Her pulse raced. Her mind told her to return to the car and drive all the way back to Manchester.

The door opened and Faith Penrose appeared. At first, she stared at Blake as if she were a stranger. Then Blake started crying. Faith smiled sadly and opened her arms. Blake fell into them and eighteen years of grief came pouring out.

34

THEY SAT at the kitchen table, Blake with a warm blanket wrapped around her shoulders and Faith with a warm smile etched on her lips. Mugs of hot chocolate sat untouched in front of them.

Blake's mind was a maelstrom of conflict. She had been so intent on coming here, but now she wished she'd gone straight home. Years had passed since she'd last talked to Faith. Years had passed since she'd sat with Demelza, Christine, and Judy in this very kitchen, drinking juice and eating cheese sandwiches, or lounged in Demelza's bedroom, talking and laughing for hours about college and friends and the exciting lives they were planning to lead. She didn't know how Faith could stand to continue living in this house, surrounded by memories and haunted by the dead.

"I'm sorry. I shouldn't have come here so late," Blake said. "I don't even really know why I did."

Faith's smile grew wider. "Don't be sorry. I'm glad you're here. But tell me what's got you so upset."

Blake stared at the table. Droplets of water had dripped from her hair to splash on its surface. "It's Dad. The police have arrested him on suspicion of murdering Lucy and abducting those girls from Truro." She looked closer. The droplets hadn't come from her hair, but from her eyes. "They've made a mistake. Of course they have. My dad may be a few things, but he isn't a murderer."

Faith's smile wavered then collapsed. "Lucy was such a sweet and kind young woman. She didn't deserve what happened to her. No girl ever does. By the way, how is your mother? I heard about the accident. Who's with her right now?"

"My cousin Kenver." Confused, Blake looked across the table. Why hadn't Faith rushed to Ed's defence? In fact, she'd barely reacted to the news. "The police haven't charged Dad with anything yet. So, there's still a chance to prove them wrong. Or maybe they'll let him go when they realise they don't have any evidence."

Faith leaned back further on the chair and cocked her head to one side as she regarded Blake. "You really have grown into quite the beautiful woman. You know, I've thought about you over the years. Even though I haven't seen your mother in such a long time, I do try to find out how you are. I was surprised that you'd become a private investigator. I think it's really quite wonderful. What made you decide to go down such an unusual path?"

What was happening? It was as if Blake hadn't mentioned her father's arrest at all. "Well, I suppose, it was because of Demelza. The not knowing made me want to seek out answers. I've been thinking about her a lot lately. Ever since Lucy . . ." She glanced away. "I'm sorry, I don't mean to compare."

"I feel so sad for Christine. To lose a child like that, and in such a violent way, there really isn't a pain quite like it. I suppose the one small recompense Christine has, is that she can lay her daughter to rest and she'll always know where to find her. I apologise if that sounds a little callous, but it *is* a blessing in such terrible circumstances." She paused to expel a deep breath. "I sometimes try to fool myself that Demelza's still alive somewhere, living her life. Or I'll pretend that one day the police will uncover a clue that will lead them straight to her, and they'll find her very much alive, but with no memory of who she is or what happened to her. She'll return home and a hypnotist will help her to regain her memories, and then life will return to normal." She paused, staring at Blake. "It's why I go to the police station sometimes. I convince myself they're still looking for her. That's why I went the other night."

Blake's face burned with guilt. "I'm sorry I haven't been to see you in such a long time. I can't even explain why."

"I can. It's because you know the truth about Demelza, and, like me, you don't want to admit it."

"The truth?"

"That she's dead. She has to be, because she was never a cruel person. Her father and I may have been overbearing parents, and she may have found it stifling at times, but my daughter would never have left me in pain all these years with no closure."

Blake removed the blanket from her shoulders and used the corner to mop up her tears from the table. When she was done, she draped it carefully over the back of the chair.

"I wanted to ask you about Lucy."

"Are you sure?" Faith asked. "You might not like what you hear."

"Christine told me that Lucy was fascinated by Demelza. I've since learned she was trying to find out what happened to her. I also heard that she befriended you at the foodbank."

"As I said, Lucy was a sweet girl. In some ways, she reminded me of Demelza; she was full of so much light and kindness. She did ask a lot of questions, but I didn't mind. I like to talk about my daughter. In a way, it helps to keep her alive. When Lucy first came rushing up to me at the foodbank, I was quite overwhelmed. I'll be the first to admit that I've become quite the hermit over the years. I've never really believed in the phrase 'misery likes company'. I find pain is better dealt with alone. And I've been on my own for a very long time. Ever since Demelza vanished, and my marriage ended. You hear about it sometimes, don't you? Relationships falling apart after the loss of a child? If I'm honest, our marriage was already strained. My ex-husband wasn't the warmest of people. After Demelza was gone, I realised she was the only thing holding us together. Now, I like being alone. You don't have to feel scared that you're always doing something wrong, and you don't have to worry that, one night, your only child might not come home."

Blake could feel the grief emanating from Faith in thunderous waves. Grief never lets you go, she thought. No matter how much you try to bury it or make peace with it, grief is always hiding under the surface, waiting for the ice to thaw.

"You and Lucy became friendly?" she asked.

"She was like a light in the dark," Faith said, smiling. "She would come for dinner and we would talk. She would tell me about her hopes and dreams, about her friends and her job at the hospital, and about how Christine was getting on. For a short while the house felt alive again. I'd have little daydreams that Lucy was mine, or that I was her favourite auntie that she always liked to visit. But then she crossed a line."

Blake leaned forward. "What do you mean?"

"The week before the anniversary of Demelza's disappearance, Lucy was here having lunch after volunteering at the food-bank. I happened to tell her about Demelza's memorial plaque at the churchyard. I told her how every year without fail a bunch of white roses mysteriously appears. I certainly didn't put them there. Demelza's father hadn't put them there, either. I asked everyone I knew who was close to Demelza, but no one could tell me anything about it."

"I didn't know about the flowers."

"Of course you didn't. Why would you?"

Blake flinched at the accusation in Faith's voice. *Why would you when you've spent eighteen years avoiding me?* "White roses were Demelza's favourite. I remember that."

"Yes, they were. Anyway, the anniversary arrived and just like every year before, there were the white roses lying on the grass beneath the memorial plaque. Later that evening, Lucy came running over to the house. She told me that she knew who put them there. She'd been checking on the churchyard. She told me that the day before the anniversary, she'd camped out there the whole day, waiting and waiting for someone to come. And then, just as evening fell, someone came. Just like that, the mystery was solved. When she told me who it was, I was shocked and confused. Until I started thinking about it. Then it all made terrible sense."

Faith's eyes had grown dark and angry. She stared intensely at Blake. "Did you ever wonder why Demelza suddenly decided to make you her best friend? I always felt sorry for Christine. Those two had been close ever since they were little girls, but out of the blue she was pushed to the side. Don't get me wrong, Demelza liked you very much. But it always struck me as odd how she suddenly wanted to spend all her time with you. Every day, she would say, 'I'm off to see Blake.' Christine didn't even get a mention towards the end. And it wasn't just spending time with you anywhere, was it? It was always at your house."

Unease crept over Blake like a chill from an open window.

Faith continued. "A few days before Demelza disappeared, I heard her crying in her bedroom. I went up to check on her, but as I walked in, she reacted as if she'd been caught committing a crime. She'd hidden something behind her back. I didn't see what and I didn't press the matter. When I asked her what was wrong she became defensive. She insisted she was fine, that I was making a fuss over nothing. But she was hiding something from me, and not just behind her back.

"At the time, I couldn't figure out what was wrong. Demelza didn't have a boyfriend. She was about to go off to university, which she was very excited about, and she had her whole life ahead of her. Her father put it down to teenage hormones, but I always knew it was more than that. A few days later, she was gone. I never did find out what had upset her so much. Until Lucy went searching."

"Lucy's friend told me she'd been caught with Demelza's medical records at the hospital archive," Blake said. "She lost her job over it."

"Yes, I know. I stupidly told Lucy about finding Demelza upset in her bedroom. After we found out who was leaving the roses, Lucy went looking for answers—even though I'd warned her not to. She came to me one morning, upset that she'd been fired. But she told me she'd found something. That day in Demelza's bedroom came rushing back. Suddenly, it all made sense."

Shocked, Blake looked up. "Demelza was pregnant."

"Yes, she was." Faith turned away, staring into the past. When she looked back, her eyes were wet and shimmering. "I should have asked her what was wrong. I should have pressed her until she told me. Her father would have had something to say about it. He was always such a cold man. But I was her mother. I could have helped."

Blake's mind was reeling. Her stomach churned with panic. "You didn't know she was going to disappear. None of us did."

"No, but that's beside the point," Faith said. "Anyway, I told Lucy enough was enough. I gave up volunteering at the food-bank and I told her not to come around anymore. I know she was only trying to help, but all she did was open old wounds and make new ones. I told her so, too, and she got upset. I had no idea what would happen to her next. I can only imagine that silly girl went looking for more answers."

Blood rushed in Blake's ears. She didn't want to ask the question that was fighting its way past her lips. She didn't want to know the answer, either. But deep down in a broken part of her, she already knew the terrible truth.

"Faith? Who was leaving the white roses every year?"

Faith glared at her with hatred and disgust in her eyes. Her lips curled into a sneer.

"Who the hell do you think?" she said.

35

MARY WAS asleep on the living room sofa, her leg resting on the ottoman and a blanket draped up to her chest. Blake stood in the doorway, watching her. Her mother looked at peace, as if the past twelve hours had never happened. Blake shivered violently and held onto the door jamb.

Kenver was sitting in an armchair. Hearing movement, he glanced up from his phone screen. Alarm crept over his face. Blake backed out of the living room doorway and crept along the hall. Kenver followed her.

"It's two in the morning," he whispered. "Where the hell have you been?"

It was as if Blake's voice had been frozen in ice. All she could do was shake her head.

"Auntie Mary told me everything. None of it makes sense. You don't believe your dad is a murderer, do you?"

"How's my mum? Why didn't you help her to bed?"

"Because she was worried sick and wanted to stay up until you got home. She's been crying, asking why you took off like that. I didn't know what to tell her. You know I'm not a feelings person. But she was getting more and more upset, so I may have given her one of my cookies."

Blake frowned. "Cookies?"

Pulling a hip flask from his pocket, Kenver unscrewed the cap. "You know. The herbal, nerve-calming kind."

Shock broke through the chill. "You drugged my mother?"

"Weed isn't a drug. It's a plant. Anyway, it's legal in parts of America."

"Well, you're in the UK, dickhead, and the law says you can't drug my mother just because you can't deal with her feelings!"

"She said she didn't know that I baked. She liked them. She asked for more."

"I can't believe what I'm hearing!"

"There's a few left. I brought Tupperware."

"No, thank you!" Blake snatched the hip flask before Kenver could drink from it, and replaced the cap. To her own surprise, she started to laugh. "My father's been arrested for murder. My mother is stoned out of her box. And me, what am I even doing with my life?"

Blake stared at the hip flask, unscrewed the cap again and took a swig. Rum burned her throat and heat bloomed in her chest. Her conversation with Faith Penrose plagued her mind. Demelza had been pregnant. It was so obvious now that she felt foolish for not having figured it out. But back then, she'd been so focused on getting out of Wheal Marow that everything else had paled in significance. Now that Blake knew the truth about her friendship with Demelza, she felt like the butt of a twisted and cruel joke, one that had been playing out for years.

"Did Dad's lawyer call?"

Kenver shook his head. "I don't think so. Anyway, I'm sure

they'll release Uncle Ed tomorrow. They're not going to find anything on him."

"Unless they find evidence in his van."

"Why would they?"

"His van matches the description of the one used in the abduction. He has no alibi for the night Lucy disappeared. It also turns out he doesn't have much of an alibi for the night the Truro teenagers were taken. There's other evidence as well, linking him to Lucy and Demelza."

"What evidence?"

"It doesn't matter. But it's not looking good for him. The police will be concentrating all their efforts to get a confession so they can find the girls, hopefully still alive."

"Christ, Blake. You sound like you actually believe your dad could be guilty." Kenver took back his hip flask and replaced the cap. "What's got into you?"

Anger was coming. She could feel the pressure building. Soon, she would not be able to contain it. She had been deceived. Played for a fool. All these years, she'd lived under the shadow of Demelza's disappearance. She'd grieved and blamed herself, and avoided any meaningful relationships because, like Faith Penrose, her misery had never craved company. But it had all been for nothing, because it had all been a lie.

And yet, deep down in her heart she knew her father wasn't a killer, and despite her feelings towards him, she couldn't sit by and do nothing.

"I don't believe Dad's guilty," she said. "Not of murder, anyway. But he does have some explaining to do."

Kenver was suddenly alert. "Did Judy call you? I was trying to tell you earlier this evening: she found something."

"She called when Dad was getting arrested."

"Did she leave a message?"

Blake pulled out her phone and called her voicemail service. An automated voice announced she had one new message, then Judy spoke rapidly into Blake's ear. "It's Judy. You were right! I spent most of the day making phone calls and checking into our missing women's lives. Every single one of them was a church-goer. Fifteen women. Fifteen different churches. This is big, Blake. It must be how he's choosing his targets—through the church. Call me as soon as you get this."

"Holy shit," Blake said.

Kenver arched an eyebrow. "Quite literally. So you see, it can't be Uncle Ed. The real killer has got to be connected to the church somehow. Like a reverend or a priest?"

"I'm not sure. Look at the pattern of disappearances: one woman, once a year, each taken from a different parish. As far as I'm aware vicars and priests tend to stick to one church for a good few years. Our killer is moving around. What kind of church job involves jumping from parish to parish?"

"You're asking the humanist."

"Well, we need to find out. And we need to figure out what he's doing with these women, because except for Lucy none of the bodies have ever shown up."

"Maybe Lucy was different. Maybe she got too close to the truth and was killed for it."

"It's a possibility. But why put her on display like that? Why not hide her away like the others?"

Kenver winced. "I don't think I want to know."

But Blake did. Adrenaline melted the outer layers of her anger. She knew what she had to do now. She had to find Lucy's killer and figure out what he was doing, before it was too late for Heather and Leanne.

36

LEANNE STOOD IN DARKNESS, trembling uncontrollably. She had explored every inch of every wall of her glass cell but had found nothing. No windows. No gaps. Only the door, which had no handle on the inside of the cell. In a blind panic, she had attacked its hinges with her fingers, only stopping when her nails had cracked and her fingertips had started to bleed. Then she'd cried in frustration and hopelessness. She was going to die in here. Her captor wasn't planning to let her go. Releasing her had never even entered his mind. He was going to kill her. Probably rape and torture her first, until he grew bored. She couldn't let him do that to her. She was sixteen years old. Too young to die. There had to be a way out.

And so now she stood, the handle of the metal bucket clutched in her hand, its contents expelled on the ground. Adrenaline rippled through her veins and into her muscles. Sucking in a deep breath, she drew her arm back and then swung it forward with all her strength. The bucket slammed into the front wall. An almighty boom shattered the air. The force of the collision made Leanne's arm recoil like she'd fired a gun. Pain shot up to her shoulder as she was spun around. The bucket flew from her grip and clattered on the ground.

She froze, catching her breath, shocked by the noise of the impact. Then she dropped to the ground, found the bucket, and stood up again.

She swung it again, with both hands gripping the handle. The bucket hit, the wall shuddered, and a thunderstorm raged in her ears. The kickback was less this time, only making her stagger. With a cry, she swung again. Pain ripped through her hands. She let go of the bucket and it landed noisily on the ground.

Dizziness took hold of Leanne's head, followed by a sudden weakness. She hadn't eaten in what felt like days, and all she'd had to drink was the paper cup of water her captor had pushed through the flap in the door on his previous visit. She staggered, trying to keep her balance. Then she lurched forward with hands outstretched to desperately search the wall for cracks. The coldness of the plastic glass soothed her fingertips. The unblemished surface taunted her mind. Another wave of dizziness hit and she cried out in desperation. But then her right index finger brushed over a small groove. It felt minuscule, barely half an inch wide. But she had made a chip in the glass. And if she could make a chip, she could make a crack, and cracks splintered and eventually shattered.

Hope made Leanne's heart skip a beat. Slowly getting on her hands and knees, she found the bucket. Adopting the stance of a baseball player up to bat, she twisted her upper body and swung the bucket at the wall. Thunder cracked, but the wall did not. She swung, again and again. But then fatigue tried to prise the bucket from her hands, and it was as if she was sinking into quicksand. She swung the bucket again, but this time the impact was minimal, barely tapping the wall.

"No!" She hissed between clenched teeth. She had to find the energy. To channel all her remaining strength into her arms. She swung the bucket again, her body twisting. The bucket missed its target and Leanne spun a full circle. She was falling through the blackness, the ground rushing up to meet her. She hit it hard.

Moaning, she rolled onto her hands and knees. She tried to stand but tripped over her feet and staggered to one side. Her shoulder slammed painfully into the wall and she slid to the ground once more.

She would not give up. Not now. Because to give up was to accept death.

As Leanne pushed herself up on her hands and searched blindly for the bucket, a loud click filled her ears. She froze.

The warehouse door was opening.

Terrified, she twisted around and scrambled away on her elbows. The back of her head struck the rear wall. She searched for the rectangle of daylight that always marked her captor's entrance. But it was night outside and in.

Delirious with exhaustion, Leanne pulled her knees up to her chest and waited for him to come.

And she waited.

But there was no further movement. No more sounds. Only the rapid beating of her heart.

Perhaps she had imagined it. Perhaps she had finally lost her mind. She waited another minute, before cautiously getting onto her knees again to search for the bucket.

"You can't get out." His voice was pure darkness, reverberating all around. "Do you really think you're the only one who tried?"

Leanne froze like a cat on its haunches.

"Please," she moaned. "Please, let me go."

Real or imagined, she could feel his eyes seeking her out then crawling over her flesh. The thought made her stomach twist in knots. Anger burst through her repulsion. Why was she begging for her life?

"Let me out, you fucking piece of shit! If you've hurt Heather, I'll kill you!"

He surprised her by laughing. It was cold laughter. Cruel. Like nails tearing through flesh. "I had no use for your friend. She served no purpose. But you . . . Your time is almost here. You will be cleansed and transformed, led from the path of sin to the road of righteousness."

Anger faded. Terror swept in. Leanne begged and sobbed. "Oh God, Heather! Please, no. I just want to go home!"

"Do you want to see?" His voice was closer now. "Do you want to see the glory that awaits you? What you will become?"

"Please! Please, please, please. Let me go!"

"I'll show you. Perhaps then you'll be less afraid."

Suddenly the darkness was ripped away as overhead strip lights flickered on. Leanne fell back and covered her face with her forearm. After days of perpetual darkness, the light was dazzling, as if she were staring directly into the sun. She blinked and blinked. Her heart smashed against her chest. Slowly, she lowered her forearm.

All she saw was brilliant light. And then shadows. Shadows turned into blurred shapes. Blurred shapes became textured and took on form.

Leanne's eyes grew impossibly wide. Her jaw loosened and her throat clenched.

The man stood in the corner of the warehouse, a dark stain in the light.

"Aren't they beautiful?" he said, pressing his hands together.

But Leanne didn't hear him. She was paralysed, her gaze pinned on the aberrations that stood beyond her glass cell. Her hands flew to her face and she screamed. She kept on screaming, until it was the only sound in the world. And then he was screaming along with her, mimicking her terror.

37

IT HAD RAINED LATE into the night, but Saturday morning brought a crisp blue sky and a stillness to the frosty air. Glistening dew drops clung to the lawn of the rear garden and the branches of the surrounding trees. The sun was bold and bright. Blake had already showered, dressed in clean clothes, and made a pot of coffee. Despite the lack of sleep, she was buzzing with energy. Her mother was still asleep under the blanket on the living room sofa. Setting a cup of coffee on the side table, Blake leaned down to kiss her forehead.

Mary stirred. Seeing Blake, she smiled warmly. Then it was as if all the pain from yesterday rushed over her like a tide

"Morning," Blake said. "How are you feeling?"

Mary pulled the blanket down and tried to sit up.

"What time is it?" she asked.

"Just before eight. There's coffee next to you."

Mary rubbed her tired eyes and stared down at her clothes. She frowned. "I don't know what happened last night. One minute I was chatting with your cousin, then the next . . . I suppose I must have nodded off. I can't remember the last time I fell asleep in my clothes."

Blake glanced at the plate on the table, which still contained a half-eaten cookie. "Must have been all the stress from yesterday."

She adjusted the cushions behind her mother's back, handed her the cup of coffee, then joined her on the sofa.

"Is there any news about your father?"

"Not yet. I'll call his lawyer soon."

"You'd think she would have been in touch by now."

"She's probably had a long night."

Mary's eyes grew misty. "I hope they're treating him right. They would have let your father sleep, wouldn't they? He's like a bear with a sore head when he's tired. What about his tea? They'd have given him something to eat, wouldn't they?"

Blake didn't answer. She gently patted down her mother's bed hair while avoiding her gaze.

"Where did you go last night? I was worried sick. You look like you haven't slept a wink either."

"I'm sorry, Mum. I didn't mean to scare you. Everything got on top of me, and I needed some time alone to think. You were already out for the count by the time I got home, and I didn't want to wake you."

"I see. Kenver get home all right? He's a good boy really, under all that metal in his face."

Blake shifted on the sofa. "Mum, I need to ask you something."

"Okay."

"It's about the night Demelza disappeared."

Mary seemed to catch her breath. "What's that got to do with anything that's happening now?"

"Do you remember that night? Do you remember where you were and what you were doing?"

"It was years ago. Who remembers anything from back then?"

"But it wasn't exactly a normal time, was it? That kind of event tends to stick in your mind like glue."

"I don't know about glue. I've got a memory like a sieve."

"Try to remember. Please."

Mary sighed. "Well, let me think for a minute. I expect I was at home, just like I always am."

"And Dad? Was he home with you that night?"

"I expect so. Why wouldn't he have been?"

"Sometimes he works late."

"But it was a Sunday, wasn't it? Your father never goes out on a Sunday except to church."

"Except he did last week," Blake said.

"Because he got that call, saying that someone had been seen hanging around the building site."

"And the night before you came home from hospital? The night Lucy disappeared?"

"He was at home. What's this all about, Blake? What are you trying to get at?"

Blake's knee jigged up and down. She drew in a shaky breath and let it out. "The night Demelza disappeared, did Dad get a phone call?"

"How am I supposed to remember that?" Mary looked away and scratched her neck. "I don't like these questions you're asking. It feels like you're insinuating something."

"Please, Mum."

"I said I don't remember."

"What about Demelza? Do you remember how close the two of us were? It didn't bother you that she would show up here almost every night?"

Mary's face softened a little. "I used to joke that she was my second daughter. Her parents weren't getting along so well, if I remember correctly, so I suppose she needed somewhere to get away. But Demelza was always very welcome here. You know that."

"What about Dad? Did he mind her being here all the time?"

"No, of course not. Why would he? Your father liked Demelza very much. In fact, he always insisted on giving her a ride home at the end of the night, even when Demelza said she would take the bus. Your father's like that, Blake. He's kind and caring, and thoughtful. He would never hurt anyone."

That sick feeling was bubbling in Blake's stomach again.

Trouble with a capital 'T'. Trouble with a small 't'. Your father liked Demelza very much. He always insisted on giving her a ride home.

Faith's hate-filled eyes flashed in her mind. *Who the hell do you think?*

Mary was watching her. Deep lines creased her forehead. "Why are you asking so much about Demelza and your father?"

Blake's voice stumbled in her throat. Did she tell her mother what she knew? Could she bring herself to say it out loud? Because if Faith Penrose was right, forty years of marriage would be destroyed in a matter of seconds.

Demelza. Blake's father, Ed. Trouble with a capital 'T'. Rides home at night. Medical records. White roses. Trouble with a small 't'.

Mary was still staring, but now her eyes were wide and uncertain.

Blake smiled weakly. "I'm just trying to remember, that's all. Trying to put events in order to make sense of what's happening now."

"I'll tell you what I remember most from back then," Mary said. "My daughter, so worried and upset that I was scared she was going to make herself ill."

Blake remembered those days too. The fear and anxiety that had haunted her from morning to night. And the crippling guilt. Joining the search parties hadn't alleviated it. Phoning around to every person she could remember being at the party that night hadn't helped free herself from its weight. No one knew anything. But Blake did. She knew something had been troubling Demelza. *She knew.* But no matter how much she'd tried, Demelza had refused to confide in her. Maybe Blake hadn't pressed hard enough. Maybe if she had insisted, Demelza would still be here.

She squeezed her mother's hand.

"Your father is a good man," Mary said, her voice breaking. "We may have had our ups and downs over the years, but he's a good man."

Blake leaned over and kissed her mother's cheek. "I need to go out again."

Mary started to protest.

"It's important. It could help Dad. I already texted Auntie Hester. She's taking the bus from Helston. She should be here by nine. I'll wait till she arrives."

"I don't want Hester here!" Mary cried. "I don't want her finding out about what's happening with your father."

"Mum, she already knows."

"You told her?"

"I had to. Before she hears it from someone else. She's your sister, Mum."

She watched the realisation ripple over her mother's face. Saw her cheeks flush red and her lips tremble.

"Your father is a good man," she whispered again. "He didn't do anything wrong."

"Which is why I need to go. So I can find out the truth and prove that Dad's innocent."

Mary dried her eyes with the sleeve of her cardigan.

"Then go," she said.

"I'll make you some breakfast while we wait for Auntie Hester. Then we'll get you cleaned up and into some fresh clothes."

As she got up from the sofa, Mary reached out and grabbed her wrist.

"If it helps, he did get a call that night," she said, her voice low and trembling. "He used to have a second phone for work, one of those pay and go ones, but it hardly ever used to ring. That night, your father got a call and he took it in private. When he came back downstairs, he was in a strange mood. I asked him what was wrong, but he said it was nothing, just work stuff. I wondered at the time because it didn't seem like work stuff. Ed seemed really shaken up. When I pressed about it, he got angry and told me to leave it alone. So I did. But I'm telling you, your father was here with me all night long. So whatever you're thinking, he didn't have anything to do with Demelza disappearing, or killing Lucy, or taking those two girls. He's as innocent as you or me."

Blake pulled away from her mother's grip.

Trouble with a small 't'. Medical records. White roses. Who the hell do you think?

It was all true. Her father might have been innocent of murder and abduction. But when it came to affairs of the heart, he was guilty as sin.

38

BLAKE PULLED up outside Judy Moon's house and honked the car horn. Seconds later, the front door opened and Judy hurried out wearing a long winter coat. As she climbed into the passenger seat and shut the door, she flashed a worried look at Blake.

"Your text message was very cryptic," she said. "You look terrible. Didn't you sleep?"

Blake started the engine and pulled away. "Have you heard about my dad?"

"Yes. There's a police scanner in the press room."

"Isn't it illegal to eavesdrop on the police force in this country?"

"I didn't say it was *my* police scanner."

They drove away from the cul-de-sac, leaving comfort and safety behind.

"Anyway, where are we going? I need to be back by twelve to take the girls to their dance class."

"Field trip," Blake muttered. "Is your paper going to run a story about my father?"

There was an uncomfortable silence before Judy answered. "I don't know. I told you, I only write the farm news. What I do know is that Jake, the editor-in-chief, went to school with your dad. No one in the office believes he's responsible. But you should know the tabloids are going to jump on this. Ed Hollow, friend of the Truscott family, well-respected member of the community, and alleged killer. They might not identify him by name just yet, especially with the police keeping a chokehold on the press, but they'll confirm an arrest has been made."

Blake tightened her grip on the steering wheel. "I'm guessing your little paper isn't the only one with a police scanner."

Leaving the town behind, she turned onto the A30. It was busier today, with vehicles speeding up and down the lanes.

"What do you think about the church angle?" Judy asked.

"It's good. I've got Kenver looking into different church jobs that involve travel."

"What if the killer doesn't work for the church? What if it's just your average, everyday psychopath?"

"Maybe. But that would mean he's targeting churches at random, and nothing feels random about any of this."

Judy frowned. "What do you mean?"

"If our theory is right, the killer is targeting churchgoing young women who, in his eyes, have committed a cardinal sin by drinking or partying on a Sunday. The only way he could know that is if he's been watching his victims. There are over six hundred churches in Cornwall. Most congregations are close-knit from what I hear, or at least populated by local faces. If the killer was simply sticking a pin into a map then rocking up to Sunday service to see who's been a naughty girl, wouldn't at least the vicar notice a stranger in the crowd? Which makes me think our killer is someone known to the church. Besides, everything has a pattern with him. One victim, once a year, each one taken from a different church."

"Except Lucy doesn't fit into that pattern," Judy said. "And those girls—Heather and Leanne—that's two victims, not one."

"Maybe he meant to take one of them, and the other got in the way."

The strange feeling that had struck Blake last night returned. It was like déjà vu, making her head spin. What was it that she knew?

Judy stared out of the passenger window. "Are you going to tell me where we're going or do I have to guess?"

"Ding Dong Mine," Blake said, and heard Judy catch her breath.

"What? Why are we going there?"

"Because like you said, Lucy doesn't fit the pattern. There's got to be a reason why the killer left her on display at the mine when none of his other victims have ever been found. And why the mine, when there are plenty of remote places in Cornwall to dump a body where it would never be discovered? It's bugging me. If our theory is right, this psycho has been flying under the police radar for years. Why is he jeopardising that now?"

Judy's complexion paled. She readjusted her seat belt and shifted on the seat. "Who knows why psychopaths do what they do? Maybe we've jumped to conclusions and got it all wrong. Or maybe Lucy was killed by someone else."

Turning off the A30 at Crowlas, Blake retraced the journey she'd made last night. But instead of dark and foreboding buildings, all she saw now was pretty villages and hamlets lit up by cold sunlight.

"The killer wanted Lucy to be found, but I don't know why. She was conducting her own investigation into Demelza's disappearance. She made friends with Demelza's mother at the foodbank, then got fired from her cleaning job at the hospital for sneaking into the archives and accessing Demelza's old medical records. Then she wrote something in her diary about my father that was incriminating enough for the police to arrest him."

Judy's jaw slackened. "What did she write?"

"I have an idea. But —"

"But what?"

"Nothing. Just that Detective Sergeant Turner isn't exactly forthcoming when it comes to sharing the facts."

"Then how did you know about the . . . Wait, Rory told you about the diary, didn't he? That idiot's going to get himself fired one of these days."

"Not if you don't say anything about it."

They were driving along the winding country lane that led to Ding Dong Mine, gorse-covered moorland spreading out on both sides. The ruins of the engine house rose up in the near distance. Blake slowed the car and pulled over. Switching off the engine, she let her hands drop to her lap as she stared through the windscreen.

Judy, who had been deep in thought, looked up. "So, if your father isn't the killer, how does he fit into all this?"

Blake shook her head.

"What is it? You're not telling me something."

"Are we talking off the record?"

"Shit, Blake. I'm going to punch you in the face if you ask me that again."

"This is important. Especially if your paper is covering the story."

"Okay fine. Off the record. Happy now?"

Sucking in a deep breath, Blake turned to face Judy. "Last night, I went to see Demelza's mother."

"Faith? Bloody hell. You haven't seen her in years."

"I know. She told me what Lucy had found out. Demelza was pregnant. She and my father were having an affair. All that time I thought she wanted to hang out with me because she liked me. But really she was there to see my dad. So he could give her a ride home."

At first, Judy was silent. Then her jaw swung open, and her expression grew deadly serious. "This is a joke, right?"

"No. It's not." Now that Blake had said it out loud, the pain she felt turned numb. "A few days before Demelza disappeared, Faith found her upset in her bedroom. She wouldn't tell her mother what was wrong, but Faith said she was trying to hide something behind her back. I'm guessing it was a pregnancy test. Then on the night Demelza disappeared, she made a phone call to an unregistered mobile number that the police couldn't trace at the time. I just found out that my dad used to have an old pay and go phone that he allegedly kept for work. He got a call that night. One that left him upset and shaken. It was Demelza, wasn't it? Telling my dad that she was pregnant."

"Christ," Judy said. "Have you told your mother?"

"No. And until there's absolute proof she doesn't get to know. You're the only one I've told and it has to stay that way. I mean it."

"You have my word. But it doesn't look good, does it? Ed finds out Demelza's pregnant, then Demelza disappears. Lucy finds out about Demelza and Ed, then Lucy is murdered. Poor, sweet girl."

"Mum swears he was at home with her on the night Demelza disappeared. She says he didn't leave the house once."

"No offence, but could he have slipped out later?"

"I'm telling you, my dad doesn't have that kind of evil in him."

They were both silent, staring at the ruins of the engine house. Then Judy said, "So, Ed didn't kill Lucy, but someone did. Someone abducted Heather and Leanne, too. Not to mention all those other missing young women. And what about Demelza? We have pieces, Blake. Nothing that makes a whole picture."

"I know that. But I'm certain Lucy is the key to all of this. She was brought here and put on display for a reason. Right now, the police are focusing on my father's guilt, hoping he'll lead them to Heather and Leanne, which of course he can't. So it's down to us."

They stared at each other, eyes filled with fear and uncertainty.

Slowly, Judy nodded.

"Good," Blake said, throwing open the driver's door. "Then let's go."

39

THEY MADE the short walk to the engine house in subdued silence, the crunch of the stony path beneath their feet the only sound. Blake strode ahead, her lips pressed together and her eyes fixed on the ruin. Judy hung back, her hands shoved tightly inside her coat pockets. Despite the vast blue sky, golden sun, and the clear view right across to Mount's Bay, a heavy sense of desolation clung to the air. Blake felt it wrap tightly around her as she reached the engine house then circled around it, until she came to a stop in front of the open stone doorway where she had found Lucy's body. Judy came up beside her, looking desperately uncomfortable, as if she'd rather be anywhere else but here. Blake couldn't blame her. Over the years, Judy had remained close to Christine, and she had watched Lucy grow from a baby into a little girl, then into burgeoning womanhood. Blake had watched from a distance. She felt the pain of Lucy's death in her heart, but Judy felt it worse.

"I'm sorry, I shouldn't have brought you here," Blake said, quietly.

Judy stared at the open doorway and shook her head. "It's a little late for that now."

"Why don't you go back to the car?"

"No. I'm here for Christine. So let's get on with whatever it is we're doing."

"All right." Turning around, Blake shielded her eyes with her hand and stared into the distance. "The morning I found Lucy, I'd been at Christine's. The killer phoned her landline and told her that he'd seen Lucy dancing with the devil at Ding Dong Mine. So, you see, he wanted her to be found. And I think he wanted me to find her, which means he must have been watching Christine's house before he made the call."

Judy took a step back. "Why would you say that? What else haven't you told me?"

"The friendship bracelet found on Lucy's wrist. It wasn't Demelza's. It was mine. My DNA was all over it."

"What? Jesus, Blake. That means the killer's someone you know!"

"Maybe."

"Of course it is. You said you lost your bracelet. Someone close to you must have taken it. Someone like your dad."

"I told you. It's not him." They glared at each other, until Judy dropped her eyes to the ground. "As I was saying, as soon as the caller hung up, Christine called the police and I raced here. I found Lucy in this doorway. She was covered in burns and she'd been nailed to the engine house in a strange pose. I think the burns were caused by cement. The police took samples from Dad's building site. It's extremely caustic when mixed with water. I think Lucy's killer wanted her to feel every shred of pain he inflicted, until the burns killed her."

Judy muttered under her breath and scuffed the ground with her shoe.

"Have you heard anything on the journalism grape vine about the cause of death?" Blake asked.

"No. It's being kept under tight wraps. I'm assuming the police have their reasons for that." She glanced back up at Blake. "Why cement?"

"I don't know. But it's a good question."

"You said Lucy was in some kind of pose?"

Blake stepped forward. She could see the holes in the stonework where the killer had hammered nails to fix Lucy in place. Flakes of dried blood were still visible around each one. Blake reached out and felt the roughness of the holes with her fingertips.

"Like this," she said, then twisted around so she was facing outwards. She stretched her left arm out like one side of a cross, until her hand covered one of the holes. Then she bent her right arm and placed her elbow over the hole on the right side of the doorway and cupped her upturned hand against her stomach.

Judy had turned very pale.

"That looks like third position," she whispered.

Blake lowered her arms but remained in the doorway. "What's third position?"

"In ballet there are five basic positions for the arms and for the feet. The pose you did looks like position three. My girls go to ballet class. I've seen the five positions a hundred times around the house."

"Ballet," Blake said, her mind racing. "He put her in a dance position?"

Judy wrapped her arms around her ribs and covered her hands. "I want to go home now. Back to my girls."

"One minute."

"There's nothing to see here, Blake. Please, can we go?"

"See," Blake whispered.

Shaking her head, Judy began walking away from the engine house.

"I'm going back to the car," she called over her shoulder.

Blake remained in the doorway, peering out. What could Lucy see from here?

Nothing, she thought. Her eyes were gone.

But then an idea came to her. Stepping out of the ruin, Blake rounded the corner and hurried back along the path. Judy was waiting at the car, arms still folded across her chest. Blake unlocked the doors with the fob and went around to the back.

"What are you doing now?" Judy asked, as she tugged on the passenger door handle.

Opening the car boot, Blake rifled through its contents until she found a pair of binoculars. Slinging the strap over her shoulder, she shut the boot again and headed back to the path.

"I'll be two minutes," she called.

Despite the cold morning, beads of sweat dappled Blake's brow. Jogging along the path, she reached the engine house and returned to her position in the doorway. She lifted the binoculars to her eyes.

"What did you see?" She surveyed the land. Fields and moorland stretched out into the distance. She adjusted the focus wheel, zooming further.

A second later, she saw it.

A mile or two away in the centre of a grassy clearing, surrounded by swathes of gorse and heather, stood an ancient stone circle.

Blake twisted the focus wheel between her fingers and zoomed in further. She counted eleven stones.

The sense of déjà vu returned and tried to topple her. But it wasn't déjà vu; Blake knew that now. It was a memory, hiding away in the recesses of her mind.

She was very close to the truth now. She could feel it calling to her. All she had to do was be quiet and listen.

40

DENNIS STOOD in the cramped bathroom of his cottage. The bathtub and shower attachment took up most of the space, with a toilet squeezed into the opposite corner and a sink wedged in between. A medicine cabinet was fixed to the wall above it. Having showered and dressed into a crisp, white shirt and blue jeans, Dennis stared at his reflection in the mirror door of the cabinet. His skin was still red and radiating heat from the vigorous scrubbing he'd given himself, the second of the day. But cleanliness was next to godliness, and the dirt that fell off those girls was nothing short of toxic. Removing a jar of pomade from the cabinet, he scooped out a dollop of cream and rubbed it vigorously between his palms.

A smile rippled across his lips. He was pleased with Leanne's reaction to his work. Her screams had been like music. It had taken all of his willpower to stop himself from wrenching her from the cell and cleansing her on the spot. One more day, that was all. He could resist the urge until then.

He began working the pomade into his greying hair, from the roots to the tips. Then he took a comb and applied slow, steady strokes, the teeth biting into his pink scalp. He leaned closer to the mirror, finding loose strands and flattening them down.

The terror on her face had been exquisite and deserved. At sixteen years old, she had already been corrupted, the filth oozing from her pores. Cleansing her was his sacred duty. And her terror would only serve to make the cleansing pure and absolute.

Balancing the comb on the edge of the sink, Dennis turned his head from side to side and admired his handiwork. A perfect side parting. Satisfied, he returned the comb and pomade to the cabinet.

He froze. There was a speck of dirt, caught beneath the index fingernail of his right hand. Holding the finger out, he leaned in for a closer inspection. Not dirt, he realised. Blood.

Sighing, he opened the cabinet again and took out a nail brush. Running the bristles under cold water, he shook off the excess droplets and began to scrub savagely at his fingertip.

How had he missed such an obvious stain? The mistakes he was making lately! Like the one in his basement right now. That mistake had led him to take drastic action by sending the police in the direction of Ed Hollow. It was unfortunate because he'd made other plans for that deviant fornicator. But there was still more pain for him yet to come.

Dennis scrubbed harder. It was because his work was almost complete. The excitement was making him lose focus. He couldn't afford any more errors.

His fingertip was hurting. Good, he thought. Pain was cleansing.

The blood was gone. Dennis rinsed the brush clean and

returned it to the cabinet. Leanne's screaming echoed in his mind again.

"Please, don't hurt me," he whispered. "Please, let me go."

He stared at the mirror, at the blank canvas that was his reflection.

He pictured Leanne's terrified face, then slowly wrinkled his brow and widened his eyes. Was that how she had looked? No, her eyes had been wider and her mouth had trembled. He changed his expression to match the image in his mind.

Yes, that was more like it.

He mimicked Leanne's voice again, this time louder. "Oh God, Heather. Please, no!"

That wasn't right. Her voice had been more high-pitched and whiny like that of a baby.

He drew in a breath.

"Please!" he shrieked. "Please, please, please, don't kill me!"

Yes, exactly like that.

He smiled. His face went blank again. The girl in the basement hadn't screamed as much, but he hadn't given her a chance. He wondered how loud Leanne would scream tomorrow when her time finally came.

A single strand of hair had come loose. He flattened it down, checked his appearance one last time, and glanced at his wristwatch. It was almost time for the regional news.

He made his way downstairs and into the living room, which was small and square and neatly arranged. He switched on the television and changed the channel. The urge to return to the warehouse and cleanse the girl suddenly overpowered him. He squeezed his eyes shut and pulled his hands into fists. No, he had to wait. To give in now, would be to give into lust and greed. How was that setting a good example?

Tomorrow was the Sabbath. The day for cleansing.

Dennis opened his eyes again and fixed them on the television screen. The lunchtime news had already started. He didn't have long to wait. A female newsreader dressed in a conservative blouse and jacket stared seriously into the camera.

"Police have arrested a sixty-three-year-old local man in connection with the murder of teenager Lucy Truscott and the abductions of secondary school students Leanne Curnow and Heather Hargreaves. The suspect, who is from the Wheal Marow area, was taken to Truro station yesterday afternoon for questioning. The police have yet to press charges."

As the reporter continued to speak, the camera cut to footage taken days ago at Ding Dong Mine. The CSI team crawled about the crime scene in their ghostly white suits. It cut again to three photographs superimposed on the screen and lined up in a row. Lucy, Leanne and Heather, all dressed in their school uniforms and smiling at the camera.

Dennis hissed. "Sinners!"

The news story troubled him. He had been careful to plant the samples where they would be easily found. So why hadn't Hollow been charged? Twenty-four hours was almost up, which meant the police would soon have to release him or apply for an extension for the arrest warrant. At least, that's what the internet had told him. Perhaps the samples had been found but were still waiting to be processed and identified.

He watched the rest of the news bulletin, his skin itching beneath his clothes. What if they hadn't found the samples? What if they released Hollow and started their search for the girls again? What if they found Dennis before he could complete his work?

Because it wasn't just Leanne that needed cleansing. There

was still one more left to take. He had chosen her a long time ago but was saving her for last.

The news story ended and the presenter handed over to the weatherman. More rain was on its way, along with strong south-westerly winds. Dennis switched off the television and silence smothered the room.

What should he do?

He had stuck meticulously to his plan ever since its genesis. Then Lucy Truscott had come along with her pretense of inno-cence and deceiving eyes, trying to tell him what she thought she knew and almost upending eighteen years of his work. She had made Dennis panic, forcing him to strike her down. He had taught Lucy what happened when you went looking in private places. He'd also taught her mother a lesson, allowing her to listen to her daughter's dying screams. That's what you got for raising a whore.

Putting Lucy's body on display at Ding Dong had been impulsive, but there was an intention behind it: to attract the attention of his final girl.

He had spotted her by chance in Wheal Marow. She wasn't supposed to be there, yet there she was.

Seeing her had filled Dennis with such rage and uncontrol-lable desire that he had wanted to cleanse her right there in the street. To obliterate every cell in her being. That was when he had known he couldn't wait another year. His work weighed heavy on his heart, and he was so very tired. God would be understanding as long as the work was complete.

And so he had transformed Lucy's body into a waymarker that pointed towards the past. The friendship bracelet was a lure. He'd found it all those years ago, left on the kitchen counter. He'd been holding onto it for years, waiting for the right time to hook his final girl and reel her in. He was still waiting for her to take the bait. But now time was running out.

Dennis chewed the inside of his mouth as he stared at the blank television screen.

What should he do?

He would cleanse Leanne tomorrow. If Hollow was released today and the police resumed their search, Dennis would have no choice but to drive down to Wheal Marow to take his final girl. She was a greater challenge than all the others, and potentially more dangerous. But Dennis was unstoppable. He was the Sword of God.

The urge to cleanse grew more intense. Closing his eyes, he slipped a hand beneath his jeans and squeezed.

Sinner.

"No!" Removing his hand, Dennis bit the inside of his cheek until he tasted blood. The temptation remained, calling to him like a Siren.

"Hypocrite!" He slapped himself hard in the temple. He pinched the skin of his neck and twisted it. "Miscreant!"

The urge grew stronger, spiking his blood like a jolt of insulin. He bolted from the living room and into the hall.

A white heat burned inside him. Desire. Lust. A hunger for violence.

He strode towards the kitchen door and threw it open. Then he was crossing the floor, entering the workshop, and unlocking the back door. Spittle bubbled at the corners of his mouth. His pupils dilated until his eyes were pure darkness. He was outside now, floating in mid-air and staring down at the demon that had taken control of his body, watching it stalk across the yard, heading straight for the warehouse. And then he was back inside his body, because there was no demon. Only Dennis Stott and his primal, depraved hunger.

It was a clear day, capped by a bright blue expanse. Beyond the warehouse, the cobalt ocean glittered in the winter sunlight. There were yachts in the bay. A cargo ship was slowly disappearing on the horizon.

Dennis reached the warehouse. He sucked in deep breaths, tasting bitter sea salt on his tongue. His fingers twitched by his sides, clenching and relaxing then clenching again.

"No," he whispered, feeling the salt travel through his body, cleansing and purifying. "No."

The hunger was satiated. Desire slipped away and was replaced by resolve.

"Tomorrow."

The Sabbath was his day to work. He was God's martyr, cleansing the world of filth and rot.

He pressed a hand against the steel security door, then he sidestepped to the huge sliding door beside it, which was held in place by two heavy-duty padlocks. He rattled each one. Satisfied, he pressed his ear to the cold metal of the door, hoping to hear a scream or a whimper. All he heard was the soft rush of the ocean.

Turning on his heels, Dennis retraced his steps back to the cottage. Patience was his ally now. Tomorrow would be filled with screams and pure bright cleansing. Returning upstairs, Dennis undressed and climbed into the bathtub. He had missed hidden spots last time. Now he would scrub until his skin bled. Cleanliness was next to godliness.

41

THE JOURNEY back to Wheal Marow was tense and silent. Blake hadn't mentioned what she'd seen through the binoculars. She wasn't trying to hide it from Judy. Her mind was trying to tell her something, and she knew from experience that it was always better to shut up and listen, rather than let other people's opinions get in the way.

As it was, Judy was in no mood for conversation. She hadn't uttered a word since Blake had returned to the car and they'd driven away from Ding Dong Mine. Now, she sat in the passenger seat, half turned away from Blake. Being at the murder site had clearly unsettled her. And why wouldn't it? Sometimes Blake had to remind herself that not everyone had the same hardened disposition as she did. Years of lurking in the underbelly of humanity had left her desensitised and forgetful that regular people might get upset when visiting the site of their Goddaughter's vicious murder.

"I'm sorry," Blake said, as she drove through the town's high street, where Saturday shoppers milled up and down. "I shouldn't have taken you there."

Judy turned her head slightly and shrugged her right shoulder. "I thought I could handle it. Being a journalist, I thought my inquisitive nature might help. I should stick to the farming news."

"You're too close, that's all. You saw Lucy most weeks. You watched her grow up."

"Someone needs to fill in those holes. They can't just leave them there. But I suppose even if they were filled in, they'd still be visible. I hope Christine never goes out there."

Reaching Judy's cul-de-sac, Blake parked the car and left the engine running.

"You need to be careful," Judy said, staring directly at her. "If your dad isn't guilty, then the killer is still out there. He put your friendship bracelet on Lucy's wrist for a reason."

Blake gave a nod. "Maybe the killer used my bracelet as a signal to me. Maybe he wants me to stop him."

"You'd like that, wouldn't you? To be the one to catch him?"

"I just want to clear my dad's name, and for those girls to be found safe. I know in my heart that Dad's not a killer."

"But you can't be sure, can you? If you're right about him and Demelza, then he's been lying to you and your mother for years. I don't want it to be Ed, but have you even asked yourself how the killer had your friendship bracelet in the first place? Think about it: four of us had them. Demelza disappeared. Christine's daughter has been murdered. That leaves you and me, and your bracelet was with Lucy . . . I'm scared, Blake. If anything happened to my girls, I don't know what I would do."

"Nothing is going to happen to them."

"You don't know that. I don't want to be part of this anymore. We should just let the police detectives do their jobs. And you, you should go home to your mum. I know you're used to going it alone, and living independently with no ties or commitments, but in times like this family takes priority. Mary needs you. Whether you want to admit it or not, you need her too."

Blake glanced out the window, at the identical-looking houses, all neat and lined up in a row. She shook her head. "Sitting at home and doing nothing isn't going to free my father. It won't find those girls, either."

Judy stared at her and sighed heavily. "This town doesn't need any more tragedy."

She opened the passenger door and climbed out. Blake watched her shut the door, then falter, as if she were about to turn around and say something more. But then Judy was hurrying towards her home without looking back.

A weight sat on Blake's chest, making it hard to breathe. Grabbing her mobile phone, she called her parents' landline. Mary answered in tears.

"Mum? What is it?"

"Ivy Trevara just called. She said the police are holding Ed for another twelve hours. She says it's likely they're waiting on the DNA test results to come back."

Blake went numb. And yet she wasn't surprised. "It doesn't mean they'll charge him," she said softly. "The test results will come back, they'll see they've made a mistake, and they'll let Dad go."

"I just want to speak to him. I want to talk to my Ed, but they won't let me."

"He'll be home soon. I promise he will."

"I need you here with me, Blake. You need to come home now."

Blake thought about what Judy had just said. Her heart

pulled towards home, yet her instincts told her there was still work to do.

"Please, Blake," Mary sobbed.

"I'm sorry, but I can't. Not yet."

"But —"

"I love you, Mum."

She hung up and stared out the window at Judy's house. She pictured her friend hugging her daughters and kissing her husband. Blake had never felt the urge to have children or to marry, and she'd never thought for one moment that it made her less of a person. No, the emptiness inside her had been caused by a fissure, one that had cracked open the day Demelza disappeared and Blake's relationship with her father had ruptured forever. Now she knew the truth about Demelza and her father, yet the emptiness remained. But there was a way to fill it.

She grabbed her phone from the cup holder, opened the search browser, and entered the words: 'Stone circle near Ding Dong Mine.'

The results flashed on the screen.

"Boskednan stone circle," she read out loud, as she tapped the first article.

Cornwall has more megalithic sites per square mile than anywhere else in the country, including cairns, quoits, monoliths and stone circles. First documented in 1754 by Cornish geologist William Borlase, Boskednan stone circle is lesser-known than some of its more famous counterparts. Long-since fallen into ruin, it was partially restored in 2004, leaving a total of eleven stones now standing in the circle on the West Penwith moors. This is still significantly fewer than when Borlase first set eyes on the circle back in the eighteenth century and recorded seeing a total of nineteen.

Blake's mind raced. A hidden memory was taking shape and form in the shadows.

Her eyes fell upon the next paragraph. *Boskednan stone circle is also known by another, more traditional name by locals. The Nine Maidens.*

She looked up from the screen. Her heart thumped in her chest. The memory stepped out from the darkness and flashed behind her eyes.

The world slipped away, and a terrible dread slid down her spine.

Suddenly she knew why Lucy had been posed like a dancer. She knew why she'd been left at Ding Dong Mine to stare eyelessly out at Boskednan stone circle.

Worse still, Blake thought she knew who killed her.

42

BLAKE PARKED outside a cluster of cottages on a lonely stretch of country road two miles southeast of St Buryan, a village made infamous in the early 1970s by the controversial film Straw Dogs, which had not only been shot there, but had depicted the locals as heathens, psychopaths, and rapists.

She hadn't called ahead, and as she knocked on the front door she wondered if that had been a mistake.

The door opened a few inches, and an elderly woman peered out. She was short in stature and terribly thin, but there was a sharpness in her eyes that suggested she was no fool.

She stared coldly at Blake. An overpowering stench of cat urine poured out through the gap.

"We don't get charity people out this way," the woman snapped in a rasping voice. "What do you want?"

Blake forced a smile. "I'm sorry to bother you. My name's Blake. Are you Heidi?"

"Might be. Depends what you're after."

"I'd like to talk to you about your granddaughter if I may. Demelza?"

"She's dead, you know," Heidi said. "Been gone for years."

"I know. She was my friend."

Heidi narrowed her eyes, seemingly assessing whether Blake was a threat. "Don't get visitors around here. Place is a mess." She stepped back, opening the door just wide enough for Blake to slip through. "Have to be careful with the cats, what with living right on the road."

The animal smell was strong enough to make Blake gag. She waited for Heidi to shut the door then patiently followed the woman, who leaned heavily on a cane, as she hobbled through the cluttered, darkly lit hall and into a cramped living room. The stench was stronger in here, the air stale and dusty, and over-whelmingly hot. The room was finished with a sofa and chairs that had seen better days, and a twenty-year-old television set in the corner that was playing a daytime soap opera with the volume on mute. The cats were everywhere. Blake counted three on the sofa, two more sprawled on the threadbare carpet, another two perched in the windowsill and watching the road through yellowed net curtains. As Blake entered, all eyes turned on her.

"Suppose you'll be wanting a cup of tea," Heidi said.

"No, thank you. I'll only take a minute of your time."

The woman glared at her. "Well, if you're not having tea, the least you can do is sit down. I'll stand if you don't mind. Took me long enough to get up as it was."

Blake perched on the edge of the sofa, next to a tortoiseshell cat with sharp green eyes. It opened its jaws and hissed.

"So, what do you want to know?"

"I've been thinking about Demelza a lot lately. We used to be close friends. She used to tell me how much she liked visiting you when she was younger, and going to see the Maidens . . ."

"That was a long time ago. And the girl was a liar. She wasn't interested in spending time with her granny. She only came here because she didn't have much choice about it. Her mother was the same. Stuck up cow. Too good for country folk like me."

Blake unfastened the top buttons of her coat. The heat and the reek of the cats was making her nauseous.

"As for them Maidens, who cares? A bunch of rocks in a field. I never understood the fascination. But her father was just the same. He grew up in this house, you know. I used to catch him staring at them through his bedroom window. He was obsessed. I'd tell him, 'Stare at them Maidens for long enough and you'll turn into a bloody stone.'"

Blake shot a wary glance at the cat next to her, which flicked its tail and made an unnerving, guttural sound in its throat.

"You changed your mind about that tea?" Heidi asked, leaning on her cane.

"No, thank you."

"I see."

Blake's throat was unbearably dry, and she was starting to feel lightheaded. "Why do you think your son was obsessed with the Merry Maidens?"

"He liked the story behind them. He used to go and visit them, daft boy. Used to say he was going to see his girls, and off he'd go with that dog of his. Except one day the dog didn't come back. Said it had an accident. Or it ran off. One of the two, I can't remember. That boy never did have much luck with pets."

"Have you seen him lately?"

"Not for a long time. He don't visit me no more, not since that ungrateful cow divorced him. Ever since his father died, it's just me and the cats. Except in the summer, of course, when the tourists come along wanting to see those damn bloody stones."

Feeling queasy, Blake stood up. The room spun around her. "Where does he live now?"

"Up in the Forgotten Corner. The Rame Peninsula, on the border with Devon. Unless he's moved since then. It's been a while."

"Do you have his address?"

"Somewhere. There's an address book in my kitchen drawer." Heidi leaned forward, her eyes sharp and narrow. "What do you need it for?"

"I . . . well, I'd like to pay him a visit."

"A visit?"

"To say hello."

"It'll be one more visit than I've ever had. I'll go and find it. You stay here."

Heidi turned to leave the room.

"Can I see them?" Blake asked. "You said you can see the Maidens through the bedroom window?"

"I don't like strangers wandering through my house. You can do what every other bugger does and take a walk up the road."

She watched Heidi hobble out of the room. The smell of the cats was inside her now, burning her nostrils and numbing her brain. She turned a half circle. Old newspapers were piled in a corner and covered in dried faeces. All around her the cats grumbled and flicked their tails. Blake clawed at her coat, tugging it away from her throat. She knew what was coming. She had known it back in the car outside of Judy's house, but had immediately gone into denial. But now it was here—the moment of truth—and it was far worse than she had ever imagined.

Gasping for air, she stumbled from the living room and into the hall. Her eyes shot to the front door. If she left now, she could leave everything behind. She could pretend that none of it had happened, that Demelza had simply had enough of small town life, and had taken off on a solo adventure, never to return. She could pretend that her father wasn't a liar and a cheat, and that he hadn't deliberately alienated her and destroyed her self-worth just to alleviate his own guilt.

It was easy to pretend a lot of things when you didn't want to face the truth. But no matter how much you embraced denial the truth still lingered, festering under your skin, destroying muscle and devouring bone, until all that remained was its rotten, rotten core stuck in your throat like a bite of poisoned apple.

Denial isn't just a river in Africa, Blake thought, and almost laughed out loud.

The memory returned to her. They were fifteen years old. School was out for summer, and the Forever Four were lazing on deckchairs and drinking lemonade in Demelza's back garden on a stiflingly hot Sunday afternoon. Suddenly Demelza jumped up and pulled them all to their feet. Then they were dancing in a circle, their hands interlinked as they spun around and around, going faster and faster. They laughed and they screamed. The world was a blur of green, blue and yellow. And then just as Blake thought she was going to throw up, Demelza slid to a halt. The girls collided into each other. Christine and Judy roared with laughter. But Demelza didn't. Neither did Blake. Demelza's father was standing on the back doorstep, watching them, a strange, fixated smile on his lips, his eyes sharp and cold.

"Careful girls," he said. "Dancing on the Sabbath like that, you'll get turned to stone just like the Merry Maidens of Boleigh."

The tap, tap, tap of Heidi's cane filled the hall, and she appeared from around the corner.

"Here." She held out a pocket-sized notebook, a knotted thumb keeping the pages open.

Blake copied the address into her phone with trembling fingers.

"Does he still teach music?" she asked.

"No. He gave it up after he lost Demelza. Said he couldn't stand to be around the kiddies. He fixes church organs now. I heard he was in St Buryan last year. Imagine that, my son working just down the road, and he didn't even bother to visit me."

Slipping the phone back inside her pocket, Blake mumbled a thank you and hurried to the front door.

Heidi called out in a cracked voice. "When you see Dennis, you tell him to give his old mum a call. It ain't right he's left me alone like this. That's not the boy I raised."

43

As Blake stumbled from the cottage, she gasped and sucked in the cold country air. The heat that was cooking her body immediately began to subside. Her car was parked in a narrow lay-by on the other side of the road. She staggered towards it, her stomach churning violently. Suddenly her knees buckled. She shot out a hand and held onto the left wing mirror to steady herself. Then she doubled over and vomited on the road.

Dennis Stott: Husband. Father. Killer.

Demelza had never been close to him. She had confided in Blake that he rarely showed affection, and the times he did it was always in front of others, as if to fulfil his role as a loving dad. She'd said it felt like he was going through the motions, that he wasn't interested in her life, but only wanted to control it. When it came to dating boys, Dennis acted not like a puritanical father, but like a jealous lover. Those were the words Demelza had used, and Blake had told her it was gross and disgusting. They had both laughed. Demelza had said her dad was just being the way dads can be when it comes to their daughters' love lives. Blake had called it sexist bullshit. But God, they had both been so wrong.

She recalled her own memories of Dennis Stott. He had always been distant and reserved, reluctant for Demelza to have friends over, but when he did allow it, he would always manage to remain close by, as if he couldn't trust teenage girls to be left to their own devices. To Blake, he always smiled politely and enquired after her parents, and perhaps his gaze sometimes lingered a little too long, making her skin itch. He was a church-going man, and from what Demelza had told Blake, he'd had a strict, although not abusive, upbringing. If you made the mistake of mentioning Cornish history, he would keep you for hours, his emotionless eyes suddenly burning bright, as he imparted all of his local knowledge, with the conversation invariably reverting to his love for stone circles, with his favourite being The Merry Maidens of Boleigh.

Dennis Stott had always struck her as an oddball. But not once had she thought him capable of murder.

Blake's stomach heaved and she expelled more bile onto the road. The smell of Heidi Stott's home was still poisoning her senses.

In the days following Demelza's disappearance, Faith Stott, now Faith Penrose, had been white as a sheet and detached from the world, constantly wringing her hands and pacing up and down as she waited for news of her daughter. Dennis had broken down in tears in the town hall, where the locals had gathered to organise a search party. He'd been so distraught one of the neighbours had to help him offstage.

Liar.

He had murdered his own daughter. He had killed Lucy Truscott, too.

At Sunday service, Reverend Thompson told Mary that the organ had been recently tuned. Had Lucy been there at the time? Had she learned who Dennis Stott was? Had she confided in him that she possibly knew what had happened to his daughter all those years ago?

Blood rushed in Blake's ears. She wiped her mouth with the back of her hand and glanced over at Heidi Stott's cottage, where Dennis had spent his childhood staring out of the window, slowly obsessing over the Maidens.

Blake began walking along the narrow road, sticking close to the hedgerow. Above her, the sky was ice-blue with a smattering of white clouds. A cold breeze rustled the grassy hedgerow and chilled her skin.

What about all those other missing women? What about Heather Hargreaves and Leanne Curnow? Was Dennis Stott responsible for them all?

The road bucked and twisted beneath Blake's feet. A minute later, it curved sharply to the left, revealing a small parking area next to a wide field gate on the opposite side. The road was quiet, no signs of traffic. Blake crossed over, her feet unsure of themselves. She unfastened the gate and stepped into a large grassy field.

The Merry Maidens of Boleigh stood before her, a perfect stone circle made up of nineteen granite slabs measuring less than five feet tall and spaced twelve feet apart. It was no Stonehenge, but the Merry Maidens was loved by the locals, popular with tourists, and even came with its own legend.

Blake entered the circle and stopped at its centre. Slowly, she turned on her heels, taking in the misshapen stones' cracks and grooves and vivid colours: the browns, whites and greys of the weathered granite, and the vibrant orange and pale green of the lichen spreading over each one like a virus. She continued to turn, recalling the local legend.

Long ago one Saturday evening, nineteen young maidens were returning home from a wedding party when they came upon two pipers and a fiddler playing an enchanting ditty. Bewitched by the music, the maidens began to dance, twisting and twirling in a frenzy, until all else was forgotten. But as the church bells of St Buryan struck midnight, the musicians turned and fled. One by one, they were turned to stone—first the pipers, transformed into two megaliths in a north-east field, followed by the fiddler in a field to the west. Finally, came the maidens, petrified in a perfect circle: their punishment for dancing on the Sabbath.

Nineteen maidens.

Cement burns.

Blake froze. She knew what Dennis Stott was doing.

Pulling out her phone, she called the police station in Truro and demanded to speak to DS Turner, telling the duty officer it was urgent.

She waited a minute, struggling for breath, scarcely able to believe her own conclusion. To her surprise, Turner came on the line.

"Hello, Blake." There was something in his voice. A softness she hadn't heard before.

"I know who the killer is," Blake told him, breathlessly. "It's Dennis Stott, Demelza's father. He murdered Demelza, and Lucy, and all the others."

"Blake," Turner said. "Listen to me —"

"I know what he's doing. He's making his own twisted version of the Merry Maidens stone circle. Abducting young

women on a Sunday and burning them to death with cement—
it's his version of turning them into stone."

"I don't know what you're talking about, but you need to
listen to me."

"No, you need to listen! Dennis Stott grew up right beside
the Merry Maidens. He was obsessed with it. He killed Lucy and
he nailed her to the wall in a ballet pose, like one of the Merry
Maidens from the legend, who was caught dancing on the
Sabbath. He deliberately faced her towards Boskednan stone
circle, then put my friendship bracelet on her wrist because he's
an arrogant shit and thinks he's being clever. It's all a sick joke to
him. But I figured it out."

"Blake, please."

"For God's sake, Turner. Dennis tunes church organs for a
living! He travels from church to church, fixing the organs and
choosing girls he deems as sinners. Then he —"

"Blake!" Turner yelled sharply. "The forensic test results
came back from the samples we took from your father's van.
They match samples taken from Lucy Truscott's body. Another
matches a hair sample from one of the missing girls. Leanne
Curnow. I'm sorry, but your father's been charged with murder
and abduction."

Blake stopped breathing.

"Do you understand what I'm saying to you?" Turner said.
She could hear pity in his voice.

"No, you're wrong. You've made a mistake."

"I'm not. DNA testing doesn't lie."

"No, but it can be misinterpreted and hair samples can be
planted. My father had an affair with Demelza all those years
ago, Detective. He got her pregnant. That's the only thing he's
guilty of. That and lying through his teeth to his family. Dennis

Stott must have found out and killed Demelza in a rage. Lucy Truscott was looking into Demelza's disappearance. He must have killed her too, along with all those other missing women."

A sob escaped Blake's throat. She angrily wiped away tears.

Turner sighed. "I know about the affair. Your father confessed to it. He confirmed that Demelza called that night and told him she was pregnant."

She was going to be sick again. She could feel the acid in her throat. "Has he . . . Did he confess to the murders?"

"I'm sorry, Blake. I truly am. I know it's a lot to take in, but all the evidence is there. Go home to your mother. Talk to your father's lawyer. We'll be sending someone over shortly to speak to you both."

"No. Turner, please. I'm telling you you're wrong. My father isn't a killer. Dennis Stott is. And those girls are going to die if you don't go after him now."

"Go home," Turner said. "We'll find the girls with your father's help."

"Fuck you! My father can't help you because he didn't do it. I have Dennis Stott's address right here, so why don't you —"

Turner's voice was loud and angry in Blake's ear. "Go home. That's not a suggestion. Go home and do not interfere with this case in any shape or form, or you'll only make things worse for your father."

The line disconnected. Blake stood, shaking and seething in the middle of the stone circle.

"You're wrong," she said to the dead phone. "You're wrong and I'll prove it."

They were all wrong. She knew it in her bones. No matter how bizarre and outlandish the truth was, she knew that Dennis Stott was guilty.

Wasn't he?

Leaving the Merry Maidens, Blake staggered through the field and out through the gate. As she retraced her steps back to the car, one minute burning with rage, the next freezing in panic, she made a vow to herself. She would prove her father's innocence and bring Dennis Stott to justice. And when this was finally all over, she would confront her father about Demelza, and she would make him confess it all to her face. It was the least she deserved. But right now, as much as she didn't want to, she had to prove to the police that they'd got the wrong man.

Reaching the car, Blake climbed inside and switched on the heater. She rubbed her hands together and stared at the open road. There was only one way to expose Dennis Stott. It was reckless and dangerous, but her father wasn't the only one who needed Blake's help. All of those young women were still out there. At least two of them might still be alive.

Swiping her phone screen, she opened the map application and tapped in the destination address. She started the car engine and pulled away.

Then Blake was driving away from the Merry Maidens and heading towards the Forgotten Corner, with no idea of what to do when she got there.

44

Dennis Stott sat at the kitchen table with a half-eaten sandwich in front of him and a cup of tea that had gone cold. He was agitated and anxious, his shoulders unbearably tight. For the last hour, the voice inside his head had continued to tempt him. His third scrubbing of the day had only helped to shut it out for so long. To silence it, he had taken to digging a fork into his thigh. When that hadn't worked, he'd jabbed the prongs into the palms of his hand, hard enough to draw blood. He knew he had to wait until tomorrow, but since watching the news report the voice would not leave him in peace. *They'll find you*, it said. *They'll see through your pathetic attempt to cover your tracks. They'll let Hollow go and then they'll take your precious maidens from you. You'll fail and sin will prevail.*

Dennis rolled up his shirt sleeve and jabbed the fork into his forearm. He stared at the pinpricks of blood blooming on his skin. He was so close now. Too close to allow for failure.

The house phone started to ring. He looked up and smiled. He had been sent a distraction to help him wait.

Wiping his mouth on a napkin, he got to his feet and neatly

tucked in his chair. There were stray crumbs on the front of his shirt, which he brushed away. He went to the living room, where the telephone sat ringing on a side table. He picked up the receiver and held it to his ear.

"Stott Organ Service and Repairs," he said, remembering to add a cheerful lilt to his voice.

"Mr Stott? I'm sorry to bother you on a Saturday afternoon," a friendly male voice said. "This is Reverend Matthews from Saint Augustine's in Liskeard. I'm afraid we have a bit of a problem. There's a strange rattling sound coming from one of the organ pipes. It's making quite the racket. The issue, you see, is that we have a double christening tomorrow, and I was wondering if you would be able to come out just now and take a quick look at it."

Dennis frowned. Reverend Matthews . . . He didn't recognise the name. There were over six hundred churches in Cornwall covering the main Christian denominations. Most had a church organ that required servicing at least once or twice a year, depending on size and age. But Dennis was not the only organ tuner in the county, and Saint Augustine's was definitely not one of his clients.

"Well, Reverend Matthews, I don't usually service organs that aren't already under my care. The world of organ repair is a very small arena, and the last thing I want to do is cause controversy."

The Reverend cleared his throat. "I completely understand. It's just that our usual man is unavailable. Normally I wouldn't ask, but, well, I'm rather new to the parish, and tomorrow will be my first big performance, so to speak. I would love for everything to run as smoothly as possible, which I'm afraid won't happen with this terrible rattling noise."

"I see."

"I'd take a look myself, but I have no idea what I'm doing. The organ is a beautiful specimen, over a hundred years old I believe. I'd hate to cause it any damage . . . Would you be so good to come and take a look? I believe we're not too far from you."

Dennis clutched the receiver to his shoulder and stared out the living room window. His van was just outside in the front yard. Liskeard was a thirty-minute drive. He occasionally did emergency repairs on a Saturday, and he had left girls alone in the tank before during the working week. But with the police on high alert and his work near completion, he was reluctant to leave.

"Mr Stott? Are you still there?"

And yet, he had a living to make and appearances to upkeep. A bad reputation could spread quickly in small circles, and the last thing Dennis wanted was attention being drawn to him. At least, not yet.

Dennis feigned another smile. "I can leave in five minutes. If it turns out to be a larger job, I'm afraid I'll have to come back another day. I've already made plans with my girls."

"Of course. I completely understand. Family is of the utmost importance," Reverend Matthews said. "Thank you, Mr Stott. Your help is much appreciated. Now, do you know the address? Will you be able to find us all right?"

"I'm sure I'll be just fine."

"Quite, quite. Well, I'll wait for you at the church. See you in, say, forty minutes?"

"Thirty-five," Dennis said.

Replacing the receiver in the cradle, he stared at the tiny puncture wounds in his flesh. The blood had coagulated but the broken skin was smarting. Thirty minutes to Liskeard. Twenty to thirty minutes to inspect the organ, possibly more if repairs were required. Then another thirty-minute drive home. Twenty-three if he put his foot down. It wasn't as if the police were ever on patrol around here. Even with a little extra time, he would be back before the evening news report. If Hollow had been released by then Dennis would drive down to Wheal Marow and collect his final maiden.

Leaving the room, he retrieved his toolbox from his office at the end of the hall, then grabbed his keys from the rack and opened the front door. He was about to step out to the yard when the telephone began to ring again. Dennis paused. Perhaps it was Reverend Matthews calling back with additional information. Or perhaps another one of the churches? It certainly wasn't a personal call.

The phone continued to ring until the answer machine switched on and the automated voice told the caller to leave a message. Standing in the doorway, Dennis cocked his head and listened.

45

A DEEP-SEATED fear knotted Blake's stomach as she drove along a narrow coastal road through the Forgotten Corner. Coming here was dangerous and insane, with the potential to end badly. But what choice did she have? She glanced through the side window, startled by the remoteness of the landscape. Fifty miles from Truro, the Rame Peninsula had earned its nickname of the Forgotten Corner for going largely unnoticed by tourists as they headed for more well-known holiday destinations further south. Surrounded by the English Channel and the Rivers Lynher and Tamar, the peninsula was far from people. More importantly, it was far from the nearest police station, making it the perfect place for Dennis to hide with all of his victims. And yet, its isolation was what made the Forgotten Corner truly breathtaking.

Blake focused on that beauty now as she attempted to shut out the panicked voice that was telling her to turn the car around and drive home to her mother, who had called several times only to be met with Blake's voicemail. She had already passed through quaint coastal villages with even quainter names, such as Portwrinkle and Crafthole, and now she was driving alongside the high cliffs and sandy beaches of Whitsand Bay. The English Channel was on her right, its charcoal-green waters stretching out as far as the eye could see, while rolling fields rushed by on her left. The farthest tip of the peninsula, known as Rame Head, protruded in the distance. Blake was alone out here. There was only the ocean and the land and the narrow coastal road.

She gripped the wheel, aware that her heart was beating too fast. The road veered away from the cliff, leaving the ocean in her rear-view mirror, and headed back into countryside. She drove past copses of trees and lonely looking farmsteads. The road twisted again, revealing the thirteenth century church of St Germanus and its graveyard full of sea-weathered headstones that looked unnervingly like the Merry Maidens.

The road straightened. Suddenly the ocean was everywhere, glittering and vast, filling Blake's peripheral vision on all sides as she approached the tip of the peninsula. Mesmerised, she slowed the car and pulled over. On her right, the land sloped in a downward trajectory, and a narrow dirt track split off from the road at ninety degrees, ending at a smallholding in the near distance.

Blake's heart thumped violently. Grabbing her binoculars from the passenger seat, she took a closer look. An old sandstone cottage stood in a wide concrete yard, with a small extension attached to its side. A cluster of outbuildings stood beyond, partially obscured by the cottage. She returned her gaze to the front yard, which was empty. No vehicles. No one home.

"Well done, Kenver," she muttered. "Or should I say Reverend Matthews?"

She didn't have much time. Less than an hour before Dennis Stott realised something was wrong and came racing back.

You could turn around, she thought. You could lie to the police, tell them anything that would force them to come out here.

By now, word that her father had been charged would be spreading throughout the constabulary. Blake had already told Turner that Dennis was the killer, and he had done nothing. Did that mean no one else would? Over six thousand people worked for Devon and Cornwall police, including three thousand police officers. She only needed to convince just one of them to take her seriously.

Blake lowered the binoculars and grabbed her phone from the cup holder. The signal bars were empty. It was no surprise; she was in the middle of nowhere, at the edge of the world, surrounded by water on three sides.

She returned her gaze to the smallholding. It had to be her that went in. She had to go there now.

Turning the wheel, Blake manoeuvred the car off the road and onto the dirt track that led to Dennis Stott's home.

46

BLAKE PULLED into the yard and switched off the engine. There were no fences or gates to keep out strangers, only two stone walls that ran along the sides of the smallholding to mark its borders. With just a cluster of houses way back on the road, and a small car park at the very edge of the peninsula, presumably to accommodate the occasional tourist, Dennis Stott did not have to worry about being disturbed by strangers. Or so he thought.

Blake climbed out of the car and stared at the cottage. If Stott had been inside, her arrival would have been duly noted. But Stott was on his way to Liskeard.

Glancing over her shoulder at the dirt track and the road beyond, she drew in a breath and tasted bitter sea salt on her tongue. An icy breeze blew up from the ocean and rattled the shutters on the cottage windows. On the horizon, the sun was starting its descent. Evening was not far off.

Blake walked up to the cottage and knocked on the front door. She was sure Stott wasn't here, but if she was mistaken, what did she say? 'Hi, long time, no see. I don't suppose you have two girls locked in your basement?'

But there was no answer.

Blake tried the handle. The door was locked.

She returned to the car, opened the boot, and took out a crowbar and a pair of bolt cutters. Over the years, she had mostly played by the rules, but there had been times in her career as a private investigator when the rules had stood in her way. Like now.

She moved quickly around the side of the cottage and its small extension. The ground was hard beneath her feet. At the side of the building was an old wooden door. It was flimsy-looking but secured with a padlock.

Blake rounded the corner and entered another concrete yard. A cluster of granite outbuildings stood on the north side, next to a large warehouse. The outbuildings were old and weathered, perhaps once used to hold small livestock or to store equipment. The warehouse was modern and made of corrugated metal, with a gable roof, a single steel security door, and a huge metal sliding door that was half the height of the building.

On the south side of the yard, a small garden was fenced off with chicken wire and a crude wooden gate. A concrete path led from the gate to the back door of the cottage. Plots of freshly dug soil lay on both sides. A wet, earthy smell hung in the air.

Opening the gate, Blake crept along the path, tried the back door and found it locked. She stepped off the path and onto the soft earth, trying to peer through the closed windows. It was dark inside the house, but she could just make out a kitchen. Stott certainly liked his privacy.

Blake retraced her steps until she was in front of the old door at the side of the cottage. Her throat was dry, her mouth parched. Applying the bolt cutters to the padlock, she squeezed with all her strength and was rewarded with a loud *snap*. The padlock clattered on the ground. Resting the cutters against the wall, Blake wedged the tip of the crowbar in between the door and the jamb, just above the lock. She spread her feet wide, then threw her bodyweight into the crowbar. There was an ear-splitting crack. The jamb splintered and the door popped open. Blake caught her breath and entered Dennis Stott's home.

She was inside a small workshop that was draped in shadows. Shelves lined the walls, containing pots and jars of various items. A workbench stood on one side, while in the far corner a collection of rusty organ pipes was stacked against the wall.

Another door led into the house. Blake tried the handle. To her surprise, the door swung open.

The smell hit her hard; a nauseating stench of death, rot, and bleach that burned her nostrils and made her stomach heave. Covering her nose with her sleeve, she inched forward and entered the kitchen.

In ordinary circumstances she would have admired the decor as rustic chic. A small round table stood in the centre with a single chair tucked neatly underneath. A mug of cold tea and a plate containing a half-eaten sandwich sat on the counter next to the sink. Bile climbed Blake's throat as the stink invaded her senses. How could anyone eat while swamped by such a terrible odour? But Dennis Stott was not a normal human being. For him, the stench of death was as alluring as expensive perfume.

One hand clamped over her mouth and nose, Blake pulled out her phone. She unlocked the screen, activated the camera, and awkwardly snapped pictures. Leaving the kitchen, she stepped through an open door and out to a hall. She counted three more doors, including the front, and a narrow staircase leading upward. Opening the door across from her, she cautiously peered inside. A living room; minimally furnished but immaculately tidy. She snapped another picture, then moved past the staircase, towards the door at the end of the hall. Inside was a small office with a tidy desk and a noticeboard filled with newspaper clippings. Blake took another photograph then returned to the hall.

Where were the girls?

Cautiously moving upstairs, she halted on the narrow landing. The smell was less pungent up here, so she lowered her hand. The first door on her left revealed a bathroom, which was cramped but clean, with gleaming wall tiles. The next opened on a white room devoid of furniture. She opened the final door and entered Stott's bedroom. The bed was neatly made and the curtains were open. Her stomach twisting in knots, Blake glanced down at her car in the front yard.

Dennis Stott's home was not the house of horrors that she'd been expecting. If it hadn't been for the stench of death, she would never have suspected wrongdoing.

But Heather and Leanne were here somewhere.

Returning downstairs, the smell grew stronger, until Blake could taste it at the back of her throat. She covered her mouth and nose again, then retraced her steps to the kitchen. There was a door in the corner that she'd missed before, secured by another padlock.

Retrieving the cutters and crowbar, she made quick work of shearing the lock in two and opening the door.

Darkness rushed out. The stench grew stronger, forcing its way down Blake's gullet and making her retch. A set of wooden steps descended downward. She could tell that the basement had no windows because the darkness was absolute.

Leaving her tools on the floor, she checked her phone signal. Nothing. Not a single bar.

A deep shiver trembled through her body as she found a light switch and flipped it on. At the foot of the stairs, a naked light bulb flickered to life. Blake descended the stairs.

The smell of death grew more intense, making her ill. She reached the bottom step. Her pulse raced wildly. Blake entered the basement.

It was a large room, empty except for a table in the corner and an old tin bathtub taking centre stage. A second light bulb hung above it, illuminating a bare arm and the lower half of a bare leg that flopped over the side of the tub.

Blake raised a trembling hand and took a picture. Her throat grew impossibly dry as she moved closer. And then she was at the foot of the tub, staring in horror at the dead girl inside.

She was naked, her body half buried in dried concrete. The exposed skin was blistered and charred. Her eye sockets and mouth were filled with cement. The left side of her head was caved in, while the right side of her face had burned down to the bone, revealing the skull.

"Oh God!" Blake stumbled back and tripped over her feet. She ran from the basement, hurtling up the stairs, then stumbling and falling, hitting her chin on the top step, smashing her teeth together and biting her tongue. Tasting blood, she scrambled to her feet, swept up her tools and hurtled through the kitchen, into the workshop, and out to the salty air.

She gasped desperately for breath. Her chest heaved up and down. Her lungs burned. Pulling out her phone, she called 999. But there was still no service and the call would not connect.

The only way to get the police out here was to jump in her car and race up the road, to keep on driving until she had at least one bar of signal.

But what about the other girl? One was dead in the basement. Where was the other?

She spun on her heels and stared across the rear yard at the outbuildings. Soon, Stott would realise he'd been played, and he would come racing back. What if he got here before the police did? What if he discovered the broken padlocks and killed the girl in a panicked rage?

What if the girl was already dead? What if the only life Blake was risking was her own?

"Fuck!" She couldn't leave. Not yet. Not until she knew whether the remaining girl was alive or dead.

Pushing herself off the wall, Blake staggered across the yard. Checking the smaller outbuildings and finding them empty, she hurried over to the warehouse. She tried the steel security door first. It was locked, this time with a key, and it was reinforced, which meant her crowbar would have little impact. She turned her attention to the large sliding door. Two heavy-duty padlocks held the door in place. Blake rattled each one, testing their strength.

That was when she heard the cry.

She caught her breath. "Hello? Someone in there?"

The cry came again, this time shrill and frightened. *The girl was alive.*

She began to shout and babble, but Blake couldn't make out the words.

"I'm going to get you out," she shouted through the door. "I just need to cut through these bolts and you'll be free."

She gripped the first padlock between the blades of the bolt cutters and squeezed. The cutters barely made a dent. She tried again, clenching her jaw. But it was no good. The padlocks were too strong.

"Listen to me!" Blake called out. "I can't get the locks open, but there's another door. It needs a key, which means I have to go back to the house and look for a spare. If I can't find it, I'll need to drive up the road until I can get a phone signal to call the police. So, hold on for a few minutes. I promise I'm going to get you out."

The girl continued to babble and shriek, her unintelligible words tripping over themselves.

Frustration and panic pressed down on Blake's chest. Dropping the cutters and crowbar, she hurried away from the warehouse and across the yard, back towards the house.

47

THERE HAD to be a spare key. Someone like Dennis Stott wouldn't take any chances.

Shouldering open the workshop door, Blake slid to a halt and flicked on a light switch. She began searching the place, pulling open drawers, checking hooks on walls, and rifling through each shelf. Empty-handed, she hurried through to the kitchen. The smell hit her again, this time like a punch to the gut. Covering her nose, she crossed the room and kicked the basement door shut. She wrenched open drawers and cupboards. Found nothing.

Where would he keep it?

She ran out to the hall and spied the office door. Hurrying inside, she scoured the top of the desk, emptied a pot of pens and sifted through a tray of invoices. She tried the top drawer of the desk but only found more papers and surplus stationery. Crouching, she pulled open the second drawer. There, sitting on a pile of Organists' Review magazines, was a bunch of keys.

Blake snatched it up and sifted through the keys, until she came to three with green bows. One was a silver ESP high security key, while the two others were smaller padlock keys. One for the security door. Two for the sliding door.

Her pulse racing, she grabbed the keyring and got to her feet. As she straightened up, her eyes caught the notice board filled with newspaper clippings. She leaned in closer and drew in a shocked breath. There were nineteen clippings in total, pinned in neat rows and arranged in chronological order. Set in each story was a picture of a smiling young woman.

"The Maidens," Blake whispered.

Demelza was first, the headline reading: Search for Missing Teen Called Off. Then came the second, dated one year later: Falmouth Girl, 18, Disappears from Home.

On and on they went, the innocent, smiling faces of Dennis Stott's victims peering out at Blake, with no idea that their young lives had been cut short. She scanned through the articles, counting the years and the numbers, until she came to the eighteenth clipping. It had been cut out from a regional newspaper just a few days ago: Police Widen Search for Abducted Truro Teens.

Her eyes flicked to the final clipping. The room turned on its axis.

It was different from the others. Dated seven years ago, it didn't detail a missing young woman but that of a fraud case in which an employee of a well-known charity had been caught syphoning off thousands of pounds from public donations. Blake knew the case well, because she'd been the one to crack it. But why was the story pinned to Dennis Stott's noticeboard?

She didn't want to know the answer.

Photographing the news clippings, she hurried from the office with the keys gripped in her fist.

Halfway along the hall, she froze.

With no mobile phone signal out here, Dennis had to have a home telephone. She spun around, searching the hall and side tables, then ducked inside the living room. There it was, sitting on a side cabinet next to a bookshelf. Blake grabbed the receiver and punched 999 on the keypad.

She slowly hung up. The line was dead.

And yet a red light was blinking on the answer machine, announcing a new message. Confused, Blake hit the play button.

Heidi Stott's cracked voice filtered through the tinny speaker. "Dennis, it's your mother. I thought you'd want to know a woman was here asking questions about you. Said she used to be a friend of Demelza's. She asked for your address and I gave it to her, but now I'm wondering if that was the right thing. Can't remember her name. Blake something. Anyway, it wouldn't hurt you to visit your old mum once in a while, or even pick up the bloody phone."

Fuck.

Blake peered through the window. Her car was in clear view. Beyond it was the dirt track that led to the road.

"Get out," she whispered. "Grab the girl and get out."

Half running, she exited the living room and retraced her steps through the kitchen and workshop.

Had he heard the message? Surely not. The red light was still blinking.

So why wasn't the phone line working?

She shot a glance over her shoulder as she pelted across the rear yard, then almost slammed into the steel security door of the warehouse.

"I've got the key," she yelled.

The girl was no longer crying. She was making no sound at all.

Blake slipped the key into the lock with a shaking hand. She snapped it to the right and heard the lock release.

The door popped open. Darkness leaked out.

"Hello?" Blake called.

The girl didn't answer.

Spying her tools on the ground, Blake swooped down and snatched them up. Then she was stepping inside the warehouse.

48

DARKNESS SWARMED AROUND BLAKE. Panic gripped her throat. Crouching, she placed the bolt cutter on the ground and wedged it between the open door and the jamb. The gap was small, just a few inches, but the sliver of light leaking in reassured her there was a way out.

She couldn't hear the girl. Not even a whimper.

"Heather?" she called. "Leanne? My name is Blake. You're safe now. I'm here to get you out."

She stood still, gripping the crowbar and listening closely. There was only silence, heavy and cloying, mingling with the darkness and leaving Blake disoriented.

Fear prickled the back of her neck. She checked the door again, saw it was still wedged open, then searched the wall for light switches. But it was still too dark to see.

Grabbing her phone from her pocket, she activated the light and held it up as she turned in a half circle. The beam was weak in such a vast void, but directly ahead of her, it bounced off what looked like a glass wall.

Blake edged closer, brandishing the crowbar and taking one

cautious step after another. The cell revealed itself; a rectangular tank made of plastic glass, with a single door in the front wall that was barely visible except for the hinges and the lock mechanism. The girl was inside, curled up on the ground with her back turned to Blake. There was no furniture, only a metal bucket that lay on its side.

"Hello?" Blake stopped moving and watched the girl, trying to ascertain if she was still breathing. Her gaze moved to the cell door. She still had the bunch of keys. Perhaps one of them would open it.

She inched forward, guided by the phone light. Balancing the crowbar against the glass wall, she fished the keys out of her pocket.

A loud bang shattered the silence.

Blake twisted around. The phone swung in a wide arc. Things flashed in the darkness. But Blake's mind had little time to register them, because now it was going into panic mode.

The bolt cutters had sprung loose from the door, sealing her inside.

She stared at them as they glowed in the phone light. She had wedged them tightly. She was sure of it.

But now her thoughts were backing up, trying to make sense of what she had just seen lurking in the dark.

Blake turned ninety degrees and pointed the phone light straight ahead. The light began to tremble. Her eyes grew wide. Adrenaline fired through her veins. A strangled scream climbed her throat.

And then her legs were buckling and she went down, landing heavily on her knees.

At the centre of the warehouse was a stone circle. Each stone was set on a low plinth, and each stone was a deformed mass of poured concrete and human limbs. Some were merely bones, skeletal hands clawing at the darkness. Others still had flesh, but it was withered and burned, or flaking away in ribbons from the fingers as it slowly turned to dust.

And there were faces, shrunken and half hidden behind knotted clumps of hair. Pearly skulls and sockets peering out from concrete tombs. Jaws wide open in perpetual screams.

Dennis Stott's Merry Maidens.

There were seventeen in total. Two empty plinths sat, patiently waiting to be filled.

Blake staggered to her feet. Two empty plinths. One for the girl in the cell.

And the other for . . .

A breath, hot and heavy, caressed the back of her neck.

Blake spun around. The phone light fell on Dennis Stott.

A metal blade glinted then sank into Blake's shoulder and scraped against the bone.

She shrieked. Twisted away.

Dennis stumbled forward, losing his grip on the handle.

Blake hit the ground, landing on her back. The phone flew from her fingers and slid away, the light making grotesque shadow puppets on the wall.

Pain ripped through her shoulder. Her right arm dropped to her side, limp and useless.

She heard heavy footsteps moving across the floor. Dennis Stott's silhouette appeared twenty feet away as he stooped to pick up her phone.

She had to move. Now.

Pressing her feet into the ground, Blake pushed herself backwards. Her right arm dragged alongside. The pain in her shoulder was unbearable. She tried to keep it still as she scrambled away, her feet and calf muscles working like pistons, her back sliding along the ground.

"Don't you think they're pretty?" Stott's voice haunted the warehouse. He stood, half illuminated by the phone light. "Don't you think they're so much better now? Cleansed and pure."

He switched off the light, plunging them both into darkness.

Terror gripped Blake's throat. The blade was still inside her shoulder, wedged beneath the collar bone. It would slow the blood loss, but any sudden movement could sever a nerve and leave her paralysed. If Stott didn't kill her first.

Blake didn't want to die. Not yet.

She pushed herself backward with her feet, friction slowing her down. The warehouse seemed to have no end.

Stott's footsteps echoed across the hard floor. She couldn't tell where he was.

"You've grown into a fine woman, Blake. Even if you were bred from inferior stock. And you're cleverer than I thought. I'd almost given up on you finding me." His voice was at once all around her and a thousand miles away. "But you're still a dirty sinner. I watched you at the party that night. You didn't see me, but I saw you and Demelza and those other whores. I followed you all there. I watched you all drinking and dancing and rubbing your parts up against the boys. And I knew then, just like when I knew I had to cleanse my daughter of your father's filth, that I was going to save you till last."

The numbness was spreading from her shoulder and arm, into her neck. She kept moving, her feet and left hand operating on autopilot. She had no idea if she was making progress or turning around in circles, like the Merry Maidens of Boleigh dancing on Sabbath Eve.

"You were always going to be my final girl, Blake. Always. First that whore over there, then you when it was time. But time is not on our side."

The overhead lights flickered to life. Blake was dazzled by brilliant white. She blinked and gasped, but she kept moving.

As the dark spots faded from her vision, she saw the Merry Maidens in all of their horrific glory. And then Dennis Stott was cutting through the circle, heading straight for her.

He was in his late fifties, but just like Blake's father he was strong and powerfully built.

"My final Maiden," he said. His face was empty of emotion, his eyes two glittering black holes.

Blake scrambled away, pushing off one foot, then the other. She could see the hilt of the knife in her peripheral vision, and a dark red stain.

Stott was getting closer. "Your father poisoned my little girl. He stole what was mine and planted a maggot inside her. I had to cut it out before it rotted her insides. I had to cleanse her of his dirt. Just like I had to cleanse all my pretty maidens. Just like I have to cleanse you."

Blake slammed into the leg of a workbench. Things rolled off and clattered on the ground. Her good arm shot out and her hand found a chisel. On her left was a large plastic sack filled with powdered cement.

Dennis was upon her, wrapping thick hands around her left ankle and pulling her away from the workbench. The chisel flew from her fingers.

Blake screamed and lashed out, kicking him hard in the gut. Dennis grunted and released his grip. She kicked him again and he doubled over.

Blinding pain tore through Blake's injured shoulder. She

scrambled back on her feet once more. She found the chisel and picked it up.

Dennis's black eyes burned into her as he straightened his spine.

Blake stabbed the chisel into the bag and tore it open. She stuffed her hand inside and grabbed a fistful of powder.

Dennis flew at her. He grabbed the hilt of the knife and thrust the blade in deeper.

Blake shrieked as metal bit into bone. The world flashed red then yellow. She brought up her hand and threw the cement mix into his face.

And then Stott was jerking away and scratching at his eyes. He rolled over onto his back and thrashed on the ground. As the powder reacted with the moisture in his eyes to create a dangerously caustic compound, Blake rolled onto her knees.

Half-conscious and bleeding, she grabbed a mallet from the floor.

The cement mix ate into Dennis Stott's eyes. He screamed and clawed at his face.

Blake swung the mallet blindly and heard a terrible thud.

Dennis stopped screaming and started convulsing.

She brought it down again. Unbridled fury burned inside her. Her right arm dangled lifelessly. Blake raised the mallet over her head. The world spun and the glass tank filled her vision. She saw the girl.

The mallet slipped from her fingers. Dennis was deathly still, the lids of his eyes turning red and purple.

Blake was going to pass out. But she couldn't. Not yet.

Breathing heavily, she searched Stott's pockets and retrieved her phone. Slowly, unsteadily, she got to her feet and dragged her body towards the cell. It took several tries until she found the right key, but then she was inside and on her knees, gently shaking the girl awake, who opened her eyes and tried to crawl away.

"You're safe," Blake croaked. "It's over. Are you Heather?"

"Leanne," the girl said, and began to cry. "I think Heather is dead."

"Okay, Leanne. We need to get up."

They helped each other to their feet. With their arms entwined, they hobbled towards the security door.

"Don't look," Blake said, turning Leanne away from the Merry Maidens and the two empty plinths.

But Blake looked. It was the least she could do for them. And as she passed by, she saw a skeletal arm reaching for help that would never come. And on the wrist was a faded textile bracelet that had once been filled with colour and hope and the promise of ever-lasting friendship.

Dennis remained unmoving at the far end of the warehouse. She didn't know if he was alive or dead. She hoped it was the latter.

Out in the yard, Blake handed the keys to Leanne, who quickly locked the security door. They rounded the house and staggered to Blake's car.

"Can you drive?" she asked.

Leanne shook her head.

Blake gave her the phone. "Go up to the road, turn left, and keep going until you get a signal. Call the police and tell them you're at the Rame Peninsula. The address is right here on the map screen. You see it? Tell them a man called Dennis Stott took you. Tell them he killed them all."

"You have to come with me," Leanne said, fresh tears spilling. "You can't stay here."

But Blake knew that she wouldn't make it.

"Go," she said. "I'll be fine."

She waited for Leanne to leave before climbing inside the car. She watched the girl stagger up the dirt track in the rear-view mirror. Once she was safely away from the house, Blake turned her attention to her body. The knife was still protruding from her shoulder. Blood seeped through her jacket. Her right arm hung like dead meat at her side. She tried not to think about any of it, but turned her attention to the side of the cottage. She waited for Dennis Stott to come. To rise like the undead and claim his final victim.

Dizziness took hold. Blake leaned back against the headrest. Her eyes rolled in their sockets and she fell into darkness once more.

49

THE HOSPITAL WARD reeked of disinfectant. The glaring yellow lights hurt Blake's eyes. She had been awake for an hour. A nurse had helped her to sit up. She had gently adjusted the sling that held Blake's bandaged shoulder and right arm in place across her chest, then told her a doctor would be along soon. Now, Blake's body felt at once as heavy as lead and as light as a passing cloud. A catheter attached to a cannula was inserted into the crook of her left arm, allowing a controlled flow of pain medication to be administered intravenously. Her throat was unbearably dry. She wished her mother was here to pass her a glass of water and to gently stroke her hair. Instead, she settled for DS Turner, although she wasn't letting him anywhere near her hair.

Blake glanced at the water jug.

"Let me get that for you," he said. Filling a plastic glass, he added a paper straw and passed it to Blake, who nodded her thanks. Once she'd drunk her fill, Turner put the cup on the side and sat down again.

He watched her for a moment. "How are you? I heard you had to have surgery."

Blake's voice was filled with gravel. "Apparently the knife snapped the collarbone and cut into the brachial plexus, whatever that is. There was nerve damage, which the surgeon did her best to repair. It's too early to tell if I'll get the full use of my arm back."

She stared at the sling, glad that the painkillers were also numbing her emotions.

"If it's any consolation, Dennis Stott looks worse," Turner said. "You messed him up pretty good."

"Is he here? At the hospital?"

"Don't worry. He's under tight security, and he'll be moved as soon as he's well enough. He lost his left eye, the other is pretty damaged. He has a few broken bones, too."

"Good." Blake felt no remorse.

"You're lucky to be alive. What were you thinking going in there alone?"

"It wasn't like I had much of a choice. You saw to that."

Turner flinched. "Fair enough."

"Anyway, I didn't think he was there. The bastard must have hidden his car."

"It was parked behind the warehouse, along with a white van. Forensics will have fun with the amount of samples we collected."

"What about Leanne?"

"She's dehydrated. Slightly malnourished. Traumatised, probably for the rest of her life. But she's alive and she's safe, thanks to you."

"Good. That's good."

Blake's mind flashed back to Dennis Stott's basement and the body in the bathtub. Heather Hargreaves. Sixteen years old.

A young life with a bright future snuffed out like a candle flame, along with all of his other victims.

"We also checked in with Reverend Thompson at the church in Wheal Marow," Turner said. "Dennis Stott was there to tune the church organ a few days before Lucy Truscott disappeared. It was the same day the foodbank was running."

"Lucy talked to him," Blake said. "She told him what she knew about my father. He killed her for it, then he used her body to lure me in."

Turner leaned forward a little. "Aren't you going to ask about your father?"

A flash of anger pushed through Blake's drug induced haze, but she said nothing.

Turner continued. "The scene of crime officers are still sifting through the hell that is Stott's house, but based on the evidence we've found so far, and along with Leanne's statement, it's pretty clear that your father was being set up. We found extensive notes and scribblings in Stott's office that detailed a long-fuelled hatred. And then there were the photographs . . ."

Blake stared at him.

"We found pictures of your parents, taken candidly over a span of several years. And . . . pictures of you."

"Taken where?"

"Manchester from the looks of it."

A chill slipped beneath the sheets of Blake's bed. "He was keeping tabs on me. Making sure he knew exactly where to find me—for when the time was right."

"When Stott's more coherent, we'll get a full confession. But he's clearly psychotic. There doesn't seem to be a single motivation for what he did to all of those women, other than his own disturbed delusions. As for your father, it seems like it was an act of revenge."

"Stott said my dad ruined Demelza. He said he was forced to kill his own daughter because of it."

"Like I said, psychotic."

"Did you see? Inside the warehouse?"

Turner nodded and stared at the floor. "I don't think I will ever unsee it, and I've seen a lot of messed up things in my career."

They were both quiet, terrible images haunting them.

Turner looked up again. "I'm sorry, Blake. In my defence, Stott did a good job of planting the hair and blood samples. Seems you can learn anything from the internet these days. Coupled with your father's lack of alibis and his involvement with Demelza, plus Lucy's diary, well, I suppose we made a mistake."

Blake said nothing. She shifted on the bed, staring at the IV pole, desperate for another dose of painkillers. "My dad has been released?"

"Yes. In fact, he's just outside. He'd like to see you. Shall I send him in?"

A rush of confused emotions swept over Blake. Part of her never wanted to see her father again. Part of her wanted to collapse into his arms. Either way, she needed to hear him tell the truth.

Silently, she nodded.

Turner stood up and straightened his jacket. "We still need your statement. If you're up to it, after speaking to your father, I'll send an officer in."

"Fine."

"Take care of yourself, Blake. I'm sure I'll see you again at

Stott's trial." Turner pulled back the privacy curtain. "You know, I'm sure you could put your skills to better use. You never thought of joining the police force?"

Blake shrugged her left shoulder. "I like being a private investigator. Besides, I tried out for the police force a long time ago. I got rejected."

"On what grounds?"

"Apparently, I have a problem with authority."

Turner laughed. Then he was gone, shutting the curtain behind him.

Blake tried to sit up. She stared at her arm in the sling. The idea of not regaining its full use was terrifying. But it was still early days. Stitches need to heal, and there was rehabilitation and physiotherapy to come.

The curtain shifted, and there was her father, standing at the foot of her bed. His shoulders were hunched, his head bowed. He'd aged considerably over the last few days. The whites of his eyes were tinged with red.

He smiled weakly. "How are you feeling?"

Blake stared at the bed. Ed continued to hover.

"Sit down, Dad."

Ed did as he was told, and clasped his hands together in his lap. They sat in silence, both avoiding eye contact.

"How's Mum?" Blake asked.

"She's fine. Your Auntie Hester's come to stay. God help us all."

More silence. More uncomfortable shifting. The muttered voices of other patients on the ward slipped through the curtains.

Blake grew impatient. Her father wasn't going to start this

conversation. Not because he didn't want to. He didn't know how.

She forced herself to look at him.

"I'm glad you've been released," she said. "I'm glad they've finally got the right man."

Ed's hands curled into fists and his face turned crimson. "That bastard, Stott! I should have known it was him. I should have killed him. Look what he did to you. Look what he did to all those other girls."

Anger heated Blake's chest, and she tried to contain it.

"Is it true, Dad?"

Ed turned away and bowed his head.

"Dad, look at me and tell me the truth. I know about you and Demelza. I know that you were having an affair. But is it true that she was pregnant?"

Tears slipped from Ed's eyes. They startled Blake. She had never seen her father cry until now. Ed Hollow had always been the type of man who was unable to show emotions. Unable to express worry or fear or doubt. Because to make himself vulnerable was a sign of weakness. And now he was blubbering like a baby in front of his daughter, and Blake didn't know whether to hug him or punch him in the face. Men like her father drove her insane. If only they could see that vulnerability was a strength, and that to cry or to feel afraid was intrinsically human. Maybe then the world would be a safer place to live.

"It was you, wasn't it?" she said. "Lucy saw you bringing white roses to Demelza's grave. That's how she knew. That's what she wrote in her diary and what I'm guessing she told Dennis Stott. That's what got her killed."

Ed wiped his face, but he couldn't stop the tears. "I never wanted any of this to happen."

"And it was you Demelza called that night from the party. Was that when she told you she was pregnant?"

"Yes," Ed sobbed. "She told me."

Even though she already knew it, the admission was like a knife in Blake's chest. Tears slipped from her eyes. She let them run down her face. "What did you say to her?"

"I told her to get rid of it. I told her I would pay, but she would have to go to the clinic alone. I couldn't be seen with her. I couldn't let Mary find out. I told her that the whole thing was one big mistake, that it should never have happened. But Demelza got upset and angry, and she said she was coming to the house to tell Mary. I panicked. I thought it was all over then. All because I made a stupid mistake. But Demelza didn't come. And the next morning, she was missing, and everyone was worried sick. But all I felt was relief. Because it meant you and Mary would never find out, and life could go back to normal, like none of it had ever happened."

"Except things were never normal again."

"No, they weren't."

"My whole adult life I thought I'd done something wrong. Something to offend you. Something that made you disappointed in me. I thought it had to be me, because why else had you grown so distant? Why else had you stopped showing me affection, or love, if I hadn't done anything wrong? But it was *you*. It was always you. Because you were riddled with shame and guilt, and you chose to let it destroy our relationship rather than come out with the truth. I would have hated you for it, but at least I wouldn't have spent years blaming myself."

Ed reached out a hand. "I'm sorry."

Blake pulled away from him. She clenched her teeth

together, pushing the emotions down until she was nothing but stone. "Have you told Mum?"

"Not yet."

"Well, you need to. She deserves to know the truth. All of it. I won't keep a secret like this. There's been too many lies. You need to go home and tell her. Or I will."

She turned away from him, unable to bear the devastation in his eyes. Guilt tore at her, but she refused to let it in.

"I'm tired," she said. "I need to sleep."

She twisted her head further away from him and winced at the pain. She heard her father slowly stand. She heard the curtain open and close, then Ed's footsteps shuffling away, growing quieter and quieter, until he was gone.

Blake was alone again. Alone and afraid.

50

EIGHT WEEKS LATER

Blake stood in the centre of an empty room, staring at an ominous stain on the carpet. It was either blood or red wine, she couldn't tell which. Whatever it was, she didn't like the look of it. She turned in a circle, absorbing the details of the room: the faded and peeling wallpaper; the splintered crack that ran from the central light to the corner of the ceiling; the suspect wire protruding from a small hole by the light switch; the young man wearing a cheap suit and standing in the corner. He smiled awkwardly, his eyes moving down to Blake's right arm that was still in a sling and tucked inside the left fold of her coat.

He cleared his throat. "As you can see, it's not the biggest office space in the world, but there's room for a desk and chairs. Through that door over there is a small bathroom, and through that one just here is a kitchenette. And of course, the lack of space is more than made up for by the magnificent view. Go ahead, take a look."

Blake stepped in front of the bay window. Ignoring the peeling paintwork, she peered down at the empty Prince of

Wales Pier and the yachts swaying on the choppy water, their naked masts pointing up at the charcoal sky.

"In summertime it's rather lovely," the letting agent said. "Busy, too. Falmouth is quite the tourist hot spot."

Blake nodded. "I used to come up on the train from Wheal Marow when I was a teenager. Me and my friends."

"Oh, you're Cornish? You don't sound like it."

"I've been away a long time."

"I see. And what business is it that you're in?"

"Private investigation."

The young man laughed, and then stared at the floor as he realised it wasn't a joke. "Well, it will be two months' rent as a deposit and a minimum twelve month contract, and then of course the usual rates apply. The office is available as of today, so if you want it, you'll need to make up your mind quickly."

Blake gave the room another glance. It was small, but it wasn't like she needed an arena. "Thanks. I'll call you later and let you know."

She followed the letting agent downstairs and out to the street. She waited for him to lock the door, then awkwardly shook his hand and watched him walk away. It was Saturday afternoon. Shoppers milled up and down in hats and scarves, their raincoats zipped up to the neck. Her train home wasn't leaving for another thirty minutes, so she rounded the corner and walked down to the pier. A wind was blowing, churning the waves, and dampening the pier in a fine mist.

If she took the office, it would be a thirty-minute drive from her mother. Or an hour and ten minutes on the train, with a change at Truro; travelling in Cornwall was never straightforward if you couldn't drive. And right now, Blake still couldn't. She wasn't planning on staying with Mary forever, just until her mother had adjusted to being alone and Blake had gained better use of her arm, whichever came first.

She stared at the estuary waters, wondering if she was making the right decision. With her father moved out and her mother in a vulnerable state, it felt like she had little choice. But perhaps returning to Cornwall would help revive her career. It would mean less clients than she'd find in the city, but it would also mean less competition from corporate rivals like Axis Investigations.

Her phone started to ring. She carefully removed it from inside her sling. Judy Moon was calling.

"Hello stranger," Judy said. "How's that arm of yours?"

"Slowly coming back to life," Blake replied. "The jury's still out on whether I'll get full use back, but so far the good doctor is pleased with my progress. Still hurts like a bastard, though."

"I heard on the grapevine you're out looking for office space today."

"And by any chance would that grapevine belong to my mother?"

"A journalist never reveals her sources. So, how was it?"

"Grubby. In need of a good lick of paint. I think I'll take it."

"Exciting times. I'm so glad you're coming back. Anyway, I was calling to ask if you and your mother would like to come to dinner on Saturday night. It's been a while. I haven't seen you since Lucy's funeral, and I've been worried."

Blake shrugged her left shoulder. "I've needed some time to process, that's all. The situation between Mum and Dad isn't good. At least Alfie's new baby is providing a welcome distraction. And Mum's cast came off last week, so that's something."

"And you? How are you doing?"

Blake leaned against the pier railing. Two gulls swooped

overhead, piercing the air with shrill cries. "Honestly, I don't know how to answer that. Everything has changed. It's a lot to take in."

"Have you talked to your Dad?"

"No. I don't want to."

"Blake —"

"Everything I knew was a lie. Everything. Dad and Demelza, they were both liars. Do you think she even liked me? Or was she just playing best friends so she could get close to my dad?"

Blake winced. She hated how needy she sounded, but she was trying to make sense of all her conflicting feelings. To confront them, not bury them. Not anymore.

"Demelza was barely eighteen," Judy said softly. "Your dad was old enough to know better. Maybe she was, too. But you're forgetting something, Blake. You and Demelza, Christine and me—the four of us were friends long before any of that happened. Of course Demelza liked you. She *loved* you. And her father was . . . *is* a monster. We have no idea what was going on at Demelza's house behind closed doors. All we do know is that Demelza was good at keeping secrets, and so was your father, and that none of it is your fault."

"At least it's all out in the open now. No matter how much it hurts. It's Mum I worry about. Forty years of marriage gone up in smoke."

"Do you think she'll take him back?"

"I've no idea, and I don't know how I'd feel if she did. But that's between them."

"I suppose it is," Judy said. "So come around for dinner on Saturday. Bring your mum. I want to hear all about your plans for your grand return. I'll invite Kenver, too. You know he's been babysitting the girls for us?"

Blake snorted. "Excuse me? Since when did Kenver like children?"

"The girls think he's the best thing to ever happen. My oldest asked if she could get her septum pierced, just like Uncle Kenver."

"Well, good luck with that."

"So you'll come? On Saturday?"

"What time?"

"Six o'clock?"

"That's a bit early, isn't it?"

"You're on Cornish time now, my dear."

Judy hung up. Tucking her phone back inside the sling, Blake looked out across the harbour. Her mind returned to Dennis Stott's warehouse and all the Merry Maidens entombed in darkness. She thought about her father, about how you could never really, truly know someone. All you got to see was the version they wanted to project. Everyone had secrets. Everyone told lies. Everyone held back. Blake had been holding back for the longest time, but now she was learning to let go. All she could do was trust her instincts. It was all anyone could do, really. Trust and hope that you'd made the right decision.

Turning her back on the water, Blake stared up at the buildings before her, at the office window on the second floor.

She hoped that she was making the right decision now.

A NOTE FROM MALCOLM

Dear Reader,

Thank you for reading *Circle of Bones*. If you enjoyed reading this first book in the PI Blake Hollow series, please consider writing a short review on the site that you purchased it from. Leaving a review is one of the best ways you can help authors to attract new readers, which in turn gives us the opportunity to write more books for you to enjoy. Everybody wins.

It was a joy to be writing about Cornwall again, and to explore some of its lesser-known places, such as Ding Dong Mine and the Rame Peninsula (aka The Forgotten Corner). However, Wheal Marow is a fictional small town inspired by a real town with a similar history. If you were to go looking for it on a map, you would probably find it somewhere between Redruth and Hayle.

Having been born and raised in Cornwall, and as with my previous Devil's Cove series, I've tried to present an authentic slice of what I like to call Cornwall's dual nature. On the one hand, there is the gentle pace of life and breath-taking rugged beauty that understandably brings millions of tourists flocking to the county each year. On the other, there is hardship and pockets of poverty that don't align with the romanticised ideal of Cornwall, which is probably why you rarely see it portrayed in books and on-screen.

The Cornish are a fiercely proud and resilient people, and I hope this book does them justice.

As for Blake Hollow, you can find her shoulders deep in more murder and mayhem as she investigates the suicide of a wealthy heiress in *Down in the Blood*.

Malcolm Richards

ACKNOWLEDGEMENTS

Thank you to my editor, Natasha Orme, for always asking the right questions and challenging me to go deeper into the story. This is our sixth book together, and hopefully there will be many more. Also, thank you to Virginia King, for eagle-eye proof-reading and your help with writing the book blurb.

Huge thanks to the police officers, detectives and forensic scientists over at the *Cops and Writers* Facebook group, who provided invaluable help and insight when it came to the procedural aspects of Circle Of Bones. The group is fast becoming a go-to source for aspiring crime writers who care about authenticity. The group's founder, Patrick O'Donnell, also has a fascinating podcast with the same name, which I encourage crime fiction writers and readers alike to seek out.

Thank you to all of my family and friends (you know who you are), with special thanks to Xander, Mum and Dad, and Sonia.

Finally, the biggest thanks to all of my readers, including my wonderful Read & Review team—the support and encouragement you provide is truly humbling, and I know that I wouldn't even have this career without you. From the bottom of my heart, thank you.

DOWN IN THE BLOOD
PI BLAKE HOLLOW BOOK 2

Wealthy heiress Kerenza Trezise was about to marry the man she loved—until she committed suicide in front of the entire wedding party.

Private investigator Blake Hollow is hired to find out why. Physically and emotionally damaged by a near-death encounter with a serial killer, Blake knows this case is an opportunity to relaunch her struggling P.I. business.

But as she attempts to infiltrate one of Cornwall's richest families at their impressive Frenchman's Creek estate, she learns that the Trezises have their own dark secrets to protect, and a shocking legacy of madness, horror, and death.

Worse still, they'll do anything to stop Blake's private investigation from revealing the truth, including deception, intimidation, and perhaps even murder.

They say family is forever. But *they* have never met the Trezise family . . .

Printed in Great Britain
by Amazon